dandelions in a jelly jar

**Center Point
Large Print**

**This Large Print Book carries the
Seal of Approval of N.A.V.H.**

dandelions in a jelly jar

Traci DePree

CENTER POINT PUBLISHING
THORNDIKE, MAINE

This Center Point Large Print edition
is published in the year 2004 by arrangement with
WaterBrook Press, a division of Random House, Inc.

Copyright © 2004 by Traci L. DePree.

The text of this Large Print edition is unabridged. In other
aspects, this book may vary from the original edition. Printed in
Thailand. Set in 16-point Times New Roman type.

ISBN 1-58547-465-7

Library of Congress Cataloging-in-Publication Data

DePree, Traci.
    Dandelions in a jelly jar / Traci DePree.--Center Point large print ed.
        p. cm.
    ISBN 1-58547-465-7 (lib. bdg. : alk. paper)
    1. High school teachers--Fiction. 2. Women art teachers--Fiction. 3. City and
town life--Fiction. 4. School sports--Fiction. 5. Minnesota--Fiction. 6. Farmers--Fiction.
7. Large type books. I. Title.

PS3604.E67D47 2004b
813'.6--dc22
                                                                          2004004103

for
John

acknowledgments

I am indebted to many for the creation of this book. First to my husband, John, and our children—Caitlin, Megan, Haley, and Willow—for their support in so many ways. To my partners at WaterBrook Press: Steve Cobb, Don Pape, Dudley Delffs, Laura Barker, Ginia Hairston, Laura Wright, Brian McGinley, Paul Hawley, Carol Bartley, and the crews in each department, thank you. To my readers "in the know": Jan LaFond, Dianne Pinney, and Paul Braun, your insight was perfection. And last but certainly not least, to Erin Healy, who holds my hand and helps me see so much more clearly—you are a godsend.

*The round expressionless clock tick, tick, ticked duti-
fully as seven-year-old Trudy Ploog waited. She was in
the principal's office after school again. That dumb
Jack Linder. It was all his fault.*

*She sat in the embrace of the hard orange plastic
chair and swung her legs back and forth. Multicolored
tile squares on the floor looked as though someone had
spattered red, blue, and green paint all over.*

*Trudy tried to think about anything other than what
was going to happen, but no matter how hard she tried,
she was stuck on how mad her mom was going to be.
Making her mom angry was the last thing she wanted
to do, especially when Mom had so much else on her
mind with taking care of her and baby Mae all by herself.*

*The voices grew steadily louder on the other side of
the big door with the white-glass window. Trudy's eyes
shifted. She wiped her sweaty palms on her jeans, then
grabbed her long ponytail and twisted the bright red
tresses. The door opened, and Principal Bascom
returned.*

*His face was a storm cloud. Trudy wished she had an
umbrella.*

*"Trudy Ploog," Mr. Bascom said with a defeated
sigh. He walked slowly around the wide desk and held
up a flattened, scratched, and contorted piece of
yellow metal. A filthy red plastic handle poked out. Mr.
Bascom placed the evidence on the desk in front of her*

and leaned in so the light from the window behind his bald head glared in Trudy's eyes. "Do you know what this is?"

Sweat gathered on her forehead and her heart beat wildly as she tried to swallow the lump in her throat. She twisted her hair and then nodded ever so slightly.

"I didn't hear that, Miss Ploog," Principal Bascom said as he leaned closer, hovering like a vulture.

"Yes sir," Trudy squeaked. She bit her bottom lip and said, "It's Jack Linder's lunchbox."

The scrawny man stepped back and pulled a tired and stained cloth handkerchief from his gray suit coat pocket. He wiped his moist upper lip. "Would you know how Jack Linder's lunchbox came to look this way?" His eyes were dark BBs peering into her soul.

"Um . . ." Trudy glanced around the room, wishing for a quick escape route—a trapdoor, a window, any way out of Mr. Bascom's office. She lowered her head and said, "I kicked it."

"And then?"

"The bus ran over it."

"Miss Ploog, I'm extremely disappointed by these antics of yours. Last week the incident in the boys' bathroom and now this. Why would you do this?"

"He . . . ," she paused. "He was teasing me."

"So because Mr. Linder teased you, it is appropriate to vandalize his property?" It sounded like a question, but Trudy guessed it didn't need answering. "This is the third time that you've been in my office in the past month. Trudy, I'm sorry, but since you haven't chosen to mend your ways, I'll be speaking with your parents." His icy, angry gaze locked on Trudy. She pursed her lips together and, though trembling, stared hard back at him, trying to use mind control to will him to stop even as he picked up the black receiver on the rotary phone and dialed, waiting after each number for the humming dial to revolve back.

Good luck getting ahold of my dad. She released her hair from the tight coil she had twisted around her finger. Her heart kept up its racing rhythm. She wanted to cry. Instead she blew out her cheeks. Mr. Bascom lifted his eyes over his glasses to the ceiling and, tapping a yellow number 2 pencil on the desk, turned his swivel chair to the side as he began, "Yes, Mrs. Ploog. This is Principal Bascom from school. I need to speak with you regarding Trudy's behavior lately." The thrumming in Trudy's ears grew. She could guess her mother's reaction—it was the same reaction she had to everything these days. Since Dad left. Tears. Horrible, unkind tears. Trudy hated tears. Why couldn't her dad see what he was doing to her, to them all? Trudy folded her arms across her chest.

"Oh, I'm sorry," Mr. Bascom said as he glanced at Trudy. His angry and cold expression turned to pity. She hated that Jell-O look adults gave her. Trudy wished the mean face would come back. Anything but pity. She'd had enough "poor dears" in the past month to make her puke. Mae didn't understand, but Trudy knew. People felt sorry for them because of what their father had done. Well, she'd show them. She wasn't any different from any other kid, and she wasn't going to let them think she was. A lot of parents got divorced.

Trudy gazed up.

Mr. Bascom was still talking to her mother. "I'm sorry to hear that, Mrs. Ploog. Sure, I understand." No doubt her mom was blubbering on about the whole sad story. At this rate, everyone in school would know. Trudy began twisting her hair again.

Finally Mr. Bascom hung up. He cleared his throat, and that kind face was there. "Trudy, why didn't you tell your teacher about your trouble at home?"

Trudy shrugged. "It's not any of his business."

Mr. Bascom stacked his hands on the desk. "Tell you what, I'm going to give you another chance here. But if you need to talk about anything, I want you to know that your teachers are here to help. Talk to them." Trudy felt her insides shrivel. "But this is the last time you get in trouble, Miss Ploog, or you will face detention."

Trudy nodded contritely. She was afraid her voice would crack if she said anything aloud.

Mr. Bascom stood and opened the door for her. "I don't expect to see you in here again, understood?" But he said it with such kindness that Trudy felt like punching him.

She bit her lip and mumbled, "Yes sir." She picked up her backpack and moved as fast as she could without actually running to escape the stuffy office. When she heard Mr. Bascom shut the office door, Trudy let out a pent-up breath. That stupid Jack Linder. If he hadn't been teasing her about everything . . . The big cry-baby—who cared about a silly G.I. Joe lunchbox?

Trudy headed down the hall to the art room and let herself into the darkened room. Her mom would know to pick her up here. Inside it smelled of tempera paints and clay. The scent comforted. She flicked on the lights and climbed onto one of the tall stools next to the wide table. After pulling out her pad of paper and colored pencils from her pack, she began to draw. When she drew, she entered another world, a world without time, parents, divorce, or sad-eyed looks. Shapes changed, shifted. Soon she'd drawn a house with a dog and a kitty, then a girl with a flower in her hair.

"Trudy?" It was Mrs. Zernickel, the art teacher. She had long dark hair and thick, perfectly sculpted eyebrows. She always wore groovy outfits Cher would've been jealous of. Today she had on a maxiskirt that had lots of small pieces sewn together like a patchwork quilt and platform shoes that added a good three inches to her already tall height.

"Hi, Mrs. Zernickel," Trudy said as she glanced up.

"What you working on?" She tilted her head and looked at Trudy's drawing.

Trudy shrugged. "A picture."

"I like it." She pulled out the stool beside Trudy. When she was seated she put a hand to her face as she studied the simple drawing. "You really like art, don't you?"

"Uh-huh."

"What would you say to a few lessons after school on Fridays? I'm usually here until four."

"Really?" Trudy felt like leaping.

"You'll have to ask your parents if it's okay to stay late."

"My mom won't mind. She'll probably like it." She paused, then added, "It's not so much fun at home right now." Trudy turned back to her picture and added a sun to the upper left-hand corner.

Mrs. Zernickel watched her in the quietness of the big room. "I'm sorry to hear about that," she said softly.

"My parents are getting a divorce," Trudy said.

Mrs. Zernickel placed a gentle hand on Trudy's shoulders. Tears burned Trudy's eyes and nose. She touched the corner of her eyes to stop the flow.

"Would you like me to show you how I draw trees?" Mrs. Zernickel said as she reached for a brown pencil.

Trudy grinned. "That'd be great."

The teacher leaned closer and took a piece of paper from a drawer and started to sketch. She smelled like honeysuckle. "First, I start with the trunk. Like this," she said. She worked quickly, explaining each gesture and applying several colors. Trudy watched, amazed as a tall tree slowly came alive on the paper. It was beautiful, with thick green leaves and burly oak arms. Its own stream gurgled past, and birds sailed on the wind far above.

"That's beautiful," Trudy breathed.

Mrs. Zernickel returned her hand to Trudy's shoulder. It felt warm, nice. "I can teach you how to draw all kinds of things. You could be a great artist if you keep on with it."

"Really?"

"You have a lot of talent, Trudy. You need to train it, to focus it. Then that talent can take you wherever you want it to."

See, Jack Linder, *Trudy thought,* You are wrong. Just watch me.

14

S ince Trudy Ploog could first remember, she had
lived in St. Paul. She loved life here—the bustle of
the neighborhood, people on the move, exciting events
always happening. St. Paul was a place where others
shared her love of art. It was a place where she felt safe
and accepted. She sighed happily as sounds of the
neighborhood reported their whereabouts—a bicycle
bell, honking horns, squealing tires. They all gave her
that familiar, warm feeling of home. If only Bert were
here. But he was a hundred miles away milking cows.

Trudy walked eight blocks downhill along the tree-
lined boulevard to an old Victorian house, then
climbed a staircase to her rented apartment in the
second story. Trudy had lived here for almost a dozen
years since graduating from college. She stepped in
and paused for a minute in the sunshine that bathed the
wide-open living area and kitchen with warmth.
Expansive south-facing windows set in ancient brick
walls overlooked the city from their hillside perch.
Groups of secondhand chairs and couches gathered in
cozy conversation over thick rugs. Trudy loved the
dark and brooding artwork—some of it her own, other
pieces she'd found at various art shows and sales—set
off by imported fabrics and tapestries, the beaded-door
curtain, the building's thick wooden ribs along the
ceiling. Her cheery painting studio waited for her in
the far corner of the room.

Singing came from one of the back bedrooms. She

dropped her purse on the kitchen counter and moved toward the sound.

Ellen, Trudy's roommate, stood before a full-length mirror admiring her own reflection as she belted out in a slightly off-key voice, "You make me feel, you make me feel like a natural woman . . ." Her private moment ended in an embarrassed blush as Trudy's gaze met hers in the mirror. "Hey. What do you think?" Ellen twirled. She was a tiny thing with a cute figure and hair so blond it was almost white. Her eyes were a pale blue, and her pert nose had a miniature ski jump at the end. She wore a soft lavender sheath dress that showed off her curves.

"Going out with Tony tonight?" Trudy asked. "Didn't you two go out last night?"

"You're not going to believe what happened today!" Ellen's voice hopscotched a couple of beats. "It was so romantic. Tony rode his motorcycle to work—I mean my work, not his. Anyway, he brought me a peach-colored rose. He held it above the partition to my office until I saw it. I don't know how long he had to wait, but he was so cute. I have no idea how he kept it from getting ruined on his motorcycle." She pointed to a bud vase bearing proof of her story. Trudy plopped onto the floral-print chaise longue in the corner of the feminine bedroom, which Ellen had decorated with a canopy bed and pink frilly curtains. "He had this tucked right in the middle of the flower." Ellen held her left hand in Trudy's face.

"Nice nails," Trudy teased.

"Trudy! The ring, silly. Look, it's a ring!"

"A ring!" Trudy squealed as she sprang up and gave her friend a hug. "I'm so happy for you. It's about time that bum proposed!"

"Isn't it amazing? After eleven years, I thought we'd never get married." Ellen pulled the diamond to herself, cradling it like a baby, then holding it at arm's length to admire it again. "I can't believe it. He's so perfect. How did I get so lucky?"

Ellen gazed in the mirror again. She fluffed her hair. "We're going out tonight to celebrate. You're the first one I've told. You will be my maid of honor, won't you?" She turned back to Trudy.

"Of course I will. I'm a pro at it. Have you set a date?" Trudy asked.

"We're thinking maybe Christmas. Won't that be beautiful? All that snow. We can decorate the church with mistletoe and holly, fresh greens and candles. I know it's only a month and a half away, but we've been dating for so long I don't want to waste another day, you know? I'm nabbing him while he's still willing. I've been planning this day since I was twelve. I think an ivory gown, simple with straight lines. Maybe a Vera Wang knockoff. There's a really pretty Catholic church outside of Heidelberg. I've always wanted to get married in a cute country church. They'd let us rent it, don't you think? Or maybe the Cathedral of St. Paul." Suddenly Trudy missed Bert. Ellen turned to her. "What's wrong? You don't look well."

"I'm okay," Trudy said, despite the pang in her heart. "This is a surprise, that's all. I'm happy for you. Really."

"All right, Trudy, out with it." Ellen placed a hand on her hip.

"No. It's nothing. Really."

"Out." Ellen leaned closer. "We've lived together long enough for me to know when you're bugged."

"I said I'm fine, and I am." Trudy smiled at her.

"You never open up about anything," Ellen complained.

"That's not true."

"Then tell." Ellen stamped an impatient foot.

Trudy moaned and blew a stray hair that floated into her face.

"It's just that . . . I'm going to miss you." Trudy shrugged. "I really am happy for you and the bum."

"I'm going to miss you, too." Ellen leaned in for another hug and patted Trudy's back. "I'm not moving to the moon, you know. We can still do things together after I'm married."

"I know," Trudy said. "You're right, but good roommates are hard to find."

"You'll find someone as wonderful as me, I'm sure."

"You don't know how hard it was to find you, do you? If you hadn't been arguing with Mr. Lee about the price of soy sauce, I might still be searching." They laughed at the memory. "There are a lot of kooks out there."

"Like I'm not a charter member of the kook club!" Ellen grinned, then placed finger to chin thoughtfully. "Maybe this is a good way to get Bert interested in marriage. He *is* cute. Let's see . . . Invite him to the wedding . . . let the mood carry him away . . ."

"Ellen, we've been going out for less than a month."

Trudy pictured the way his dishwater blond hair curled beneath his green seed cap, the twinkle in his blue eyes when he beheld her as if he saw something delightful in her that no one else could see, the way his brow would furrow in concentration when he played a bluegrass tune on his banjo. And there was something else, something intangible that drew her to this tall farm boy. Maybe it was his kindness, his sincerity. Bert was never false; he never played games the way most guys did. He was just . . . Bert. Her face warmed at the memory of their first kiss in the old German cemetery.

Ellen slugged Trudy in the arm. "Admit it. You wouldn't mind at all if the farmer proposed." Ellen smiled with those perfectly straight, perfectly white teeth. Trudy imagined her with a front tooth blacked out and smirked.

"Honestly, Ellen, what is it about people? Once they decide to get married they have to push everyone else into it too."

"We want everyone else to be as happy as we are."

"It took Tony *eleven years* to propose," Trudy said. "So cut me some slack."

"Not at your age!"

"Hey!" The phone rescued her.

Ellen hopped over to it and chirped in her high-pitched toddler voice that she reserved for the phone, "This is Ellen. I'm getting married. Oh hi, Mae." She held the phone out to Trudy.

"Hey, Trudes. What's this—Ellen's getting married?"

19

"Yeah. Tony the bum finally proposed." She smiled over at her roommate, who had returned to primping. Trudy took the phone into the living room, where she plopped onto one of the two overstuffed couches. She stretched her feet to the opposite end and sank into its cushy depths. "Ellen's so excited. She's got it planned for Christmas. You know how all that snow makes for great family travel."

"What's up? I know that tone—you sound bummed," Mae said.

The doorbell rang. Ellen bounced past Trudy to open the door for tall, dark, and handsome, then mouthed "bye-bye" and gave a little wave before quietly shutting the door behind her.

Trudy sighed. "Do you know how much I hate interviewing roommates? There was Judy with that awful case of tetanus. Then Organic Girl from Oregon, who wouldn't tolerate a single Ho Ho in the cupboards. And of course there was LouAnn, the army sergeant." Mae didn't respond. "After I found Ellen, I vowed never to go through that torture again, and now she's getting married."

"But that's wonderful."

"For her."

"C'mon, I doubt she's getting married just to bother you."

"I know, and I am happy for her." Trudy slumped back and twirled her long hair into a coil with her free hand.

"This isn't really about finding another roommate, is it, Trudes?" Mae said.

"What are you implying?" Trudy let the coil unwind as she sat up straighter.

"You're tired of watching all your friends get married."

"Of course I am!" Trudy said. "I'm thirty years old. Even my baby sister is married."

"Well, I know a guy who likes you a lot," Mae said.

"Go on."

"Honey, our farmer friend keeps dropping by the farm for no reason. And every time he asks how you are and if I've talked to you lately and when you might be visiting. And he gets this dopey grin on his face."

"Really?"

"He's a goner if you ask me."

"So you're saying I need to visit my sister? Or maybe I could move. You know, I'd like to be near you and Peter and all that fresh air."

"You're pulling my leg, right? You love St. Paul. You can't move on a whim."

"Why not? You moved. Why can't I?" Trudy turned on the couch and let her feet drop to the floor. "Good night, *Ellen's* getting married. We thought that would never happen, and I'm stuck holding another bouquet." Trudy stood and paced to the window that overlooked the city. "I'm tired of waiting around for Mr. Right or even Mr. Wrong. I don't even *know* what I'm waiting for! If Bert's the one, I need to lasso that dogie before he gets away."

"We're farmers, not cowboys!" Mae began laughing.

"What?" Trudy protested, but the laughter continued.

"Trudes," Mae said and took a moment to calm her

giggles. "I am behind you no matter what you do. Really. There's nothing I'd love more than to have my big sister down the road. You know that. So, whatever. Someone at Extension said there's a teaching position coming open at the school. I could find out more about it for you if you want."

"Mae, you're a gem. That would be great."

"Okay then." Mae took a deep breath. "Oh, I remembered why I called—I wanted to see if you'd like to come to the St. Paul Chamber Orchestra concert on Saturday. Free tickets. Virginia's coming too—it'll be a family event."

"Are Mom and Paul coming?" Trudy said.

"No," Mae said, "I'm not up to that yet. Don't get me wrong; I was glad they came to the baby's funeral, but it's hard for me to be around her. After all the hurtful things Mom said about Peter when we moved here . . . It still stings, you know?"

"Eventually you'll have to forgive her," Trudy said.

Mae didn't say anything, and Trudy immediately regretted her words.

"Hey, I'm sorry," Trudy said.

"It's okay. You're right," Mae said, but Trudy felt like a worm.

"No guilt from me, okay? You take things at your own speed and take care of yourself. I mean that."

"I know you do."

"Are you sure you're up to a family outing?"

"It'll be fun—really." Her voice returned to its former happiness, minus that spark. "Peter's grandma hasn't gone in ages. It's a good excuse for a get-together. So, what do you say?"

"I wish I could, but I have a date on Saturday."

"Say no more. I don't want to interfere with the roundup."

Trudy wandered into the kitchen after Mae had said her farewells. The dark evening had drawn its shades on the outside world. Trudy could see her rippled reflection in the aged window. She opened the cupboard door in search of a cup. The conversation with Mae played through her mind. She felt lonely, left behind, now that Ellen was leaving, and she missed her younger sister. She missed being part of Mae's life, especially after last summer together at their farm. She missed doing things together, nothing monumental: sipping iced tea on Mae's rambling farmhouse porch, weeding endlessly in Mae's massive garden. She wistfully remembered listening to the distant hum of traffic on Highway 36, the breeze rustling the corn in the fields, birds whistling and twittering from the telephone lines and the windbreak, horses in the neighbor's pasture, and Peter's cows bellowing for attention.

The thought of that silly calf of Mae's following them around like a puppy begging for a handout lifted the corners of Trudy's mouth. She even found herself thinking fondly of the smell of the cattle feedlot when the wind came from the east. Trudy turned on the tap and let the water run cold while she filled the glass with ice from the freezer. She took her glass to the Formica table. Condensation dribbled down its side.

Trudy frowned. She'd heard the pain in her sister's voice, and yet she'd handed out clichés like candy corn. Why had she gone and hurt Mae? She knew that Mae had been struggling since she'd put that tiny baby in the grave. Mae needed her to be her anchor, to be strong. Sure, Peter cared and was there for her, but Trudy couldn't betray the bond only sisters shared.

Maybe moving to Lake Emily would be just the thing.

two

The brown autumn landscape surrendered to noisy interstate. One car zoomed past the next on I-35E north to St. Paul, each vehicle competing to be first in line. A rusty Ford Mustang merged mere inches from Bert's front bumper. He rode the pickup's brakes to give himself room. He hated driving in the cities, but some things couldn't be avoided. Not if he wanted to see Trudy. He'd thought of her every time the pace of work on the farm had slowed since their date last weekend.

He'd never felt this way about anyone, not even Emma Kruger. Trudy brought such energy with her. She could light up the darkest cave with her laughter, her smile, her kisses. It was as if all oxygen were sucked from the room whenever she left.

Trudy'd been secretive about her plans for this evening. No doubt she'd planned something exotic and wild; she had a knack for that. Nervous excitement coursed through him. He ran a hand through his freshly cut dishwater blond hair and took a deep breath. He glanced at the bouquet of daisies beside him on the pickup's bench seat. *Sure hope she likes daisies.*

Finally Bert saw the building—a large, renovated Victorian house that had been divided into four apartments. He drove around the block trying to find a parking spot, then found one a block and a half away. He grabbed the flowers and climbed out of his pickup. Houses in a variety of styles lined the walkway—a Cape Cod with ivy vines now bare in the autumn frost; a white-and-green bungalow with Mission-style light fixtures; an English Tudor with a steep lawn, its many plants dormant, brown stalks bearing testimony to former abundance. It seemed more like Lake Emily than the middle of St. Paul. The wind had started blowing during his drive. November could be so fickle. Cold nipped at his nose. He hunched his shoulders and made his way through the leadedglass door of Trudy's building and into the foyer. He pushed the intercom button.

"Hello-o." Trudy's honeyed voice sounded distant through the speaker.

Bert pushed the button as he talked. "Uh, it's me. Bert." His palms were sweaty again.

"You're here! Come on up, second floor." The lock buzzed as Trudy activated the release for the interior doors. He opened them and then made his way up the stairs and down the brightly lit hallway. When he reached her door, Bert knocked tentatively. A moment later Trudy appeared in a pale green sweater. Bert's heart raced. Her carrot mane was pulled back in a loose ponytail. Curled tendrils caressed her freckled face.

"Hey," he said, handing her the bouquet of daisies.

"Hey, yourself." She gave him a peck on the cheek. "I love daisies, thank you!" Trudy took his hand and pulled him into the small apartment. Bert stood in the living room while she disappeared into the kitchen to find a vase for the flowers.

"I'm still getting ready. I won't be long, I promise. Make yourself at home," Trudy shouted as she disappeared into the bedroom in the back.

Bert wandered around and gazed at Trudy's artwork and knickknacks. One wall was covered with a congregation of black-and-white portraits—some of past presidents and celebrities, others of everyday people. One caught his eye—a heavyset woman with a scarf tied around her head sat at a counter beside a thin, weatherworn man. They seemed to have a story to tell. Both wore beaming smiles, his front tooth in silver. The couple reminded him of his grandparents—hearty people who understood the satisfaction of a good day's work, who knew how to laugh and enjoy each other's company without ever wanting for more. He wondered why Trudy had chosen the shot. Were they people she knew? There was so much about her he had yet to learn, so much mysterious territory still to chart. He often wondered how long it would take to fully know her, or if it was even possible, but he longed for that intimacy.

An eclectic group of paintings—both big and small, some modern, others more folksy in flavor—covered the rugged brick walls. An old upright piano with yellowed keys held an assortment of family pictures, including a toothless seven-year-old Trudy, her curly bright red hair making her easy to identify. That same spark was there, even way back then. Mae and Peter Morgan's wedding portrait in a silver frame sat next to it. Mae gazed down at a bouquet of long-stemmed yellow roses. Peter had a wide grin on his face as he stared into his bride's smiling face. They had become Bert's friends in the past months. No longer city folk come to fulfill some country fantasy, they had proved themselves ready for the long haul, neighbors of the best kind.

Above the piano hung a multicolored tapestry that appeared to have its origins in Asia somewhere. Bert wondered if Trudy had done some traveling to acquire such a piece. Another discovery to make. He meandered into the kitchen to get himself a drink of water. He opened a cupboard door to search for a glass. The cupboard held bottles of vitamins and basic "healthy" food—rice cakes, wheat germ, granola, whole-wheat bread. Bert opened the next cupboard and found juice glasses that looked to have been jam and jelly jars in a previous life.

Bert turned on the water and let it run cold. On the sill above the sink an assortment of fragile ceramic birds perched. Two clear cobalt bluebirds touched beaks. A jay clung upside down to a tiny water spigot as it tried to get a drink from its dripping spout. Bert's gaze was drawn to the cupboard doors, painted a pale aqua with purple accents, where a note read, "Don't wait for tomorrow—live today!" in Trudy's looping script. Bert smiled.

"Hey, I'm ready." Trudy's voice sounded over his shoulder. He faced her and immediately felt his pulse quicken.

"What do you think?" Trudy turned in a slow circle, showing off her Asian-style outfit in red silk with covered buttons in the same fabric. Her purse matched too, in the same red silk with gold medallions. Her hair was loose, a curly mane of red that brought out the faded red of the freckles sprinkled across her nose and cheeks.

"Wow." His face grew warm with the word.

"I think that's the nicest compliment I've ever had," Trudy said.

"Is this a hint about our date tonight?" he said. He drew her to himself in a tender embrace. His finger traced the curve of her cheek.

"I think you're going to like what I've planned," Trudy said. They moved toward the door and stopped at a tall hat rack studded with hooks. On it hung every imaginable style and color of purse. Trudy reached for a gigantic bag made of straw with "Mexico" embroidered on its front in bright pink with embroidered flowers accenting it in shades of green and blue and red. She rummaged through the monstrous bag, pulled out her wallet and keys, and slipped them into the smaller silk purse.

"The right purse for the right occasion, you know?" she explained. Then she put on a long black wool coat and a hand-knit scarf. She locked the door, and they left.

The cold November air chafed their cheeks as a blast scuttled a whirlwind of leaves along the downtown street. Bundled pedestrians edged along, backs hunched against the cold. Trudy grabbed Bert's hand, and they jogged to his truck.

"You found a spot pretty close," Trudy said as she scooted into the passenger seat and rubbed her hands together briskly. Bert got in, then turned the key in the ignition.

"Where to?" He raised a questioning brow.

"There's a great place on Larpenteur. Do you like sushi?" Her eyes sparkled.

"Never had it," Bert admitted as he pulled away from the curb. He'd heard things about sushi, nothing too favorable, but he didn't mind taking a chance. What was it about her? She could tell him they were going to the moon, and he'd happily drive her there.

"Then this'll be fun." Trudy slipped her arm inside the crook of Bert's elbow. "You taught me to milk cows at the fair, so now it's my turn to broaden *your* horizons. Take a right up here," Trudy instructed. "So." She tilted her head and inspected him. "You look great. I've missed you so much!"

Bert blushed and glanced down at his flannel plaid shirt and dark blue Levi's. "This restaurant isn't fancy, is it?"

"No. You're dressed fine. Did I tell you my room-mate Ellen is getting married in December? They've been dating eleven years, can you imagine? That is one slow-moving turtle! Oh." Trudy pointed at a strip mall. "It's right up here—Sumo Yoshi Sushi House." The sign above the hole in the wall had faded to pale shades of red and salmon so the words were hard to read. Bert parked and came around to get Trudy's door. She hopped down and settled her hand again in the crook of Bert's elbow. She smiled up at him sweetly and gave him a peck on the cheek. Bert felt as if he would burst. How had this happened? How had he won this mysterious woman's attention? Any moment now she would discover that he was just a simple farmer and leave him.

The restaurant was dimly lit and sparsely furnished. Bert and Trudy were met at the door by the hostess, a petite young Japanese woman in a flowered lavender kimono. She placed her hands together and dipped her head in a bow, then showed them to a low, long table surrounded by mats and said, "Can I get you somesing to drink?"

"Pepsi for me," Trudy said, looking to Bert.

"I'll take a Pepsi too," Bert said as he tried to figure out where they'd put the chairs.

"You sit on the floor," Trudy whispered. "Take your shoes off first." Bert obeyed hesitantly. He glanced at the hostess to see if she'd noticed the hole in his white sock. She smiled benignly. The girl handed them each a menu, then poured some water and left to retrieve their pops. Bert glanced around and realized they were the only ones in the place.

"Not real busy, is it? For a Saturday?" Bert said.

"No . . . but isn't this great?" Trudy leaned across the squat table toward Bert. Freestanding folding screens in Asian patterns gave the restaurant a private feel despite its strip-mall facade. Soft music played a foreign melody.

"Great." He repeated her word and gazed down at the menu. "Does 'seaweed' mean real seaweed?"

Trudy laughed. "Would you like me to order for you? I promise I'll be kind!"

"Sure," he said and smiled gratefully into her eyes.

The waitress returned with their drinks, and Trudy gazed down at the menu. "I think we'll share the sampler plate. Does that have octopus?"

The dark-eyed woman said, "Yes. Some octopus but is not cook. Okay?"

"Can we get it without the octopus?" Trudy said. Bert felt his stomach lurch at the thought of eating anything raw.

"Yes." The waitress bowed again and was gone.

"The sampler plate will give us a good taste of everything. I didn't want to freak you out with the octopus— the suction cups are really chewy. Do you like horseradish?"

"Yeah. I guess."

"The California rolls with sticky rice and seaweed are my favorite." Trudy stopped talking and peered into his eyes. "You doing okay?"

"I'm great," Bert lied.

"Mae invited me to one of Peter's dad's concerts, but I told her I'd rather be with you." Trudy reached for his hand and simply held it. "I worry about her."

"Mae?"

Trudy nodded. "Ever since the baby died, she's been so quiet. I know something's going on in there, but she's not talking. That's not like her. We talk about everything."

"You're good friends. Fred and I used to be, a long time ago, but we've grown apart through the years. I envy that about you two."

"Mae's my best friend." She squeezed his hand and sat back. "That's why I've been thinking about moving to Lake Emily."

"You're what?"

"With my roommate getting married I'm kind of in a housing crunch. There's no way I can handle rent alone. It's outrageous here. My half of the rent is seven hundred dollars!"

"You could buy a house in Lake Emily with a mortgage payment that was less than that," Bert said.

"Exactly," Trudy said. "And I could be nearby . . . for Mae, you know?" Bert wondered if Mae was the only reason. Embarrassed by his thought, he stared down at his plate. When he glanced up at her, her red hair haloed her smiling face.

The food arrived—a large platter of bite-size, unidentifiable foods bundled with rice and held together by something green. Bert wondered if that was the seaweed. The waitress then set two smaller plates down. Bert took Trudy's hand and said a brief prayer over the meal, then watched as Trudy added soy sauce to a tiny bowl of green sauce and mixed it. Then she reached for the chopsticks, removed them from their paper wrapper, and lifted a piece of sushi. She deftly dipped it into the mixture and placed it on her tongue.

Bert unwrapped his chopsticks, unsure what to do next.

"Have you ever used chopsticks before?" Trudy asked.

"No," he admitted.

"Hold the first one like this," Trudy instructed. She held it between her thumb and first two fingers. "And then slip this one into the crook of your thumb. Use your top fingers to get a good scissors action going." She took the chopsticks and dipped a piece of sushi into the sauce, then lifted it toward him. He leaned in and let her place it on his tongue. Their eyes held. He stared, wanting nothing more than to kiss her. Then he was aware of a tingling sensation in his mouth, followed by burning fumes coursing through his nasal passages, stinging his eyes until they watered.

Trudy smiled and said, "I forgot to warn you that it has a kick."

Bert held up his hands and wiped the tears that streaked his cheeks. "It cleared my sinuses."

"That's the horseradish."

Bert hiccuped, and he took a drink of pop.

Trudy laughed. "It really got you, didn't it? Try this." She handed him another chopstick's worth of food. He raised an eyebrow as he inspected it. "It's safe, honest," she said. "Crabmeat. Cooked too." He tasted and had to admit it wasn't too bad. "I knew this would be fun," Trudy said.

Bert smiled uncertainly.

"You hate it," Trudy said with no hint of being offended.

"Well," Bert began, "cooked fish would be my first choice, but the company makes it worthwhile."

Trudy grinned, then cleared her throat. "So. I was saying about moving . . ."

"You're really serious about this move to Lake Emily?" Bert's hope soared at the thought of having Trudy living so near.

"Once I make up my mind about something, it's pretty much set. Now all I need to do is find a teaching job. Teaching is one thing I won't give up."

"Why is that?"

Trudy ran a hand through her long hair and twisted a strand as she talked. "I feel like it's my 'calling,' you know? Like if I can really make a difference in the life of just one kid, then I'll have done my part. When I was a girl, I had a teacher named Mrs. Zernickel. She'd stay with me after school and show me all kinds of great art techniques. How to throw pots and do sculpture. She was a teacher who cared. She was the only person who told me I could draw. It was during a really hard time in my life." Her voice grew quiet, and she chewed her lower lip as though she wanted to say more.

"It's great that she was there when you needed someone," Bert prompted.

"Yeah." Trudy fell silent. She stirred the rice on her plate, her gaze a thousand miles away.

"Tell me about your parents' divorce," Bert said.

"Not much to tell. It was all unfair as far as I was concerned." Trudy took another bite of rice and fish, then lifted the corners of her mouth in a smile. "Dad left us when I was seven. We tried to move on." She lowered her gaze to her plate. "Mrs. Zernickel died a couple of years ago. Complications from her diabetes. She was a great person. I visited her as often as I could, but life gets busy. She was always so kind and wanted to see whatever art I had been working on between our visits. She kept one of my drawings framed in her living room." Trudy drew in a deep breath and nodded as she gazed off into the distance.

Bert leaned toward her. "There's more to you than you let most people see."

"Who, me?" She smiled coyly, the sassy spark back in her emerald eyes. "I don't know. What you see is pretty much what you get."

DAVID MORGAN

The big Greyhound bus was already half an hour late. David Morgan sat in silence next to his father, Roy, on the bench outside Miller's Texaco Station on Main Street with a jumble of mismatched luggage heaped beside them. The green awning shaded them from the hot September sun. Still, David's tweed suit coat was stifling. He wished he'd worn the blue linen. He was sure that tweed was out of style at Juilliard anyway. He lifted his hand and chewed on his thumbnail.

He glanced over at his dad. Roy twisted his seed cap in his hands as he sat bent at the waist, elbows on knees. The blue of his overalls matched his pale eyes set in a weathered face, sculpted by years of farm life. David wondered why he hadn't noticed those wrinkles before. His father seemed so old suddenly. "It's comin', Son," Roy reassured. David sighed. He wished his nerves would give him a break.

A station wagon pulled up to the pumps with the accompanying ding ding. Todd Miller came out of the office. He wiped his greasy hands on a rag as he neared the car. He tucked the rag into the back pocket of his dirty coveralls before he leaned over the driver's window. "Fill 'er up?" he asked. The elderly woman nodded.

"Did Mr. Miller say how late the bus would be?" David asked his father.

"Nope. Just that it was late."

"My first concert is in October; do you think you and Ma will be able to make it?"

"Already on the calendar," Roy said.

David twisted his gray felt hat.

"Nervous?" Roy asked, putting his cap back on.

"A little," David confessed. "You think Ma will be okay?"

"She'll be fine."

They watched the woman pay for the gas and pull out of the station. Mr. Miller gave them a nod and returned inside. Another station wagon passed on Main. It turned and disappeared up Ferry Street.

"Dad? Take care of Laura for me. I want to marry that girl, you know."

"We know." Roy grinned and patted his son's knee.

"It's going to be harder for you to bring in the harvest this year."

"I'll find a way." His gray eyes crinkled into a smile.

"I could wait to start school next semester, after the harvest."

"There's always something to hold folks back from their dreams," Roy said wistfully. "No. Now's your time. You can't let this dream get away from you."

David felt a surge of gratitude push back his anxiety.

"You have a gift, Son," Roy said. "It's a God-given gift. It wouldn't be right not to use it. There's always sacrifices—no matter what path in life we choose. You have a chance that few people get, so make us proud. We'll come visit soon. Your ma'd like to come next weekend."

The blue-and-white bus with yellow accents and a chrome grille came into view. The passenger compartment rose above the driver's seat like a cockpit on an airplane. Its brakes groaned as it stopped before them. Roy patted his son's back and reached for the luggage. The driver opened the door. He hefted his big frame down the narrow stairs.

"I guess this is it," David said. He stood.

"It's just the beginning, Son." A tear slipped down the older man's cheek, traveling through the crevasses of time. David couldn't remember ever seeing his father cry. His father turned away and carried suitcases to the driver, who placed them in the storage beneath the bus with the rest of the luggage.

"Looks like you're the only pickup in Lake Emily," the driver said to David in a scratchy voice. David handed the man his ticket, then faced his father. The sky was so blue behind him and the sun so bright he had to squint. David lifted a hand to shade his eyes.

37

"Say good-bye to Ma and Sarah," he said. Roy nodded, and the two embraced. "I'm going to miss you, Dad."

Roy patted his back and held him fiercely. Finally they pulled apart, and David boarded. He took a window seat and waved to his father. Even from here, David could see the trail of tears on his face. Then the bus pulled away.

three

The lights in St. Paul's Ordway Theater dimmed, and a hush fell over the audience. The maestro strode to center stage and gave a bow, and applause filled the hall as the burgundy curtain parted behind him to reveal the orchestra in black. The conductor tapped his baton, and the musicians set bows to string. A moment later Wagner's *Tannhäuser* Overture began with its paced yet grandiose sensibilities.

The performance was captivating. Peter Morgan stared at his father, David, whose body moved back and forth with the melody. He was so strong, so happy. Pride welled in Peter. Mae, Peter's wife, placed her hand on his arm. He absently patted it, but his gaze remained on his father, who was absorbed in the music. His face held that transcendent quality that was so familiar to Peter, as if the music were taking his father to a world of his own making. Peter watched the expressions there; he could have read the music's tenor from his father's face alone.

Peter traveled back through time as the masterpiece

flowed, back to a childhood filled with many orchestras and countless concerts. Familiarity warmed him, comforted him. This he found surprising.

Through his childhood he'd often resented the orchestra. It had represented unwanted change. Friends left behind. Never a place to call home. Moving from one city to the next. But that had all changed in these past months. Peter had found his place, with Mae at his side now, on his grandparents' farm, making their own way with the land. He'd found a heritage in Lake Emily, something bigger than himself to work toward, a hope to pass on to his own children. Yes, they'd had their setbacks. But they held firm to each other despite losing a baby only weeks ago, when that hope flickered and faltered like a candle's flame.

The orchestra began a second piece. David's eyes danced across the page as his fingers darted like sprites through a wood.

Peter considered his father's own struggles. He'd lost his beloved wife after fifteen years of marriage and then his father last year. But through each loss David had found a way to survive and even to thrive. His father's example buoyed Peter, inspired him to hang on to God in life's storms, though Peter knew the strength of his grip was determined one day at a time.

In the Irvine Park area of St. Paul, quiet whispers of diners in intimate conversation floated through Forepaugh's restaurant. The historic manor had been meticulously renovated to create a formal yet comfortable ambience. Long tapered candles cast playful shadows on white tablecloths as waiters in black glided from table to table. A fireplace along the wall radiated its crackling warmth into the chilly November evening.

"This is wonderful," Mae said as she took her seat. Peter pushed her chair in and then took the seat to her left. Virginia—Peter's grandmother—and David sat across from them.

"I don't know if I've ever had French cuisine before. David, you'll have to tell me what's good," Virginia said with a wink. She turned to place her napkin in her lap, then said, "The orchestra was enchanted tonight. It reminded me of that first concert at Juilliard." She grew thoughtful at the memory. "You were so nervous, remember?"

David placed a hand on top of his mother's. "Of course I remember. You and Dad drove all that way. I wanted to be certain everything was perfect!"

Their waiter arrived bearing menus and offering beverages before disappearing again. "What do you recommend, Dad?" Peter said as he studied the menu.

"The *Moules marinière* is excellent. If you like mussels. The *Caneton grillé à la sauce au miel* is my all-time favorite." He leaned toward his mother. "Roast duckling with honey, lime, and wild rice. I usually order that."

"Mmm, I love duck," Virginia said. She said to Mae, "We had duck every Sunday after church—I'd butcher one every Saturday. Remember that, David?"

"Of course I do. Why do you think I order it?"

"I think I'll take the duck too," Peter said, glancing

up at Mae, who was absorbed in the menu. He looked at his father.

David rubbed his thumb and then massaged his fingers before taking a drink of his ice water. "You okay, Dad?" Peter asked.

"Fine. A cramp is all. I've been practicing a lot lately."

"Well." Mae cleared her throat. "We have something special to celebrate tonight. As well as our anniversary and a wonderful performance, I mean." She turned toward her father-in-law with that amazing smile of hers. Deep dimples formed perfect parentheses in her cheeks. Her dark eyes were alight. She looked at Peter and said, "The harvest is in. We've done the books, and while we won't be getting rich anytime soon, the Morgan farm did make a profit." Her gaze moved to Virginia. "Peter and I want to buy the farm."

Peter felt as though his face would crack from the smile those words produced. He'd hoped for this moment all summer, and now it was finally a reality despite the obstacles.

"Oh, that's wonderful! I knew you could do it. Roy would be so proud," Virginia said. She placed a hand over her heart, and her eyes had a misty quality. "You've had a go of it this past year." She patted her grandson's hand. "I didn't always think you'd want to stay."

"It wasn't easy," Peter agreed. "But we love it. It's *home* for us." He smiled at his bride of one year. "I can't imagine living anywhere else."

Mae leaned her shoulder into her husband's and

said, "I was surprised because I love it too. I had to learn a few lessons about living in the country—like keep your hair out of the fly strip." She smiled. "But I also learned what family is really all about." She gazed meaningfully into Virginia's pale blue eyes. "I hope it's okay that I think of you as my grandma."

Virginia patted her hand. "Of course, dear. With Sarah and her girls so far away in California, I need another granddaughter."

"This *is* cause for celebration," David said, clapping his hands together. "Too bad my violin's in the car!"

"No, Dad," Peter said. "Don't make me relive my childhood!"

David laughed. "Maybe I could play for tips."

"This is celebration enough," Mae said. "Being with all of you here."

The waiter returned to take their orders. Peter changed the subject when the waiter left. "You know, now that the harvest is in and I'm back to milking twice a day, I feel as though I need more to do."

"You got used to those twenty-hour days," Virginia said. "Don't worry, you'll get the rhythm soon enough! I always loved November because Roy and I had time for coffee and such. We'd go out to eat at the Chuckwagon in the middle of the afternoon some days. Oh, my! It was a honeymoon every year."

"We're enjoying it too," Peter said with a sly smile toward Mae. "But I'm thinking I should find a part-time job between milkings. We still have medical bills to pay . . ." He thought to say, *from losing the baby,* but decided it would be better to leave that unsaid. He wondered how long he would be leaving things unsaid. Mae never wanted to talk about the loss, and yet it was always there, between them, weeks of accumulated unsaid thoughts.

"You'll have a time finding a job flexible enough to accommodate your milking schedule, especially with all the things that forever seem to come up," David said, pulling Peter back into the conversation.

"I could deliver papers, sell insurance, drive a school bus."

"Driving school bus wouldn't really work with milking," Virginia said. "But most farmers take on extra jobs to make ends meet. Roy used to sell honey, and of course I had my eggs. Lew Olsen drove truck for the pea and sweet corn pack."

"But delivering papers won't pay the medical bills," Mae said, meeting him in the eye.

"No," Peter said.

"That reminds me—the county called this afternoon," Mae said. "There's an opening for a receptionist at the courthouse. Remember I put an application in when we first moved?"

"You want to go back to work?" Peter asked.

"It's a thought. Like you said, we could use the money. It'd be easier for me than for you to get away from the farm. It's a government job, so it has full benefits—medical, dental, all that. Maybe even a pension plan. But it's full-time. That could put you in a bind when planting time comes."

Peter glanced over at his father and grandmother. "I guess we forgot you were all here," he said.

David waved the comment aside. "Don't worry about it. You know, a lot of farm wives work outside jobs these days."

"We can talk about it later," Mae said. Peter wondered if they would or if this topic would go in the basement of their marriage with all the other unsaid things.

four

Trudy couldn't remember when she'd had a nicer evening. She stood before the mirror in her bathroom, staring absently at her face as she applied cold cream to her cheeks and nose. Her hair was tied up, and loose red curls fell in stray strands.

What was it about Bert? When his eyes met hers, he didn't see the outward her, he saw *her*. And he still liked her. She couldn't remember any man accepting her that way. Especially not her father. The aged pain returned.

Bert's words resonated. *There's more to you than you let people see.*

She knew what he said was true, and yet it was almost impossible to let another person see her inner secrets. She didn't like to peer into that closet herself. There was too much pain hiding in there, too many old stories that led to tears. And what good did that do? She'd gone to support groups for children of divorce, to Emotions Anonymous. All she'd done there was wallow. For months on end she rehearsed the same story only to confirm she couldn't *do* anything about it. So she moved past it and lived. That was an accomplishment she was proud of—she wasn't going to let her father's desertion ruin a perfectly good life.

She twisted the cap back on the jar and turned out the bathroom light. Ellen was sound asleep in the other room. The only light that shone was the one in the hall closet. Trudy went to turn it off and caught sight of the cloth-covered box on the top shelf. Dad's letters.

She pulled the box down and inhaled its woodsy scent. The smell of pipe smoke lingered after all these years. Trudy ran a hand lightly across the lid and took the letters into her bedroom. She sat on the bed and reverently opened the time capsule—filled with memories from twenty-some years, all from her father. She wondered again why he had written to her but never to Mae. Was it because Mae was so little? Or didn't he care about Mae? If he didn't, what kind of person did that make him? It would hurt Mae if she ever found out about the letters. Trudy had never told anyone, sharing her secret only with the mailbox, always checking the mail first thing when she got home while her mother was still at work. Always hoping for a word, hoping for much more than a letter, hoping for a sign that he loved her and Mae. Oh, her father said he loved them, but even as a child Trudy knew words came cheap. She wanted proof. She needed him to come back home. But he never did. He just sent letters, full of words, hollow promises.

She opened the first letter. "To my daughter . . ." The words pulled at her. Tears trickled down her cheeks. "I wish I didn't have to write these words. I wish I could be with you, holding you as a daddy should hold his daughter, but sometimes there are things that make that impossible. If I could make things different, I would. I'm sorry about that. How many times have I told you that? But I am truly sorry. Your mother and I can't work things out. I always tried hard to make things work for your sake and for Mae's, but sometimes things are hard to explain. Someday, when you're older, you'll understand. Love, Daddy."

"Sure, Dad," Trudy whispered bitterly. "I get it now."

How many special moments in her life had he missed? It wasn't just the big things—her first prom, graduation, or leaving for college—it was the everyday stuff of life he'd missed. When she had a bad day at school or went on her first date or had her heart broken; when she got braces, pimples; when she came home to an empty house because her mother was working. He'd missed it all, and all he had to say was that he was sorry.

She gingerly slipped the letter back into its envelope, rubber banding it together with the others, and placed it in the box. "Enough of that," she said. She lifted her wet face to the ceiling and drew in a deep cleansing breath. "At least you were there," she whispered to God.

The letters had stopped when Trudy was fourteen. She wondered where he was now. If he was even still alive. She wiped at her cheeks and quickly pushed the box under the bed until the next time she needed someone to be her daddy.

five

T he porch light cast an amber hue on the back of the square brick farmhouse, flakes of new winter snow igniting under its touch. Midnight had come and gone. Peter turned off the car and sat for a moment as the November winds whistled. Even in the cold it was good to be home. And it *was* home. No longer his grandparents' place, but his. He wondered often if his prize would remain as satisfying now that he'd won it. Life here had certainly been good enough for Grandpa Roy. Then again, he was a much different person than his grandfather. What if he had inherited a part of his father's wandering spirit?

He looked over at Mae. Her head was turned to the side on the headrest where she slept. She was so beautiful, his bride of one year. She was more than beautiful; she was a gentle, tender companion. His best friend. She'd given her all to make his dream a reality, and it had cost them dearly. He scolded himself. He knew it was wrong to blame himself for losing the baby, but still he did. Mae wouldn't be so sad now if he'd paid closer attention then to how hard she'd been working, or if they'd stayed in St. Paul . . . Peter brushed her cheek with his fingertip.

"Hey, sleepyhead," he whispered. Mae opened drooping eyes. "We're home."

"Mmm." She stretched her back and slowly reached for her purse between the seats. "It was a nice night," she said.

They entered the kitchen and flicked on the light. Peter hung the keys on the hook by the doorway. It was a bright, cheerful room with white cupboards and an old porcelain sink. Open shelves held a collection of Yellow-ware bowls and ceramic chickens.

Mae unclipped her long hair, and it fell around her shoulders in a cascade. "That feels better," she said, running her fingers through it.

"Are you headed up to bed?" Peter asked.

Mae stretched. "I might be getting my second wind after that nap."

"I'll put on some water for hot chocolate," Peter volunteered.

"Sounds good." Mae slid into the built-in seat in the cozy breakfast nook. "I think your dad was proud to have us there. Did you see the way he was grinning at you? There was something magical about tonight, wasn't there?"

"There was," Peter said. He mused a moment before going on. "Do you ever look at someone and suddenly see them differently? Like you're seeing them for the first time?"

"Maybe. What do you mean?"

"I never thought about what Dad went through. I mean, I thought about it, but I never realized how much strength it took for him to go on after my mom died. I guess I was always thinking about what I was going through—that's sad to say, isn't it? I can't even begin to imagine what it would be like for me to lose you."

Mae was silent. Peter knew she was remembering

their own loss. He waited patiently.

Finally she said, "They really loved each other."

"He still wears his wedding band," Peter said.

Mae twisted her own wedding band around her finger and gazed into Peter's eyes. "Will you wear your wedding band twenty years after I die?"

"Always."

The kettle whistled its shrill call, and Mae got up to fix the hot chocolate. "Why didn't you mention the job at the county before?" Peter said as Mae stirred hot chocolate.

"Oh." Mae hesitated. "I guess I'd forgotten about it. I'd kind of given up on job hunting."

She brought the steaming mugs over and slid into the other side of the booth.

"Do you want to interview?" Peter watched her eyes.

She ran an index finger along the rim of her mug. "I guess." She lifted the cup and blew gently across the surface. "We could use the money."

"It would be hard here in the spring without your help."

"I know. Right now I can't see any solution to that. But it's the only thing that's opened up. I could take it until something part-time comes along or until you need me here again. We have all those doctor bills."

Peter lifted her hand from the table and kissed it. "You do whatever you think is best. Medical bills or not. God has taken care of us so far." Tears shimmered in Mae's eyes. Peter gazed longingly at her and didn't let go of her hand. "We need to talk about things," Peter said.

"We have talked, Peter. There's nothing more to say." Mae's eyes met his. She was so fragile. "I don't want to keep rehashing the past, Peter, and I don't want any more sympathy. I'm tired of it. I don't want people telling us we should have another baby. I want to heal."

Peter ran his hand along her cheek. "Okay," he said. He felt inept and guilty all at once.

"We're still newlyweds." Mae went on, "We need to be *us* for a while, you know?"

"I like being married to you, Mae Morgan. That's enough for now."

six

The fields alongside Highway 36 were bejeweled in glimmering white snow. Trudy checked her makeup in the rearview mirror for the dozenth time, hoping she wasn't too late, then glanced at her watch. She wondered what Bert had planned for the evening. After their sushi attempt, it was Bert's turn to plan their date. Bert had been so secretive that she didn't know how to dress. After endless outfits, she'd settled on a white cotton poet's shirt with drooping sleeves and slim-fitting jeans that flared below the knees. Platform clogs rounded out the ensemble.

Trudy pulled into the Biddles' long gravel driveway. Bert stood waiting, a single yellow rose in his hands. Trudy waved and stopped her car. Bert smiled, revealing that deep dimple in his cheeks.

"You look gorgeous," he said, climbing into the passenger seat. "Would you rather we took my truck?" He pointed a thumb over his shoulder.

"No. I can drive; show me the way."

"Oh, I almost forgot." He handed her the rose.

"Whah, thank you, Mr. Biddle," Trudy said in a soft drawl. She took the flower from him, smelled it, and gave him a peck on the cheek.

"I hope I'm not underdressed," Trudy said, pointing at her outfit.

"You're fine."

"So, Mr. Mysterious, where are we going?"

"Head toward Lake Emily."

"Where? The Chuckwagon? The bowling alley?"

"Uh . . . no. High-school hockey game. Lake Emily is playing Blue Earth at the indoor rink."

"Oh?" Trudy said. "I've never been to a hockey game before . . ."

"If you don't want to—"

"No. It sounds like fun. I want to go. It'll be a cultural experience. I hope I brought the right purse for hockey!" she joked.

"High-sticking!" the overweight man next to Trudy shouted as the buzzer blared. He had stained yellow teeth and a bulge in his lower lip and a Minnesota Wild jacket. He sat a little too close to Trudy on the bench. His breath smelled of cigarette smoke. Trudy scooted closer to Bert.

The Lake Emily hockey rink was an indoor skating oval with white boards and stands of bleachers on

51

opposite sides. Some boards carried painted advertisements; Ott's Drugstore, Clusiau's Clothiers, the Farmers' Elevator, and State Farm Insurance were among the most prominent.

A heavyset woman behind Trudy shouted, "Let's go, Bulldogs!" and clapped her hands furiously. Trudy hadn't known hockey could be so loud. Either everyone was shouting at the players, or buzzers were blaring in her ears. She had to sit on her hands to keep them warm; otherwise she would have covered her ears.

The team in white had the puck—she figured maybe that was the Lake Emily team. She strained her eyes to see where the disk was. No. The team in blue had it. A flash of white and blue skated past again.

One bruiser with a big 52 on his back slapped the puck toward the crouched guy who was wearing some sort of Halloween mask. Trudy glanced at Bert. His gaze was locked on the game, and a smile crinkled the weathered corners of his eyes.

With a loud crash 52 slammed a blue-clad player into the sideboards, his hockey stick pressing into the other boy's helmet. Trudy gasped and grabbed Bert's arm. Then the two boys started throwing punches. Within seconds a pile of players were swinging at one another, and officials blew whistles like playground monitors. The crowd was on their feet, shouting at the miscreants. Trudy wondered if all these parents were supportive of their children's violent actions.

She tugged Bert back down to the bench. "What now?" she whispered to Bert.

"Fifty-two will get a penalty, no doubt."

Trudy watched as the pile dispersed and number 52 skated to an enclosed box along the side of the rink.

"He gets a time-out? He tried to hurt somebody, and all he gets is a time-out?" she said too loudly. Bert nodded. "He could have put that kid in the hospital!"

The man beside Trudy glared at her. Trudy sat up straight and returned his defiant expression.

By the time the final buzzer sounded, signaling Lake Emily's defeat, Trudy felt completely drained. She couldn't remember ever witnessing anything so violent. And it seemed pointless to watch a little black disk slide back and forth on the ice. Half the time she had no idea where it had gone. A big man with black wavy hair graying at the temples picked his way through the crowd toward them. Bert waved to him and said to Trudy, "There's someone I want you to meet."

The man, who appeared to be about the same age as David Morgan, seemed even larger up close. He had a deep dimple in his chin that he could've hid peanuts in. Trudy had noticed him with the players during the game.

"Bert Biddle!" his voice boomed. He extended a thick hand to Bert. They shook. "Best goalie to come through Lake Emily," he said to Trudy. Bert turned red.

"Glen Miller," Bert said, "this is Trudy Ploog . . . my . . . uh . . . girlfriend." Trudy's insides warmed as she smiled at Bert's sudden fit of embarrassment. "Glen is the high school athletic director."

"Nice to meet you," she said, offering her hand.

"Did you know that Bert was state MVP in 1981?"

"No, I didn't know that." Trudy glanced at Bert, wondering what MVP meant and what other secrets she didn't know about him.

"We did awful tonight," Glen said to Bert. "These boys have no discipline. You know, Bert, I could use an assistant coach, someone who knows how it should be, someone to inspire them." He patted Bert on the shoulder. "What do you think?" Bert glowed in the praise.

"Well . . . ," Bert began. "It's kind of hard with my milking schedule."

"School's out at three. What time do you start your evening milking?"

"Six, six thirty."

"That'd be perfect." Glen glanced over at Trudy. "We're done with practices by five or five thirty and have one or two games a week, usually around seven. You wouldn't have to come to the away games." Trudy hadn't seen anyone this persuasive since . . . herself!

"I guess Fred could cover for me once in a while," Bert said.

"So it's a deal?" The coach grinned.

"It's a deal."

Bert smiled at Trudy, and she lifted her eyebrows in surprise, not sure whether to congratulate him or question his sanity.

August Cleworth sat on the end of the rumpled bed and stared at the dresser. Nothing was real. He breathed in and out, in and out. His tears had dried, leaving only a dull hollow. He could still smell her scent on her pillow—his Willa. His wife of fifty-two years. He lifted his eyes to the ceiling and said a prayer for comfort, but the hollow remained.

He placed his hands on his thighs, stood, and moved to the closet. The funeral director had said to bring her clothes to the funeral home when he came at eleven. He opened the door and stared. Her scent was there too, in the clothes she would never wear again. They waited for her, poised, perfectly pressed, arranged by color, skirts together, slacks with crisp creases, dresses on padded hangers. He touched her white silk blouse with the pleats down the front, the one she'd worn to church last Sunday.

"Willa," he whispered, "I don't know what I'm going to do without you. I don't know if I can do this." The phone rang, and he reluctantly answered it.

"Hello," he said.

"Dad, it's Maggie," his daughter-in-law said. "Did I wake you?"

"No. I'm up."

"Would it be okay if I come over?"

He glanced around at the small apartment. Willa never would've let it get this messy. "The place is a wreck."

"I thought we could pick out Mom's clothes, maybe have breakfast."

August felt his tears returning. "Some company would be nice," he conceded.

When Maggie arrived at his door, she looked as tired as August felt, but she still had a smile for him. Always a smile from that girl his son had married. She leaned to give him a hug around the six-month-old baby boy in her arms.

"I brought Ben to cheer us up," she said. She came inside and surveyed the disheveled apartment. "It's not so bad in here," she said. "Just needs picking up." She placed a hand of comfort on her father-in-law's arm. "You sleep okay?"

August shrugged. "Kind of hard to sleep."

"Why don't you sit down in the recliner while I tidy up? Can you hold Ben for me?"

He obeyed, and Maggie handed over his grandson. The baby shifted. His tiny lips made a sucking motion as he slept. August pictured Willa holding Ben in this chair just last week.

Maggie moved around the place like an angel, doing dishes that had piled up in the sink, making his bed, throwing a load of darks into the washer, sweeping the floor. August watched her work and felt the warmth of his grandson's body through the blanket of sadness. He had much to be grateful for, he realized, still so much to be grateful for.

Maggie disappeared into the bedroom for a while. When she came out she had Willa's white silk blouse and pink skirt on hangers, and some jewelry and makeup. *"I thought this would be a good outfit, or did Mom have a preference?"*

"No, no preference," August said.

Maggie pulled out the locket that bore Willa's mother's initials and a pair of pearl earrings. "I thought these would be good too. She always wore them."

"They're perfect," August said. Ben shifted, and August gazed lovingly at him. Wide, dark eyes stared up at him. *"Hey, sailor,"* August said through renewed tears. Ben smiled and answered with a coo.

"He's lucky to have you for a grandpa," Maggie said.

"No. I'm the lucky one."

seven

Mae waited in the wide marble hallway of the county courthouse. Hundred-year-old light fixtures and white tin panels decorated the massive building's high ceilings. Mae ran her hands through her sleek, dark hair, smoothing it back yet again. Her stomach churned. She hadn't had a job interview in ages.

A woman with a full skirt and frosty blue silk blouse gave her a polite smile. "Are you still waiting for Mr. Cleworth?" she asked.

Mae nodded, afraid her voice would crack if she spoke. The woman looked toward the closed door, then disappeared into a maze of five-foot-high tan cubicles.

Mae stared at the second hand on her watch to be certain it was working. She blew out her cheeks.

Was she doing the right thing getting a job? She wasn't sure of much these days. She'd spent the past month wondering what to do, often sitting in the now-empty nursery, weeping as she buried her face in the baby blanket Minnie Wilkes had made for Laura. She'd seen the concerned expression on Peter's face, the worry in his brow, the too-kind tone he used with her as if he were afraid she'd shatter. At least now she was doing something, anything. It felt good. And she was helping with a real need—paying the medical bills that had piled high and put a strain on the farm's resources.

The door beside her opened, and a stoop-shouldered, gray-haired man stepped out with a balding fortyish man. The two shook hands and said farewell, then the gray-haired man turned to Mae. "I'm August Cleworth. You must be my three o'clock. Have you been waiting long?"

"I'm Mae Morgan, and, no, I haven't been waiting long," Mae fudged.

He offered his hand, then pointed her to a wooden chair in his office. The dark, heavy woodwork and elaborate plaster moldings contradicted the contemporary, functional furniture. Mae smoothed her black slim-fitting skirt as she perched on the chair's edge. Mr. Cleworth took his seat behind the massive maple desk. His pale eyes twinkled as he gazed down at her résumé.

"So. You have a music degree?" He lifted his head.

"Yes. I play the cello." She wished the nerves in her stomach would settle. She folded her hands together and crossed her ankles. "You probably don't have a whole lot of call for that."

August Cleworth had an easy smile. Mae found herself liking him almost at once. "Do you have any experience as a receptionist or secretary?" He turned the page and adjusted his glasses.

"Not exactly," Mae said. "I like to help people. My last job was at a flower shop in St. Paul. I waited on people, made bouquets, took orders, that kind of thing. I'm a quick learner and a hard worker. I graduated magna cum laude—"

"I saw that," he interrupted, leaning back in his chair. "So, what brings an intelligent, educated woman from St. Paul down to Le Sueur County?"

"That's a long story." She laughed. "My husband took over the family farm."

"Really? What place?"

"Roy and Virginia Morgan's."

"Yes, I know it. Good for you. Do you like farming?"

"Sometimes. It's a lot of work, but it grows on you."

August nodded. "And what made you decide to apply for this job?"

Mae thought of the multitude of reasons and finally decided on the easiest. "Frankly, we could use the income. There aren't a lot of jobs to be had. Something steady would help, especially with benefits. And I like the social element of being a receptionist, being around people."

Mr. Cleworth smiled encouragingly. "The woman you'd be replacing had a baby. She couldn't keep up her responsibilities once he was born. He'd be sick, or the sitter would cancel. She did her job well, mind you. I liked her a lot, and I certainly understand the problems of being a single mom . . . but, well, you know how those things go."

Mae put on a smile and hoped the jab his words sent to her heart didn't show in her eyes. "We don't have any kids," Mae said. "We've only been married a year, so it'd be quite a while before you'd have to worry about that." Mae winced, sure she had shared too much.

"I wouldn't say it's something I fret over. Just the course of life. I have a grandson of my own, and I know how precious those little ones are." He smiled and settled back in his chair. He reached into a desk drawer and withdrew a manila folder. "I'll tell you, Mae. You're the best candidate to come through that door. I like your openness and your willingness to learn, and I know that the Morgans are solid folk. I'd like to offer you the job. It doesn't pay much to start, but it does come with benefits, the usual package— 401(k), health, dental, life insurance. Vacation time won't accrue until after six months. It's all laid out for you here." He slid the folder across the desk to Mae. "You can have some time to think about it if you'd like."

She swallowed and lifted her eyes to his. There was that twinkle again. For a moment she wondered if he knew about the baby and was acting out of sympathy.

But just as quickly a joy bubbled up in her that she hadn't felt in weeks.

"Thank you," she said. "But I'll take it now. When do I start?"

"Next Monday, eight o'clock?"

"I'll be here."

A pile of shoes lay like pick-up-sticks on the floor of Mae's bedroom. She stared at them, trying to decide which pair to wear. She'd wanted to get out the door by 7:40 so she could make a good impression on her first day, but everything was conspiring against her. First the water pressure in the shower had been torturously low. Peter must've been filling the cows' water tank. Mae stared at the showerhead, praying that it wouldn't stop altogether. Finally it worked its way up to a stream. Mae squeezed the shampoo out of her hair and impatiently rinsed off. And now the choice of what to wear.

In the end she chose a simple green skirt with straight lines and a classic white blouse, which she topped with amber-and-silver jewelry. She glanced at the clock alongside the bed—7:42. "Dratted water pressure," she said. She popped back in the bathroom and quickly blow-dried her hair, brushed her teeth, and added the finishing touches to her makeup. She scrambled down the stairs as the scent of frying bacon wafted up.

Peter stood before the stove humming "How Deep Is Your Love?" along with the Bee Gees on the radio. When he turned, Mae noticed that he was wearing one of her yellow gingham aprons. He held a pancake turner in his hand.

"What smells so good?" Mae said.

"Hey," he said. "I thought I'd make breakfast for your first day."

"That's so sweet!" Mae checked her watch—7:45. "I've gotta go. I'll make it up to you, but I need to run if I'm going to get to the office a few minutes early. Why aren't you milking?" Peter shrugged. She hurried to put on her coat and scarf, then looked outside the back door's window. A thick crust of snow had fallen during the night. "Rats, it snowed! Do I have a scraper in the Jeep?"

"I already scraped the windshield and warmed up the Jeep for you."

"Oh, you're an angel!" She leaned to kiss his cheek. "Thank you. I owe you big." She looked toward the set table with its steaming platter of eggs and pancakes and stuck out her bottom lip in true contrition, then picked up her purse and hurried out the door.

Peter followed and watched as Mae got into the Jeep. Snow sprayed up behind the car, then she was gone. He lifted a defeated hand in a last good-bye.

"Bye," Peter mumbled to no one.

Without Mae at home, he felt out of sync. He finished his huge breakfast alone, washed dishes by hand, and let them dry in the drainer.

His thoughts turned to what his grandmother had said about afternoons at the diner with grandpa once the harvest was in. Suddenly he felt gypped. It would've been nice to have that luxury with Mae. This was the time of year they'd worked so hard for, the time when they could be together.

This train of thought would only lead to discontent, Peter knew. He needed to forget about how he felt and give Mae her space. Wasn't that what loving husbands did?

He meandered to the living room and flicked on the television. It blared mindlessly. He flicked the set off and wandered through the house, not sure what he was hoping to find. When he got to their bedroom, he saw that the bed remained in rumpled disarray. He stripped the sheets and blankets and glanced around. The curtains seemed dingy too, so he took them off the rods and brought everything down to the laundry room in the basement.

He picked up the detergent and read the instructions on the back of the Sam's Club bottle. He had done laundry all the time when he was single, but he couldn't remember if sheets were washed in cold or hot water. The directions said cold for colors. There were certainly plenty of colors in the floral sheets, but then it said hot water for whites, and the sheets had a white background. He gave his head a scratch.

After some consideration, he decided warm would be a good compromise. He put the sheets and curtains in the washer along with a few other whites that had come down the laundry chute. That done, he returned to the living room.

Welcoming sunlight streamed through the lace curtains. He sat in the warmth and gazed through the opening at the fallow fields surrounding their farm. The sky was a crisp, pale blue with wispy clouds streaked along the horizon like distant crop rows. The galvanized shed roof of the Huber farm in the next section glimmered in the morning light. Peter listened to the hum of the refrigerator in the kitchen.

He sighed and looked at the magazines displayed like a fan on the coffee table—*Country Home*, *Knitting*, and an assortment of other women's fare.

Two hours had passed already. He had to get out of the house. He put on his black canvas chore coat and ventured into the brisk November air. His breath came out in puffs. Scout, his yellow Lab, bounded over. His pink tongue drooped from the side of his mouth, and he pushed his head into Peter's leg. Peter reached down and gave him a scratch.

"It's you and me, boy," Peter said.

The dog smiled up and licked his hand.

Cows lay in the barn like overturned boats, their huge bellies to the side. The ladies chewed their cuds and studied Peter curiously. A couple lifted their rumps to stand and then ambled to the big, round feeder in the center of the open area of the barn where bales of hay were piled high. Peter watched them for a few minutes, then went into the milking parlor.

He grabbed a large scoop shovel and pushed aside manure that had accumulated, then squeegeed the remainder away. He sprayed the floors and wiped the equipment with disinfectant. The cold wetness bit into his hands. He woke the old green Oliver tractor out in the Quonset hut where it hibernated and brought bales of straw into the barn in the Oliver's bucket. He laid a new layer of the bedding, which would grow to be a couple of feet deep in the winter. The thick pack provided warmth in the coldest of months. On it the cows would calve and rest until spring was roused from its slumber.

The cows, stirred by all the activity, seemed grateful for the fresh linens and meandered around seeking the perfect spot to recline. Some girls stood in the sunny doorway, their faces soaking up the warming rays like teenage lifeguards on a summer day.

By the time lunch rolled around, Peter felt like himself again, his self-esteem bolstered by the hard physical labor. Ed Smee, the driver for the Lake Co-op Dairy, pulled up in the long silver truck to collect the last two days' milk. At the purge of the truck's air brakes, Peter stepped outside to meet him. The stout man with a barrel chest climbed down from the truck's cab and joined Peter at the door to the parlor.

"Hey, Ed," Peter said.

Ed looked around the parlor as he crossed to the large silver tank that stored the milk between pickups. "Looks like you've been busy."

"Mae took a job in Le Center, so I had some extra time on my hands," Peter explained.

Ed nodded, then performed his ritual—testing the milk, then pumping it into his truck. "Heard mention that you decided to buy the place from Virginia permanent," Ed said, standing back at an angle to Peter, his arms folded across his chest.

"Yep. It's all ours, or the bank's for the next thirty

years," Peter said.

"H'm," Ed said. He nodded his bald head.

Peter didn't know what to say after that. Truth was, he didn't know a thing about Ed Smee, other than that he picked up the milk every other day. Peter glanced at him, suddenly self-conscious. Ed seemed content to stand with Peter and stare into the distance silently. Peter crossed his own arms. The pump and idling diesel engine of the milk truck filled the silence.

"Well, congratulations on getting the farm and all," the man said when he'd finished emptying Peter's tank. He tipped his gray cap with "Lake Co-op" stitched in red. "See you day after tomorrow."

Peter nodded. Ed climbed into the tall cab, backed the truck up, and pulled around the loop of driveway and left. Peter stood watching it rumble along the snow-packed road.

"Yep. Congratulations to me," he said.

When Mae pulled her Jeep into the driveway after four thirty, Peter was in the barn getting set up to milk. Dusk eased its will onto the landscape like a thick fog. Through one of the four-paned side windows, Peter saw her climb out and walk toward the house. Mae pulled her knit scarf tight against her cheeks as she climbed the steps to the back porch. Even in her thick winter coat she was lithe, sleek, beautiful. His earlier frustration dissipated.

"Hey, working girl," Peter called as he swung open the barn door, "how was your first day?"

Mae turned and waved, then came to meet him in

the small room that held the milk tank. She gave him a cold-lipped peck on the cheek.

"I'm exhausted," she said. "And all I did was watch another girl answer the phone and direct people to the right office. How am I going to do it? There is so much to learn."

"You'll get used to it."

Mae sighed and smiled a contented smile. "Everyone was so kind. I think it's gonna be a good fit. How was your day?" She gazed around at the sparkling barn. Eight cows stood waiting in their stanchions, the headstalls locked tight against their thick necks. They strained their curious big brown eyes to see Mae. The pumps filled the room with their steady noise.

"I missed you," he confessed. "Kind of dull without you around."

"You'll get used to it."

Peter laughed. "I'm not sure I want to get used to it. Hey, those curtains in our bedroom are washable, aren't they?"

"I think so."

"Well, they were dirty, so I went ahead and washed them when I washed the sheets."

"You're kidding me."

"I didn't have anything else to do."

"Oh, honey. That was so considerate of you." Peter shrugged; he hadn't done it to be considerate. Mae glanced toward the house. "I suppose I better go make us some supper. We'll be eating even later now that I'm working."

"I made Spanish rice and chicken before I came out to milk."

"Mr. Morgan,"—Mae lifted a dark brow—"if you're trying to romance me, it's working."

"Aw shucks, ma'am."

eight

T he weather was a fickle girl. The next week she couldn't make up her mind if she should bring on winter's blankets of snow or change the sheets and let fall slip back under the covers. One day temperatures were frigid with icy winds that bit cheeks and fingers; the next the snow was melting and the mercury soaring to forty-two.

Trudy ducked her head to look through the bottom of her AMC Pacer's windshield. The wipers had left a streak of grayish snow on the upper half, and with each swipe of the blades the mess only got worse. Trudy slowed as she turned onto the dirt road to the Biddle farm. She rolled down the window, then as the wiper reached the apex of its arc, she grabbed it and gave it a quick snap, trying to dislodge the ice that clung to it. Instead of fixing the problem, she had flipped the wiper outward and up so it flailed like the dislocated arm of a dairy princess flopping back and forth in a parade.

The cold breeze gusted into the car, and Trudy pulled her arm in and blew on her fingers to warm them. "Brr." She rolled the window back up and let the wiper flop. Today she wouldn't let anything ruin her mood.

Trudy pulled into the long circular driveway and killed the motor. The old car sputtered and finally died. She loved this car. It had seen her through her twenties and into her thirties, a trip to Yellowstone, through a dozen boyfriends and as many breakups. She got out and glanced at the scenes painted across its lime green surface. There was Mickey's Dining Car in St. Paul, the Metrodome, Foshay Tower, and of course Mae and Peter's farm.

She glanced at the farmhouse. She couldn't wait to tell Bert her news. She hoped he'd be as happy as she felt. It was as if everything was coming together, as if God was making all her plans work for once.

The back door of the rambling Biddle house creaked open, and Lillian Biddle came outside. She wore a purple quilted overcoat, and her curler-wrapped hair was covered by a scarf. Muck boots reached to her knees.

"Lil," Trudy said. "Good afternoon."

Lillian cleared her throat. "What are you doing here? It's a weekday, you know. Don't you have a job?"

"Of course I do. I'm a teacher." She said it slowly and watched, amused, as Lillian's nostrils flared.

"I suppose you're here to see Bert," Lillian finally said. Then her gaze landed on the Pacer. "What happened to your car?"

"I was trying to get some ice off the wiper, and it did that."

Lillian raised an eyebrow. "Your windshield wiper painted graffiti on your car?"

69

Trudy laughed. Lillian didn't crack a smile. "That's a hoot!" Trudy wiped her eyes. "I thought you were talking about the . . . Oh, never mind." She waved a hand of dismissal. "Where's Bert?"

Lillian's mouth opened as if she were a trout in search of flies. "I'll get him," she huffed. "He's in the barn. Wait here." She disappeared into the shaded depths, and Trudy readjusted the wiper blade. When she finally lifted her head, Bert was beside her. Trudy gave him a big hug and watched Lillian march heavy footed back into the house.

"I have the greatest news," Trudy said. He tugged on her mittened hand and led her into the barn, away from the cold, blowing winds. It was dark inside. The noise of the November blasts yielded to the sounds of creaking siding. It was warm and humid in the barn, heated by the cows and heifers in their winter retreat, and smelled of musty hay and manure.

Trudy's eyes adjusted to the dark. She peered up into Bert's dancing gaze. "You know that teaching job in Lake Emily?"

"Yeah. What about it?"

"Well . . ." She took a deep breath and smiled. "They hired me today! I start at the end of Thanksgiving break." She watched, riveted to see what his reaction would be, glad that at least he wasn't heading for the hills.

"That's soon." Bert scratched his head.

"But what do you think? Is it okay with you? I mean, I was afraid you'd freak out when you found out I was actually moving here."

"No." He pulled her into his arms. "If you want to move to Lake Emily, that's fine by me."

"I know it's quick, and I hate to leave the school in St. Paul in a lurch," Trudy went on, "but they have other art teachers who can cover for me, and Lake Emily has no one. I have to move when the moving's good. It works out perfectly. I'll be out of the apartment even before Ellen is."

"Where are you going to live?"

"Principal Rosen gave me several leads. If nothing else, Mae and Peter have room, although I don't want to impose on them. Confidentially, I think Peter doesn't like company anyhow." Bert's smile grew.

"What are you grinning about?" she said as she took a step back. Bert shrugged. "Are you sure this is okay with you?"

"It's more than okay," Bert said, drawing her into his embrace.

"You're what?" Peter said, looking up from the ironing board as Trudy plopped onto the couch.

"Is Mae around? Because that was not exactly the reaction I was hoping for." Trudy pulled a nail file out of her purse and began touching up her nails.

"She works, remember?" Peter shifted the fabric around the ironing board and moved the heavy iron back and forth across it. The steam sputtered.

"And what are you doing?" Trudy pointed with the file to the floral-print dress.

"I'm being helpful," Peter defended.

"Where is a camera when I really need it?"

"You're jealous because you don't have a man waiting on your every whim," Peter said good-naturedly.

"Ouch!" Trudy held up her hands. "You really are touchy, you know? I came to tell you that I got the job in Lake Emily and I start November 28."

"November 28?" He looked panicky.

"Is there an echo? Don't worry. I'll find a place to rent in town. I prefer town anyway. It's too quiet out here. I'd get bored sitting around with you ironing and waiting all day for Mae to come home."

"Hey, I do more than iron," Peter said.

"Oh yeah. I bet you do tubs, too."

Trudy parked the Pacer in the cobbled driveway of her mother and stepfather's St. Paul home. She gazed at the three-story brick mansion. Bare vines clung like skeleton fingers to the pristine exterior, each bone white from the previous night's snowfall.

Trudy took a deep breath. She wasn't looking forward to this, not after all the flak Mae had taken when she'd announced her move to Lake Emily, but she might as well get it over with. She climbed out of the car and reached for the seven-layer bars she'd made for the occasion.

Paul Larson, Trudy's stepfather, met her at the back door. He was a tall, good-looking man in his mid-fifties. Hair that had been California Beach Boys blond was now a distinguished gray, making his bright blue eyes even more striking.

"Hey, Paul," Trudy said, leaning in to give him a

quick, polite hug before handing him the bars. "A little chocolate." She lifted her eyebrows.

"Uh-oh," he said. "You don't bring food unless something's up." He closed the door behind her and set the treats on the kitchen counter off the white-tiled entry.

"*Moi?*" Trudy feigned innocence. "I'm here to visit my dear old mother and stepdad."

"Is that you, Trudy?" Catherine said as she entered the room.

"Hey, Ma," Trudy said.

Catherine gave her a scolding stare, then leaned in for a hug.

"Mother," Trudy corrected herself with a smirk toward Paul.

"I'm glad you finally pulled yourself away to come for a visit. You've been so preoccupied with this new boyfriend of yours."

"His name is Bert, Mother."

Catherine waved her words aside like a gnat. "Whatever his name is, I haven't seen you in forever. Have you lost weight? You seem thin to me."

Trudy snorted. "Oh, yeah, Mom, I'm wasting away." They walked into the large open kitchen. Trudy pulled out a stool at the center island. Copper pots and pans hung from an overhead rack, and a large cluster of garlic, like grapes on the vine, held the spot near the wall between the stainless fridge and the dark-paneled pantry. Catherine pulled a frosty pitcher of fresh-squeezed lemonade from the top shelf of the fridge and poured three glasses, adding a slice of lime to the rim of each. The smell of a rib roast slow cooking in the oven made Trudy's mouth water. Paul brought the snack over and opened the lid, revealing the chocolate-butterscotch-and-coconut bars.

Catherine said, "Are those seven-layer bars?" and Trudy nodded. "Ooo, my favorite."

Trudy stuck her tongue out at Paul, who rolled his eyes. Catherine got down some plates and served herself a treat.

"So," Trudy began once everyone was settled again. "I have some news."

"Big surprise," Paul mumbled.

"Really, what?" Catherine said.

"I had a job interview last week. Lake Emily needs an art teacher to switch-hit between the elementary and high schools." Catherine's face fell.

"You're considering moving? This isn't a good idea," Catherine sputtered. She dabbed the corner of her mouth with her napkin. "You love living in St. Paul. You have a good job here, friends, family. You've always said you enjoy the city, the culture and theater. This doesn't sound like you."

"I do love St. Paul," Trudy said. "I know moving is totally insane." She shrugged her shoulders. "But Ellen getting married really hit me, you know? I'm not getting any younger, and I really like Bert. If there's a chance we can take our relationship further, I want to do it."

"I haven't even met this person. Has he proposed?" Catherine shot her husband a glance that said, *Jump in and help anytime here.* Paul poured himself more lemonade.

"No," Trudy complained. "Don't you understand? Life isn't always about being nice and safe. It's about . . . living."

"So you're willing to pull up roots and move a hundred miles for some *farmer?*" She emphasized the word like an expletive.

"Yep. I'm tired of living the same life I've always lived."

"And what's wrong with that?"

"Do you want me to be alone for the rest of my life? That's awfully selfish, isn't it? Besides, if you miss me too much, you can move to Lake Emily too," Trudy suggested. "Then we'd all be together." She grinned at Paul.

Catherine sighed and gave Trudy her you're-impossible-but-I-can't-do-a-thing-with-you look.

Trudy put an arm around her mother, who softened at the gesture. "If it doesn't work out, I promise that I'll move in here with you and Paul." She kissed her mother's temple. That put a smile on Catherine's lips, and Paul took another sip of lemonade.

BOB OTT

There was nothing like the roar of a hog engine, the wind squeezing tears from your eyes, and a two-lane highway to clear the mind, to unshackle a person from the nagging burdens at home. Lately that was all home was for Bob Ott—a burden. The late-afternoon sun was warm on his face as he rode his 1963 Harley-Davidson westward. *The July air stung his cheeks and eyes as it whipped his long hair back from his face. He pushed his sunglasses up on his nose and gazed at the looming snowcapped mountains of Glacier National Park ahead. He'd never seen anything so awe-inspiring. He inhaled deeply. This was freedom. No responsibilities. No one harassing him.*

Robert, your hair is too long, *his mother's voice said.*

What's gotten into you lately with this nonsense about "finding yourself"? *his father's voice harped.* Stay here and help me with the pharmacy. You can make a life for yourself here, Robert, a life that counts for something.

Yeah, right. Working day after day for a paycheck to buy stuff he didn't need anyway—how was that better than this? No one understood, at least no one in Lake Emily.

Except Marion. Marion Krenik shared his passions, his enthusiasm to see the world. And yet she was wise—she understood his need for a little time away even if he didn't. He'd begged her to come along on this westward pilgrimage, but she'd said, No, you need to do this on your own. This is your time, Bobby. *Then she'd smiled at him and tucked her long red hair behind her ears. She had gazed at him with those clear blue eyes, and he'd felt accepted for once in his life.*

He'd promised to come back for her once he was settled in California. They'd make a way without the narrow-minded traditions of their parents.

He pulled the loud Harley up to the 76 station and killed the motor. A woman with a beehive hairdo at the pump in front of him stared disdainfully at the bike and its grimy rider. Bob ignored her. What was it about people? He was tempted to roll up his sleeve so she could get a good look at his tattoo. Instead he turned his back to fill the tank and then went inside to pay. He heard the woman say under her breath as he passed, "Get a haircut." His blood boiled. He wondered if things would ever be different, if he would ever be judged for who he was on the inside instead of how he appeared on the surface. Once in the store, he slapped his money onto the counter and stalked back out to the Harley.

He pumped on the kick starter. The Harley roared to life, and Bob eased away from the pump and onto the highway, running through the gears to eighty miles per hour. Twilight drifted across the sky in airy tufts of neon pink and red.

Bob lifted his face to the view, determined not to let the woman at the gas station get to him. She was an old biddy, he told himself. He'd find people who saw the world the way he did, and when he did, he'd make a real home for himself and Marion.

He never saw the El Camino run the stop sign, never heard the brakes squeal. But it was there. In an instant the Harley-Davidson exploded into the car. The sensations of flight and incredible pain were the last things Bob was aware of.

When he awoke, a familiar voice, a mother's voice from his childhood, spoke, "Bob. Oh, thank God." She stood next to his bed, haloed by the light from the hospital window. Everything was a blur. He felt her warm hands caress his cheek. There was a contraption surrounding his skull like something from a Frankenstein movie. It tugged at him and kept him from turning his head.

"What happened?" he said. The pain returned then, darts that shot up and down his shoulder in agonizing shafts. He grimaced.

"There was an accident. A terrible, terrible accident." She was crying, and he tried to reach for her but couldn't move his hands.

"What's wrong with me?" Bob asked.

"You broke your back, Son," his father's voice sounded from his side. Bob strained to see him. He seemed so old and fragile as he moved behind Bob's mother. His eyes were lined in dark bags despite the smile he gave his boy. "You had us scared there for a while, but you're going to be okay. Now that you're awake you can start to heal."

"Where are we?" Bob asked.

"We're in Helena, Montana. They said we can't transport you back home."

"Is Marion here?" With those words he felt like crying. Did she know about the accident? What would become of them? He closed his eyes to block the churning thoughts.

"I'm sorry, honey. No." Nothing would comfort him now.

W hat can I do for you, young lady?" Bob Ott, Lake Emily's resident pharmacist, lifted his face and wiped a bandanna across his shiny forehead. His shoulders were slightly hunched, and one hand rested on the low counter where the prescriptions came in. He wasn't necessarily a big man, only five feet seven or so, and he appeared to be in his early fifties. He had a ready smile and a twinkle that never left his eyes. The top of his head was shiny as a bowling ball, except for some strange-looking scars tucked under the fringe of hair. He wore a pale salmon-colored cardigan with buttons shaped like Easter eggs in the same hue.

"Mr. Rosen, the principal at the school, mentioned that you had a place to rent?" Trudy said.

"Ah." His face took on a smile, revealing a deep dimple in his right cheek. "I'd be happy to show it to you, if you're interested. It's right upstairs."

"That'd be great," Trudy said.

"Janey," he called to the teenage girl working behind the soda fountain's counter. The girl lifted her freckled face. "I'm going to show this young woman the apartment upstairs. Keep an eye on things for me?"

"Sure, Mr. Ott," Janey said, her smile revealing shiny silver braces.

The pharmacist led the way to the back door of the pharmacy. It was an ancient building, no doubt built in the early 1900s and remodeled in the late '50s, given the contrast between the exterior and interior décors. Shelves were tucked close together, loaded with pharmaceuticals, first-aid treatments, cosmetics, and perfumes. There was even a jewelry counter filled with ancient watches. Along one wall a soda fountain served malts and shakes. And a large hand-painted sign read, "All the way to state, Bulldogs!" A group of teenagers sat giggling and talking as their parents and grandparents no doubt had on these same chairs years ago.

Bob Ott led the way, his cardigan swinging, accentuating a wide gait that had a trace of a limp. The back door opened on to an enclosed foyer and a staircase that ran up the outside of the building like an enclosed fire escape. The stairs, built of wood and painted a deep brown, creaked as Trudy and Mr. Ott made their way to the second-story apartment.

Mr. Ott unlocked the door as they stood in the small landing between two apartments. They stepped inside, and he turned on the light. The apartment was long and narrow, in a shotgun style with all the windows on the east side of the building.

"You get a lot of sunlight in the morning, so it's usually cheerier than this," Mr. Ott said.

"No sunsets, though, huh?" Trudy said.

"Afraid not. The apartment on the west side gets the sunsets. I have my office in there and seasonal items we stock for the pharmacy. So you wouldn't have any neighbors to worry over, except for my occasional puttering. The bathroom's there." He pointed to a door to the left of the couch. Bob waited in the living room while Trudy peeked at the tiny space that consisted of a pedestal sink, toilet, and tub. There was barely enough room for a bath mat, but it had a minimalist quaintness that Trudy liked.

"There's no washer and dryer," Bob said when she came out.

"That's okay. I can do laundry at my sister's."

The mauve velour couch and maple coffee table outfitted the living room. The galley-style kitchen was also petite, but it more than made up for size in style. The cupboards had raised-panel doors with porcelain knobs that matched the white porcelain sink. The counters were the same salmon color as Bob's sweater. Trudy immediately felt her excitement bubble.

"Does the furniture come with the apartment?" Trudy asked.

"Unless you don't want it," Bob said.

"No. I can use it," Trudy said, thinking a chenille or a floral slipcover would add a homey touch to the couch. "The place I'm in now came furnished."

Trudy peered out the window above the kitchen table that sat opposite the big white porcelain sink. "Nice view of Main Street," Trudy said, turning her head to see the Elevator's massive galvanized bins on the cross street. Sounds of pedestrians on the sidewalk and the growl of trucks shifting gears wafted through the slightly open window.

"You can do whatever you like as far as decorating—I'm not too picky," Mr. Ott said. "I know the white walls are dull."

Trudy nodded, wishing she'd brought Mae to share in this fun. She inspected the next room, a bedroom with high shelves above the bed, which was built into the wall with drawers for storage underneath and alongside it.

"This is lovely," Trudy said, pointing to the intricate trim on the shelf's edge.

Bob took his sweater off and draped it across his arm. He wore a short-sleeved shirt underneath, and Trudy thought she saw a glimpse of a tattoo peek beneath the sleeve's hem.

"Getting hot in here," Bob explained.

"Shady past?" Trudy pointed at the tattoo. Bob glanced at it, then smiled awkwardly.

"Some things we want to forget," he said, "but some reminders are permanent." He pointed to the scars Trudy had noticed earlier. "I'll tell you the story some-time." He moved ahead, then faced Trudy again. "My grandfather built the place in 1912. The Otts have been pharmacists here in Lake Emily for four genera-tions. Course I'll be the last." He cleared his throat.

"You never had children?"

"Never got married. There was a girl once. But she turned out to be . . . not the one."

"I'm sorry," Trudy said.

Bob shrugged. "That's life. My dad grew up in this apartment. Back then the whole upstairs was one big place. He died from prostate cancer a few years back—he was a good man." He paused, gazing at some invisible spot before going on, "He divided it into two apartments when he and my mother built their house in Ridgewood Heights. Extra income, you know."

"I like it," Trudy said and entered the last room. Windows on two walls overlooked Main and Ferry Streets. Built-in bookshelves lined the west wall, and an armchair and floor lamp with a yellowed shade sat in the corner next to it.

"This is great." Trudy faced him. "How much for rent?"

"Four fifty a month . . . unless you think that's too high."

"No. That's more than fair, and, more important, I can afford it. I'll take it." She inhaled deeply, feeling satisfied. "I always wondered who lived in places like this. Now I know—me!" A painting of a seaside village with a large Dutch windmill held the spot above a small eggplant-colored velvet loveseat. Trudy gazed closely at its delicate strokes. "With more light this will make a great studio. I'd lay a drop cloth," she assured, looking up at her new landlord.

"A studio?"

"I'm an artist—I paint, do a little pottery, sculpture . . . But for money I work as a teacher," she added quickly. "I'm the new art teacher at the schools here in Lake Emily, as soon as Thanksgiving break is over anyway."

"Really?" Mr. Ott laid a hand atop the reading chair. "I'd heard they weren't going to be able to hire new teachers, with the failed referendum and all."

"Well, I suppose every school needs an art teacher,"

Trudy said defensively. Mr. Ott smiled agreeably, but his comment left her feeling strange.

"I have references, if you want to give them a call before you decide," Trudy said, shaking off her doubts. She reached into her purse to retrieve the sheet of paper on which she'd typed Mae's and Ellen's phone numbers and addresses.

"That won't be necessary," Mr. Ott assured her. "I'm a pretty good judge of character. I think you'll be perfect for the place."

"You sure?"

The bald man simply shook her hand and gave her the key. "Move in as soon as you like. Rent is due the first of every month."

As soon as Bob Ott's bent back disappeared into the pharmacy, Trudy dug in her macramé purse for her cell phone and dialed Bert's number. She sat in the driver's seat of the mural-covered Pacer on Main Street. The phone rang twice, three times. An elderly couple strolled past, eying the car suspiciously and moving to the far side of the sidewalk. Trudy smiled and waved, but they averted their eyes. Finally someone picked up the phone. It was Lillian.

"Yep." She sounded winded.

"Hi, Lil. Is Bert home?"

"Is this Trudy?"

"It is."

"Didn't he tell you he's coaching hockey? I about killed myself trying to get to the phone."

Trudy thought of a retort, then decided against it.

"Could you have him call me?"

Lillian grunted and hung up. Why couldn't she have a civil conversation with that woman? And more, why did it have to be that just when she was moving to Lake Emily to be near Bert, he chose to fill his schedule with stupid hockey?

ten

Snow fell in quiet, lazy circles. Virginia threw open the door of her white Cape Cod as David came up the front walk. She pulled off her blue gingham apron and tossed it across the coat rack inside the door, then watched as David drew closer. The snow was already so deep that the path resembled a deep fjord between two mountains. David walked with his usual vigorous gait, his arms swinging slightly behind him. It was Roy's walk to a T; Virginia felt a pang at the realization.

"You're here!" she said as she reached out her thick arms for a hug from her fifty-three-year-old son. He kissed her on the temple.

"Ma," he breathed. Virginia basked in the word. He turned to gaze down the walkway. "Last year we barely got any snow, and now it looks as though it'll reach the rafters by Christmas. I hope you didn't shovel that yourself."

"Peter did it for me," Virginia said. "Now come on in out of this cold. I want to hear all about Nova Scotia."

"The word 'damp' comes to mind. Those Canadians

are made of tough stuff," David said as he came in the front entry. Virginia helped him off with his coat. He shook the snow from his graying hair and breathed deeply. "Something's baking." David inhaled. "Mom, it smells good, but you're going to make me fat."

"It's a good thing you go on your concert tours, then. Gives you time to slim down between visits." David chuckled. He paused at the menagerie of Hummel figurines gathered on the built-in shelves in the living room at the left of the stairway. There were all kinds— boys and girls with puppies, holding umbrellas in the rain; music box Hummels and Hummels on swings. They had all been gifts from Roy during the war and afterward, a reminder of his thoughtfulness.

"I always stared at these when I was a kid and wondered about the places they came from," David said, "what experiences Dad had there."

Virginia moved next to him and placed a hand on his back. "Maybe that's where you get your love of travel."

"Maybe." He turned with a sad smile to his mother. "I miss him."

"That goes for both of us." Virginia sighed. "It's the little things that haunt me. You reminded me of him when you came to the door."

"I did?"

"You have his walk." They both honored the moment with silence.

"So how was Thanksgiving?" David broke the spell. "I'm sorry I wasn't here."

"Shh," Virginia scolded. "It's part of your job,

giving concerts over the holidays. Don't apologize for what you do. I had a fine holiday with Peter and Mae. That girl is a pretty fair cook."

"That's high praise indeed coming from you," David teased.

She smiled and patted his hand. "Come on. Let's get a snack."

David followed her to the petite, bright kitchen. She pulled a cookie jar shaped like a bear from the counter and filled a plate with cookies. Then she poured two glasses of milk and handed one to her son. "Like when I was a kid," David said. "I think that's even the same cookie jar."

"You're back in Minnesota, David. This is how we survive the winter." He lifted a chocolate-chip cookie from the plate, took a bite, and gave his mother a satisfied grin.

"My favorite!" He led the way into the dining room, and they sat down at the small table.

"I'm making tuna hotdish with peas for supper. You always liked that, too."

"So . . . tell me what's new around these parts."

Virginia reflected for a moment. "Jerry and Mary Shrupp are grandparents. Their Terri had a boy."

"Good old Jerry. I bet he loves being a grandfather. I would've liked sharing that title with him." His face saddened as memories of their own recent loss flooded back. "How are Peter and Mae doing?"

"That's hard to say. Outwardly they seem fine, but—" She halted, feeling awkward about saying more.

"But what?"

"It seems to me Mae's filled her time with this new job so she doesn't have to face the memories. I don't blame her. But I don't know if it's the healthiest way to handle her grief."

"Busyness isn't always a bad thing." David took a sip of his milk. He set the glass down and rubbed his left hand with his right. It reminded Virginia of when he'd done the same thing at the French restaurant. "Some people need the busyness, or they'll go mad with remembering," David went on. "It reminds them that they have other things to live for. Like I had Peter when Laura died."

"You're right," Virginia said. "I worry about them though. Sometimes there's a look in Peter's eyes, as if he feels guilty about what happened."

"We all blame ourselves. I blamed myself when Laura died, but he'll get past that. Before you know it, he and Mae will have four kids, and this will be a distant memory."

The tiny cuckoo made its four o'clock appearance. Virginia glanced at it and got up. "I better get that hotdish in. Mind taking our talk to the kitchen?"

David brought the plate of cookies while Virginia placed the empty glasses in the sink. "Could you get my relish plate down?" Virginia asked, pointing to one of the high cupboards. "One of the drawbacks in this kitchen—I need a stool to reach anything."

David opened the door and pulled out the crystal dish. He reached to hand it to his mother, but it slipped from his grasp and shattered on the hardwood floor.

"Oh, I'm sorry, " he said. He bent down to pick up the pieces. "I don't know what's wrong with me these days. I'll get you a new one." He grabbed the broom and dustpan by the back door and began sweeping up the shards of glass.

"I have plenty of dishes but only one son." Then she paused as something occurred to her. "Have your hands been giving you trouble lately?"

David glanced up, surprised by her question. His gaze was troubled, his brow lined.

"I remember the way you were rubbing your hand after the concert," she explained.

He examined his long, straight fingers. "It's probably all in my head. I certainly haven't gone easy on my hands; constant practicing has to take a toll."

He sat down on the tall kitchen stool and gazed earnestly into his mother's eyes. "I've been trying to ignore whatever it is," he finally admitted. "I had to give up solos a few months ago." His eyes betrayed how hard those words were to utter. Virginia's heart sank. "I couldn't bring myself to tell you. My fingers ache constantly. I keep missing notes. I never used to miss notes. The conductor has been great about it, but I don't know how much longer he'll put up with me. I don't know what's wrong. I keep hoping that it'll get better if I take it easy, but so far it hasn't."

Virginia laid a hand on her son's cheek. "You should see a doctor, David. You never know, it might be something simple that they can cure."

"That's what I'm afraid of, Ma. What if it can't be cured?"

eleven

The brightly colored hallways of Lake Emily Elementary resounded with the voices of children. Trudy loved the familiar sound. It held an energy adults couldn't even begin to emulate. A sound that believed in good triumphing over evil. It believed in endless possibilities. It was unjaded. Unadulterated joy. She stood by the long table in the art room as her third-grade class poured in. The children whispered to each other and gave Trudy covert glances as they took their seats. The bell rang, and Trudy waited for silence.

"Good morning," she began. "I'm your new art teacher, Miss Ploog." She wrote her name on the blackboard. A tow-headed boy missing a front tooth raised his hand. "Yes," Trudy said.

"What happened to Mr. Wuerrfel, our old art teacher?"

"Mr. Rosen said he's been kind of sick, so he decided to take a break from work for a while."

"He's on dialysis," a dark-haired girl with tight pigtails said expertly. She sat a little too straight and spoke in a grown-up voice. "And the stress was more than his weary body could handle—I know because he's my uncle."

"Oh," Trudy said. "Okay, and what's your name?"

"I'm Emily Pritchett. Is that your real hair?"

"Yep, it's my real hair." Trudy gave her hair a tug as proof and then turned to the rest of the group. "I know it's not ideal, switching teachers midyear, but we're going to have a lot of fun. I have all kinds of fun stuff for us to do." She paused and glanced across the eager faces. "So, rumor is you guys were learning about clay."

"Mr. Wuerrfel showed us how to wedge the clay. He said we were going to make pots and stuff. We didn't get to actually make any yet though." This again from Emily.

"Okay," Trudy said. "Then we'll work on making pinch pots today, but right now I want to show you how to throw a pot."

"Throw a pot?" a boy with curly dark brown hair asked, a mischievous gleam in his eyes.

"You don't actually throw it, not like that anyway." She smirked at the boy. "You won't be ready to do it yourself until you're older, but I want you to get an idea of the kinds of great things you can do." She took a wire, each end tied to wooden handles, and slid it through a block of clay she'd set up on the big table in the center of the room. The kids watched, mouths agape. "You already know how to wedge, so I don't have to explain that part, right?" She threw the clay onto the table and kneaded it with the heels of her hands until she'd formed a smooth ball free of air pockets.

"Come, gather around the wheel," Trudy instructed. The kids made a circle, vying for a spot from which to see her clearly. When they seemed about settled, she said, "Here's where the *throwing* comes in." She tossed the round ball onto the center of the squat wheel that had concentric circles across its surface. Then she dipped her fingers into a bowl of water that rested on a tray alongside the wheel. With her foot she pushed the treadle that powered the wheel.

"First, you find *center*," Trudy said above the noise of the motor. The clay bumped against the heel of her hand as the wheel spun. The outside edge of her other hand rested on the wheel as she wrestled the clay. Eventually the lump no longer bumped but spun in a smooth flow, its fight gone, indicating that the clay was perfectly round. Trudy smiled. "Now I'm centered," she said and sat up straight. "Once you find center you can do anything—make whatever kind of pot you like. But without finding center you'll always have a hard time and end up fighting the clay." Trudy dipped her fingers into the water again. "One of those lessons where art imitates life." The kids gave her blank stares.

"Now I'm going to make a cylinder. I put my fingers in the middle." She pushed the pedal to get it spinning again, then placed her fingers into the mass. Magically the clay parted. The kids oohed and moved in to get a better look. "Move back," Trudy scolded, although she was pleased at their enthusiasm. Then with thumb and forefinger she pulled the clay up into a tubelike shape. She did this a few more times, wetting her fingers in between until the walls of the cylinder were as thin as her pinkie. She picked up a tool like a rubber spatula with no handle and held it up for the kids to see. She put the tool inside the cylinder with one hand while using the other on the outside to support it. The cylinder shifted, its walls bowing and bending to Trudy's every whim.

Within a few moments she stopped the wheel so the kids could survey her creation. There was a general murmur of amazement as they gathered closer. "Don't touch," Trudy instructed. "It's still very soft. But you see it's a lot of fun, isn't it?"

"Can we do that?" a small voice from the back asked.

"Jessie?" Trudy asked. The other kids stared at Jessie as if wondering how the new teacher had been able to guess her name.

"Yes, Miss Ploog," Jessie Wise said.

"You've grown a couple of inches since last summer." The girl's face flamed a deep red. Trudy cleared her throat. "It'll take a while before you guys are ready for the wheel. But if anyone wants to learn more—about anything we cover in class, not just pottery—I will happily stay after school to help you." She winked at Jessie. "Why don't you guys go put on your smocks, and we'll get down to business."

Trudy moved to the big block of clay and began distributing lumps to each child. Soon the happy chatter took over. Trudy felt her insides warmed by it. She wandered around the room to gaze at projects and help as needed, stooping over shoulders to inspect, whisper encouragement, and learn names. When she reached Jessie, she said, "Why didn't you tell me you were here?"

The girl shrugged. "I didn't know if you'd remember me."

"Of course I remember you. You're Virginia Morgan's book buddy. You took your rabbit to the fair and won a ribbon." Jessie smiled. "And as I recall, you said something about liking to draw pictures." Jessie seemed so happy that Trudy thought she might pop. "Do you still draw?" Trudy said.

Jessie nodded. "Virginia got me an art pad for my birthday."

"Why don't you bring some of your pictures to school? I'd love to see them." Trudy patted the girl's shoulder. "And your pot is great."

The tantalizing scent of chocolate-chip cookies filled the house. Virginia Morgan pulled the batch from the oven and set it on the counter. A green-checked apron was tied about her heavy waist, and a faint dusting of flour traced her work-worn hands. She'd been baking all afternoon, goodies she could do without, but she knew Jessie loved them.

The front doorbell sounded, and Jessie's voice called down the hall, "Virginia, I'm here."

The nine-year-old came around the corner. "Something sure smells good."

"They're for you," Virginia said, handing Jessie a plate of the warm cookies and a glass of cold milk. Jessie took them into the dining room off the kitchen.

This was their afternoon ritual. Virginia had come to depend on it. There was nothing like the ecstasy on Jessie's face when she took that first bite. Jessie had changed from the rumpled, sad girl Virginia had met last summer after the death of her mother. It was as if she'd come back to life, full of the excitement of learning new things and ever eager to share her discoveries.

Jessie tilted her head as the old cuckoo came out for its three-thirty bow. "Where's Snip?" she called to the kitchen.

Virginia waddled into the dining room, slid into the bay window's built-in seat alongside the table, and picked up a cookie. "I haven't seen that cat since I fed him this morning. I'm sure he's hiding somewhere. How was school?"

"Okay, I guess. Mr. Odegaard wasn't too crabby. Oh, guess who I had for art today?"

"Can't say as I know," Virginia said.

"Miss Ploog. Remember from the fair?" She dipped the cookie into her milk and took a big bite.

"You mean Mae's sister, Trudy Ploog?" she said, feigning surprise.

"You knew!" Jessie protested. Crumbs dribbled from the corner of her mouth.

Virginia handed her a paper napkin. "So what did you think of her?"

"She isn't boring like most teachers, you know? She showed us how to toss pots."

"You mean throw pots?"

"Yeah. Miss Ploog made a really cool one. She said to bring my art pad to school so I could show her my drawings. Maybe she can help me with a picture for 4-H. Can I show Flopsy again?"

"You can show your rabbit every year, if you like."

"I need to go feed him."

She started to rise, but Virginia placed a hand on hers. "You can feed him later. Let's talk." Jessie sat back down. "You've done really well with your bunny," Virginia observed. "You've been very responsible, and you've kept up his care wonderfully. Do you think you'd like to raise a larger animal now? It's up to you, of course. But it might be fun." Virginia lifted a hand to wipe a cookie crumb from Jessie's lip.

"I never thought much about it. What kind of animal? Where would I keep it?" Jessie pushed her blond bangs out of her eyes.

"I've been giving that some consideration," Virginia said. "Sheep or goats would be pretty easy to raise. I'm sure Peter would let you keep them out at the farm, and I could drive you out to take care of them."

"Sheep would be fun. They're so cute and cuddly," Jessie said. "Where would we get one?"

"Well, it's a big commitment." Virginia raised her hands to calm her enthusiasm. "Why don't you think about it? I can watch the paper and ask around. Something's bound to turn up. We might have to wait until later in the spring if we want a lamb that's weaned— which means a lamb born in March would be ready in May or June. Can you wait that long?"

"That's okay," Jessie said, then her face fell. "Did you ask my dad about it?"

"Do you think he might object?"

Jessie was silent for a moment. Virginia saw that her brow was knit into a frown.

"Dad says things," Jessie said.

"Oh, really?"

"Sometimes I don't think he likes 4-H all that much."

"Why not?"

Jessie shrugged. "It's nothin'." She scooted out of the seat and said, "Is it okay if I go feed Flopsy now?"

Virginia nodded. Jessie left to put her coat back on, then went outside to feed the brown Rex in the rabbit hutch behind the garage.

Virginia wondered what Jessie had been like before her mother's accident. Virginia sighed. There were times when she saw glimmers of the way things used to be, in the laughter father and daughter would share over a joke, in the wistful way Steve smiled at his little girl when he didn't think anyone was watching. But there was always a cloud overhead, and with it a defeat in the man's dark eyes.

Virginia moved to the kitchen and stirred the beef stew that bubbled on the back burner. She opened the Frigidaire and retrieved the baking-powder biscuits she'd rolled out earlier in the day. She peeled off the Saran Wrap, set the oven at 350 degrees, and slid them inside. Then she wiped the dining room table before laying out three place settings—her favorite Limoges china, embroidered cloth napkins in shades of pink and green, and delicate crystal water goblets. Gazing at the simple yet elegant table, Virginia realized that even if life wasn't fair, she could at least treat Jessie and Steve Wise to a good meal.

Virginia glanced at her watch, then out the kitchen window toward the backyard. Jessie stood under the big elm, holding her bunny up against her neck. She stroked the soft fur, and her lips moved as she talked to Flopsy. Her eyes were filled with some new tale, no doubt about her new teacher and all the things she'd done today. The rabbit yielded to the girl's demands and seemed to enjoy the attention. Virginia recalled the times she'd watched her own children from her kitchen window as they played in the snow or had water fights in the summer.

By the time Jessie came inside, Virginia had made hot chocolate since she was certain the girl would have frostbite. Her cheeks and nose were blotched with red.

"I was wondering how long you were going to stay out. Come over here." Virginia bustled to take off the girl's hat and scarf. "Let me feel your face." She pressed her hand against Jessie's cold skin.

"I'm fine. I wasn't out that long."

"You lose track of time when you're with that rabbit." She stood back to examine her again. "At least your cheeks aren't white."

Jessie smiled. "I'm okay, Virginia. Can I go do my homework now?"

"Why don't you get started in the den? I'll come help as soon as I take these biscuits out. Your dad will be here before too long."

Jessie rolled her eyes. "You sound like my mom. She used to say things like that all the time."

"Good." She gave Jessie a squeeze. Then said, "Do you think about your mom a lot?"

"Do you think about Roy?"

"Always." Virginia placed a hand on the girl's

shoulder. "Tell me what your mother was like." She pulled the biscuits from the oven and placed them in a basket lined with a pale green linen napkin.

Jessie lifted her eyes as if trying to remember. "She was pretty. Not real fancy, but nice. You know? She had blond hair like me and blue eyes. She played the piano sometimes. I remember I'd get home from school, and I'd hear her singing and playing. Dad sold that piano right after the accident." She turned sad eyes to gaze at Virginia.

Then Virginia said, "People grieve in different ways. Some people hold on tight to the memories; others seem to do everything they can to forget, even the good memories. Your dad copes as best he can."

Jessie shrugged as if she'd heard it before. "He never used to drink before," she said. "Now he drinks all the time."

"Does he . . ." Virginia paused, resisting the urge to pry and yet needing to know. "Are you ever afraid of him?"

"No!" Jessie stepped back. "My dad loves me. He'd never hurt me or anything."

"Of course he loves you."

The doorbell rang, and Virginia was glad for the excuse to go to answer it. Steve Wise stood on the stoop. He looked much older than his thirty-eight years. His eyes were glazed and his clothes rumpled.

"Hello, Mrs. Morgan. Is Jessie ready?" he said.

"Come on in," Virginia said. The faint scent of alcohol lingered. "I made beef stew for supper. Remember, I invited you and Jessie for supper tonight?"

He gave her a confused stare, then smiled as if embarrassed that he'd forgotten. "Yeah, of course," he said. He came in and hung his coat on the rack by the door.

"Daddy!" Jessie came around the corner and grabbed him by the waist. He bent his head over hers in a hug.

"Hey, punkin. How was your day?"

"Good. I have a new art teacher, and Virginia said I could get a sheep if it's okay with you."

He looked at Virginia. "A sheep?"

"We can talk about it later," Virginia said.

"How was your day, Daddy?" Jessie asked.

He paused, and his eyes shifted as if there was something he didn't care to discuss in front of Virginia.

"It was okay, Jess," he said as he patted his daughter's hair and spied the pile of outerwear she'd left lying on the bottom step. "Why don't you go put your boots and mittens in your backpack. You shouldn't mess up Mrs. Morgan's nice house."

"Oh, this house needs a child's messes," Virginia said. "I'm glad she feels at home."

Mr. Wise shifted unsteadily on his feet. "Still, I want her to be respectful."

Jessie hurried to gather her clothes. Virginia's heart sank. She wanted to help Steve get his life together, but she had no idea how. She'd hoped her help with Jessie would somehow encourage him, but so far it seemed to have no effect. She shot a prayer heavenward that God would give her wisdom. Finally she left to set the stew and biscuits on the table.

When she returned to the den to call them for supper, Jessie and her father were talking in hushed tones. Jessie lifted doleful eyes. Tears streaked her cheeks.

"Supper's on. What's wrong, dear?" Virginia asked.

Steve ran a hand through his hair, then said, "I . . . uh . . . I lost my job today."

"Oh, Steve, I'm sorry." Then she said kindly, "You'll find another. Maybe I can ask around town for—" He shook his head, and her words fell away.

"I appreciate the offer, but I'll find something."

"Come on, you two, supper's ready," Virginia said. She led the way to the alcove dining room.

When the three of them were seated around the table, they lowered their heads.

"Dear Lord," Virginia prayed, "we thank you for another day on this earth. We ask that you'll help Steve in this hard time without a job. Help him to find something else. Thank you for Jessie and her good day at school. And thank you for your tender mercies. Bless this food; may we be truly grateful. Amen." Silently she hoped that losing his job would help Steve Wise realize his need to stop drinking, to be a real father.

"Don't be so nervous," Bert said. Trudy sat beside him in the crowded lunchroom, twisting a section of her long hair into a coil and letting it unwind. Bert grabbed her hand and gazed into her green eyes. They had flecks of gray in their depths. "They want to wel-

101

come you to Lake Emily."

Trudy let out a breath and said, "You're right. It's not like I put Jack Linder's lunchbox under the bus tires again."

Bert raised his eyebrows in puzzlement, and she waved away his question. "It's a long story."

"I'd like to get this meeting going, if everyone will take a seat," Don Lind, the school board president, said. He had perfectly coifed white hair and a smile that never quite convinced Bert. The crowd grew quiet.

Don began by going over last month's minutes and old business. Then he said with a nod toward Bert and Trudy, "We'd like to welcome our new art teacher, Trudy Ploog. She comes to us from St. Paul very highly recommended, and we're lucky to get her. Trudy, would you like to say a few words?"

He held out a hand to her. The audience applauded, and Bert felt his pride swell. She walked up to the podium that faced the school board.

"Thank you," Trudy began. "I'm really excited about being here in Lake Emily. I had a great first day today." She glanced at Bert, who gave her a thumbs-up. "The kids seem really excited about learning. That's so important. There are a lot of new techniques in art that the older students especially can benefit from. I'll be teaching raku pottery and Impressionist art." Bert glanced around. He could've heard crickets for all the blank looks her comments received. But she seemed to be gathering steam.

"I'd like to eventually offer an art history class. I

know a lot of people enjoy learning about some of the greats like Leonardo da Vinci and Renoir as well as Western artists like O'Keeffe." Someone in the audience coughed. Trudy said, "Well, thank you again for your warm welcome. I look forward to a great partnership as we prepare young people for the future." She dipped her head to indicate that she was done speaking.

"Thank you, Miss Ploog," Don Lind said. "I'm sure our children will benefit greatly from your expertise."

Trudy took her seat, and Bert reached for her hand again.

After the meeting the crowd stood in conversation. Bert and Trudy were off to the side as each of the board members and some of the residents of Lake Emily came by to greet her and shake her hand.

"Don?" It was Sandy Thompson. She and Don stood a good fifteen feet away, but she had one of those voices that seemed to carry more than others. She was a heavyset woman with a couple of spare chins, feathered '80s hair, and a long flowing dress. She had been Bert's Sunday school teacher in fourth grade; she still called him Albert. He hated that. And she always told him he played banjo as good as Roy Clark from *Hee Haw*. He hated that even more.

"Yes, Mrs. Thompson." Don took a sip of his steaming coffee.

"The referendum failed three weeks ago. Why is it Miss Ploog was hired without the consent of the rest of the board?"

Mr. Lind blanched, and Trudy leaned toward Bert. "What's she talking about?" she whispered.

He didn't have a chance to answer before Mr. Lind began, "Every school needs an art teacher. The fact that Miss Ploog is willing to teach at both the elementary and high schools means this was a good economic choice. Mr. Rosen and I felt, given that, it wasn't something the entire board needed to—"

"But without additional state funds we are facing massive cuts. We'd already talked about cutting the art program. It would be prudent of us to examine *every* area—"

Don held up a hand. "Yes, we need to look at what we can cut, but it's too early to start indiscriminate slashing. In the meantime, with Mr. Wuerffel leaving, the kids need art. I'll still have a committee determine what our options are for cutting there. But we have time on our side."

Trudy glanced at Bert again, and he shrugged. "I had no idea," he apologized.

twelve

November blustered into December. Snow fell in howling heaps, making travel hazardous. The cows were cloistered in the barn almost full-time now, protected from the elements by its sturdy walls and the body heat of their sisters.

Peter bent his head against the wind and wrapped his scarf tighter around his cheeks as he fought his way toward the warm sanctuary. The humid breath of the animals hung in the air. Some cows lay on the ground in discussion groups. Others meandered, tasting summer's preserves, or simply stood in the long wait for spring. Peter flicked on the lights of the milking parlor and retrieved six five-gallon pails, which he filled with water and disinfectant.

It had been so quiet these past weeks without Mae home during the days. He had tried to fill his time with jobs around the house—cleaning kitchen cabinets and replacing ancient shelf paper—but that had soon grown old. So he'd taken to doing the books for the farm, reading up on farming techniques, and puttering in the shop.

Sometimes he'd call Mae at work for no particular reason other than to hear her honeyed voice.

"Le Sueur County. May I help you?" she said.

"No," he said. "I wanted to say hi."

"Hi," Mae said. "What's going on there?"

"Nothing. I think I might repaint the combine."

"Why would you do that?"

"Oh, I don't know, something to do."

"Peter, you need to get a hobby or learn to nap!" He laughed.

"Hey," Mae said when she got home that night. Peter was bent, wiping an udder with a brown paper towel. He straightened stiffly to kiss her. "How's it going here?" Mae said.

Peter shrugged. "Cow kicked me. My knee's a bit stiff now. I guess she didn't like cold hands."

The cow shifted her weight to get a better look at

Mae. "You remember me, don't you, old girl?" She patted the cow on the rump.

"How were the roads?" Peter said, stretching his knee.

"Nasty," Mae said, her gaze trained on the animal. "But I drove slowly, kept my distance from the other cars. It's not nearly as risky as 494 at rush hour. Back roads to Le Center are a breeze." She turned toward Peter. "Want some help?"

"You can't milk in those duds." Peter scratched his bottom, then pointed to her dress slacks and blue chenille sweater that peeked from the neck of her black peacoat, then returned to scratching. Mae raised an eyebrow.

"Peter, are you okay?"

"What do you mean?"

"You keep scratching your . . . um . . ."

"Yeah. I don't know what's going on. It's like I've got poison ivy or something."

"Do you have a rash?"

"No."

"Huh. Well, I'll go change." She pointed over her shoulder toward the house.

Peter nodded, and Mae left to put on jeans and a grubby shirt. When she returned, they settled into their former routine. Peter rounded up cows while she pulled the bars that released the clanging headstalls from the cows that were finished being milked. They sprayed and wiped udders, then attached the black spiderlike tubes.

Mae wiped an udder. It was particularly dirty, so she

flicked the muck off the teat and gave it an extra spray with the curly blue hose. She wiped it again and attached the suction cups. Peter had gone into the open section of the barn to round up a few more girls to replace those who were done. He was still scratching.

"Say, did you wash your underwear with the bedroom curtains?" she yelled to Peter.

He stopped to think. "Yeah, what about it?"

She paused for effect. "They're fiberglass."

Peter stood as still as the cattle. "Well, that explains a lot! I thought I was going insane."

Mae started laughing and couldn't stop. She bent at the waist, holding her aching sides, wiping tears from her eyes. "Do you want to go change?" she asked.

"I can finish milking," he protested.

"Suit yourself!" She laughed again.

It felt so good to laugh. Mae wondered if that meant she was healing. She smiled toward Peter's back. Two big cows ambled into the parlor and stepped up into their positions. Mae reached for the hose. It seemed as though everything was coming together. Her job was going well; Trudy was nearby. And then there was her mother. Even that relationship seemed better. She'd come to the baby's funeral, shown Mae that she did care.

Mae glanced out the side window. It was snowing again. Christmas was only weeks away.

Peter rejoined her in the milking parlor. Mae spoke over the sucking sounds of the milk machine. "I've been thinking about Christmas. What do you think of having Mom and Paul out?"

He stopped and turned to her. "Are you sure? We had Thanksgiving here last week."

"I know. And it was nice to spend it with Virginia, but I want to see my family." She knew he only meant to protect her from being hurt by her mother again.

"Your mom hasn't exactly apologized for all the nasty things she said about our marriage and leaving St. Paul."

Mae sighed. Part of her yearned to forget, to pretend that she and her mother were as close as she wanted to be, but the pragmatist in her knew Peter's caution was warranted.

He led her to the small room that held the milk tank to get away from the noisy parlor. "We're doing so well now," she said. "We have come through so much together—surely Mom has to see we love each other, that we aren't about to get a divorce like she said we would." The forgotten tears returned.

"Your mother still sees things her own way. Her coming to the funeral didn't change that." Peter reached to hold her. "I don't want to see you go through that pain again."

"She's my mother, Peter. I want a relationship with her; she's part of who I am. I love her." She lifted her head to look him in the eyes. "You and Paul and Trudy will be here. We can invite Bert, too, and of course Virginia—I don't want her to be alone for the holidays. Surely there's safety in numbers. I think it's a good starting point—Christmas."

Peter searched her eyes. He touched her hair and

said, "If that's what you want. I know about wanting to be close to family." He kissed her forehead and then tilted his head toward the parlor, and they returned to the waiting ladies. One cow swatted Peter with her tail, and he scratched her side.

"It'll be good," Mae said. "Our first Christmas together on our own farm. We'll be like the Waltons."

David Morgan wished he could walk out the door and forget the appointment, but it was too late for that, and he knew his mother would ask about it. He sat in the bland tan-and-green waiting room while CNN droned from the corner television near the ceiling.

He ran his hands across his face. His hands. Traitors. He looked at the backs of them. Veins in blue rose here and there. His nails were cut short. His wedding band still encircled his left ring finger. He twisted the ring.

Some men put their wedding bands away within weeks of losing a spouse, yet he'd never been able to do it, had never even had the desire to do it. It felt like a betrayal of the vow he'd spoken all those years before. And yet he knew Laura would have wanted him to move on. He had moved on, hadn't he? He'd raised Peter to be a man she would've been proud of. He'd pursued his musical gifts with an even greater passion than before. No, he hadn't found love again, not that he'd tried. To hope for the kind of love he'd had with Laura would be hoping for more than he deserved. Twice in one lifetime—that just didn't happen, not a love as deep as theirs.

"Mr. Morgan," a nurse in blue scrubs and white shoes called from the entrance to a long hallway. David followed her to a cubicle of a room with a paper-covered padded table and sat in a chair in one corner. The room smelled of rubbing alcohol and disinfectant. She took his blood pressure and temperature and told him the doctor would be in shortly. A few minutes later the doctor came in and introduced himself, shaking David's hand. He was a tall man with sandy-colored hair and a white lab coat.

"David Morgan," he began. "That name's familiar. You aren't by chance related to the violinist in the St. Paul Chamber Orchestra?"

"One and the same," David said.

"I've patronized the orchestra for as long as I can remember."

David's gaze fell to his hands.

"So." The doctor turned a page in his chart. "What seems to be the problem?" He scooted the wheeled stool in front of David.

David nervously held out his hands for the doctor's inspection as he spoke. The pain deep within them echoed. "I've been having pain in my hands, a problem gripping things, fingering."

The doctor's brow furrowed. He reached for David's left hand and stared at it. "Is it a tingling sensation?"

"No. More of an ache."

"Your whole hand or certain fingers? Your palm?" He ran his fingers along David's palm.

David thought. "My joints mostly. It comes and goes, but all my fingers hurt, especially when I haven't been using them. And I have a crunching sensation sometimes."

"The reason I ask is it could possibly be carpal tunnel syndrome, which is fairly treatable, or arthritis, which can sometimes be treated depending on what type and how bad it is. My guess is we're dealing with some form of arthritis."

"Is this good news?"

"Depends. Carpal tunnel would start with some tingling, especially in the thumb, index, and middle fingers. Sometimes a simple Advil can reduce symptoms, or therapy can help. Surgery is even a possibility. But your symptoms don't seem to lean that way. We can take some pictures to see what we're up against." He looked at David's hands again and turned them over to see the back side. "Your knuckles seem enlarged."

"I'd noticed that a while back," David admitted.

"Let's hope for the best. First we'll take some x-rays."

David sat in the cold examination room. He hated not knowing—it was like waiting for a judge to pass sentence. He stared at the criminals: his stiff, aching hands. He'd always prided himself on his ability to fly across a parade of sixteenth notes effortlessly. Now even eighth notes posed a hurdle.

At first he'd hoped it was a fluke, some passing ailment he would soon be over. That had been six months ago. He gazed up at the ceiling and begged God to make it something treatable. At least then there would be hope; he could recover and get back to what he loved most.

The doctor came into the examination room with David's file in hand and took a seat. He seemed too quiet, and his face was grim. David braced himself for the worst.

"It's not good news." The doctor leaned toward him. The compassion in his eyes broke David's heart. "I'm afraid you have osteoarthritis. I'll want to take more x-rays every few months so we can get a feel for how quickly things are deteriorating, what kind of cartilage loss and bone damage there is. As for treatment, we can start with Advil."

The room seemed to swirl with the verdict. David heaved a long sigh and lifted his head to the ceiling. "I've been taking Advil like candy for a long time already."

"That's not good for you either." The doctor ran a hand through his thick hair. His eyes met David's again. "Let's put you on Celebrex. It's a COX-2 inhibitor. It blocks the inflammation. See if that does anything. I can't guarantee that we can help you with your violin playing." He paused. "I have to be honest with you, David. Osteoarthritis can be very debilitating. Most likely it's only going to get worse."

"You mean eventually I'll lose the ability to play at all."

The doctor nodded. "For some it becomes a challenge to hold a pen, turn a doorknob . . . I'm sorry."

"I appreciate your honesty," David said. He rose from his seat and reached out to shake the doctor's hand. "Thank you, Doctor."

Numbly, David headed outside and climbed into his car. There he sat. The world outside had gone silent. He gazed at the hands atop the cold steering wheel. So that was it. Within time his hands would become gnarled tree limbs, no good for even opening a jar. It seemed cruel of God to give him this gift and then snatch it away like some bully on the playground.

What was he supposed to do now? Those hands had been his whole life. They had touched Laura, held Peter as a baby. They had brushed away tears and enchanted audiences.

He wondered how long it would be before he was forced to resign the symphony. Truth was, he knew he was already past that point. Deep down he'd known it for a long time. The orchestra deserved a musician who could keep up. He was already failing.

thirteen

The Morgan farm glistened like a Currier and Ives print. The old retired wooden wagon waited expectantly for visitors at the end of the drive. It sparkled with delicate white lights shining from the snowy depths of potted white pines in a starry effect. Peter had lined the drive with kerosene lanterns that hung from welded steel holders ranged like sentinels. The wraparound porch with its intricate gingerbread trim held swags of fresh evergreens dusted with a light snow, making the red bows at the apex of each drape Martha Stewart perfect.

Inside, the cinnamon and pine scents of Christmas

filled the air. Mae's ceramic houses were carefully placed here and there throughout the house. The light shining from their miniature windows still enchanted her as they had when she had started collecting them as a young girl. A bright fire glowed in oranges and reds. It crackled and hissed, itself a yuletide carol.

Mae had found a scraggly four-foot Charlie Brown fir in the woods along the north field. The tree stood alone in a galvanized bucket in the corner of the living room. Strings of cranberries and popcorn circled it in swooping loops.

They didn't have many ornaments yet, not nearly the number Mae's mother had garnered over the years. Mae had some simple glass balls that reflected the firelight and a few precious ornaments she'd inherited from her grandparents: bright painted glass birds that perched amid the branches, and tiny antique bulbs in reds and greens and golds.

"Next year I pick the tree," Peter said from behind her as she stood admiring it. He slipped his arms around her midsection and kissed her neck.

"I like this tree. It needed a home."

"Why ours?" Peter teased.

Mae swatted his hands. He reached around her and lifted an ornament off one of the branches. It was a simple eight-penny nail with a ribbon tied at the top.

"What's this?" he said.

Mae took the nail from his hands and held it up. "A reminder of what a Christmas tree stands for—that Jesus was born to die." Mae leaned into Peter's embrace. It felt good to be held by him.

"It's going to be a good Christmas," Peter said. "You ready for tomorrow?"

"I think so. I'm a little nervous," Mae confessed. "But I'm looking forward to seeing Mom too. I want her to see how happy we are here, that moving to Lake Emily was good for us. We're doing well in spite of everything—she'll have to see that."

"Don't get your hopes too high," Peter said.

"I know. But I can't help but hope."

Christmas Day dawned cold and blowing, with a blizzard predicted for most of Minnesota. The old house creaked and groaned in protest, and frost covered the corners of the windows in crystalline designs. Mae was in the kitchen, putting a turkey in the oven. She wanted every detail of today's celebration to be perfect. The white tablecloth had been pressed, the silver candelabra shined. Her wedding china and silver service were already set on the long dining-room table. A cluster of red poinsettias served as a centerpiece with long white tapers on each side.

Peter had gone out to milk half an hour early so he could lend a hand with preparations. He was back inside by seven thirty, looking like a snowman with frost atop his shoulders and woolen hat.

"It's bad out there today," he said as he stamped his feet and dusted himself off. He placed his coat on its hook in the back entry. "It's blowing something fierce. Drifts are already knee-high. I wonder how the roads are. I should get back out to plow the driveway, but first I need a cup of coffee."

Mae handed him a cup, then walked over to the big picture window in the living room and gazed out through parted lace curtains at the blowing whiteness. "Do you think we should call and tell Mom and Paul not to come?"

"Knowing your stepfather, it wouldn't make any difference."

"I think I'll turn on the radio." Mae returned to the kitchen and flipped to her regular station out of St. Peter. When Peter had finished his cup, he returned outside to fire up the tractor and began the work of plowing back the advances of the storm. Mae watched him work through the windows as she listened to the announcer's deep voice on the radio. "There's a travelers advisory for Le Sueur County," he said, "and there have been some rollovers on 169." Mae wondered if her family had taken 169 instead of the back way.

The phone rang. Mae answered, "Merry Christmas."

"Merry Christmas," Virginia said. "Would you be offended if I didn't venture out today?"

Mae's heart sank. "Oh, but it's Christmas. Peter can come get you."

"I appreciate the offer, and I do wish I could come, but if anyone got stuck in this mess, I'd never forgive myself."

"I hate for you to be alone on Christmas."

"I won't be alone. Ella decided not to go see her kids either. She'll come over, and I thought I'd see if Jessie and her dad would be willing to walk a few blocks for Christmas dinner with us."

"Well . . ." Mae glanced up as Peter came stamping

in from the arctic day. "If you insist, Virginia, but we're really going to miss you."

"I'll miss you too. But I'd rather know that you're all safe. Besides, we can celebrate after the storm clears. Really," Virginia insisted.

"Okay," Mae conceded. "We love you."

"I love you too. Tell Peter to save some of that wild rice stuffing for me."

"Okay," Mae said and hung up the phone.

Peter raised his eyebrows questioningly. "She isn't coming?" he said. Mae shook her head. "What about Trudy?"

"She hasn't called. Should I try her?" Mae dialed the phone only to get a busy signal. She hung up with a sigh and returned to the window to stare out at the storm.

"Hey, it's Christmas," Peter pointed out. "Worrying won't help anything."

She leaned into him and said, "But what if something's happened?"

"I'll call Catherine," he said. "Maybe they haven't left yet." He picked up the phone to dial and waited, his gaze trained on Mae, who sat down at the kitchen table. Finally he hung up. "They must've left already. I'll try Catherine's cell." He reached her voice mail. Mae could hear the automated message from where she sat. "She must have turned her phone off," he offered.

Mae twisted a paper Christmas napkin into a tight roll. Peter set it aside and reached for her hands.

"You know," she said. Peter waited for her to continue. "I've felt so hurt by Mom and so angry. I want to be close to her. But she is so . . . distant or threatened, maybe, to let us be close. And yet I love her, you know?"

"Of course you do," he said. He leaned across the table and kissed her forehead. "Come on. There's nothing we can do now except pray about it." He reached for her hands and said a prayer for safety and comfort. When Mae lifted her eyes, the weight on her chest seemed a little lighter.

Peter squeezed her hand. "Why don't we open our presents to each other before everyone else gets here?" he said, smiling like a schoolboy. He led her to the tree. They sat on the hardwood floor, and Mae handed Peter his gift. He lifted it to his ear and gave it a shake. "It doesn't jingle," he said with a lift of his brow.

"Open it!" she said.

Inside were a hand-knit scarf and hat in black and gray.

"These should keep you warm. I worked on them during my breaks at work," Mae said, touching the thick wool pile.

He pulled the hat onto his head and wrapped the long scarf around his neck. "Mmm, toasty! How do I look?"

"Stunning," she said, her smile returning. "I'm sure the ladies in the barn will be very impressed." Peter grinned and gave her a loud smooch on the cheek.

"Now for yours," he said, presenting her with a heavy square box.

Mae moved onto her knees and gazed at the large, heavy box before finally tearing the paper off. "A—" Her voice fell. "A bread machine." She smiled at him uncertainly.

"You don't like it?" Peter said.

"I love it," she said, trying to sound excited.

"It was between that and the vacuum cleaner," he said. Pausing then, he reached into his pocket and pulled out a small rectangular box.

Mae punched his arm. "You were in serious trouble for a minute," she said.

"I know!" he smirked. "The bread machine is for me."

She took the small box from his hands and gazed at the foil wrap, then delicately opened it. Inside was an antique peridot bracelet with petals molded in silver around each stone.

Mae gasped. "It's beautiful."

"I had to take out a loan to buy it," he joked. He leaned to gaze at the bracelet as she draped it around her thin wrist.

"Thank you." She turned to hug him. They kissed, a slow, tender kiss that sent shivers up and down Peter's spine.

The back door rattled open. "Hello!" Trudy's voice sounded from the kitchen. She traipsed in before they could get up. "Is this the kind of welcome we get? You'd think you were still newlyweds or something." Catherine and Paul were coming in the back door. "We're risking life and limb while you two are making out!"

Mae jumped up and ran to give her older sister a hug. "I was worried sick," Mae said.

"I could tell." Trudy tilted her head toward Peter, who came up behind Mae. "Merry Christmas, Sluggo."

"Merry Christmas, Pippi," Peter said. He gave his sister-in-law a quick hug.

"I don't like that nickname," Trudy complained.

"All the more incentive," Peter said.

Trudy rolled her eyes at Mae. "I'm so glad we made it," she whispered to Mae with a glance at their mother who was hanging up her coat. "She white knuckled it the whole way here. Complain, complain, complain. Poor Paul had to listen to her griping all the way from St. Paul. He's on my list of nominees for sainthood!" she whispered.

"Shh," Mae scolded and greeted her mother and stepfather. "Mom," Mae said with a catch in her voice when their eyes met. She bit the inside of her lower lip, determined not to let anything ruin their holiday.

"Merry Christmas," Catherine said and leaned in for a hug. Mae wondered if she, too, was recalling their last time together after the baby's funeral. "The roads were horrible," Catherine groused as her gaze shifted to Paul. Some communication passed between the two; what exactly, Mae couldn't tell.

Peter placed a comforting arm around Mae's back and said, "Heard there were some rollovers."

"Highway 169 was a demolition derby," Paul said.

"If we'd known the roads were so bad we would've stayed home," Catherine said. Paul shook his head and mouthed *no* behind her back. Mae smiled at him. Catherine strode into the kitchen. "I brought some *lefse* and *krumkaka*." She set the tray of Norwegian delicacies on the counter. "I would've brought *lutefisk*—"

"Eww!" Trudy and Mae said in unison.

"Trust me, Mom," Trudy said. "We're all glad you didn't."

"I thought you liked *lutefisk,*" she protested.

"Must've been your other kids," Trudy said, laughing.

Paul went out to rescue Catherine's purse and Christmas packages from the car. Then he meandered to the living-room fireplace to warm up before the glowing fire. Soon the sounds of a football game could be heard from the television set in the den.

"How are you?" Peter whispered to Mae while Trudy and Catherine peeked at the goodies she had prepared.

Mae smiled. "I'm doing wonderful now that I know everyone's okay."

The comforting aromas of sage and rosemary filled the kitchen as Mae carved the golden turkey, Trudy stirred gravy, and Catherine mashed potatoes.

"So, Trudy, when is Bert supposed to get here?" Catherine said.

"He was going to open gifts with his family, then come over," Trudy said. Today was Bert's day to stand trial before her mother, but Trudy didn't care. All that mattered was that she thought Bert was perfect.

"Did I hear that you raise chickens?" Catherine was asking Mae.

Mae nodded.

"Really? You kill them yourself?" Catherine said. "This turkey wasn't part of the flock, was it?"

Mae's cheeks flushed. "No, I bought the turkey at the grocery store."

There was a long silence. Mae leaned over the turkey as if it demanded her full concentration.

"So." Trudy jumped in. "Ellen's wedding was beautiful."

"Tony actually went through with it?" Mae said.

"He didn't pass out or anything. And it was so pretty, all in candlelight . . ."

"Tell me about your new job," Catherine said to Mae.

"It's not much really. I'm a receptionist for the county."

"A government job," Catherine said. "Good potential for a bright girl like you, more potential than slaughtering chickens." She laughed.

Mae sighed and placed another slice of turkey on the heaping platter.

"Mmm. Something smells good," Peter said, coming in with an empty plate that had held crackers and cheese.

"We're almost ready," Mae said too cheerfully. Trudy watched Peter, wondering if he could feel the tension. Peter placed a hand on Mae's shoulder, and she smiled into his eyes.

A twinge of jealousy pricked Trudy's heart, a

longing for Bert to know her the way Peter knew Mae.

As Mae was placing the gravy boat on the white tablecloth, Bert pulled into the driveway in his tall John Deere tractor. "Ooh, Bert's here," Trudy squealed. She threw the back door open as he clambered up the steps. He carried a paper grocery bag filled with gifts, and his hair was wet with snow.

"Trudy, you're letting in the cold air," her mother scolded.

Trudy hustled Bert in and closed the door. "What happened to your truck?" she said. She brushed off his winter coat before placing it on a hook.

"Wouldn't start," he said. He wore a new pair of Levi's with a Western plaid shirt in navy and white. His curly hair was combed back neatly.

Trudy rose on tiptoes to kiss Bert's cheek, then she took a deep breath and reached for his hand. "You ready?" she whispered.

"No," he said. She squeezed his arm, then led him to the dining room where everyone was finding a seat.

"Mom, Paul, I'd like you to meet Bert Biddle. Bert, this is my mother, Catherine, and her husband, Paul Larson."

Bert held out a hand to Catherine and said, "Happy to meet you," as they shook.

"Mr. Biddle," Catherine replied. Trudy rolled her eyes.

After Peter offered grace, Catherine said to Bert, "You're a farmer like Peter?" She unfolded her napkin and placed it in her lap.

Bert nodded.

"Has your family been farming for long?" Catherine said.

"The farm's been in the family since the end of the Civil War," Bert said.

"Really?" Even Catherine seemed impressed.

"Of course in the beginning the Biddles raised hogs. We've only done dairy for the past fifty years."

"Hogs?" Catherine said.

So much for being impressed.

After supper the men retreated to the den and the television while the women cleared the table and got dessert ready. Mae was making coffee, and Catherine cleared dirty dishes while Trudy sliced pie.

"Bert seems nice," Catherine said. She set the empty gravy boat on the counter by the sink.

"He is," Trudy agreed.

"Of course, you two have little in common," Catherine said.

"I don't know," Trudy said. "We both eat food, sleep in beds, breathe—"

"Be serious, Trudy!" her mother said. "His family has been in farming over a hundred years; you're—"

"A redhead?"

"Trudy!" Catherine's nostrils flared.

"It's Christmas, Mom. Take a Valium. It's not like he's proposed or anything. You said yourself, he's a nice guy, and I haven't met one of those in a long time."

Catherine sighed. "I don't want to see you get hurt."

"I'm a big girl." Trudy patted her mother's shoulder

and gave her a kiss on the cheek. "Thanks for caring—it really does mean a lot to me."

"Well, remember I told you so when your differences add up and start to pull you apart."

"Cross my heart," Trudy said with a smile toward Mae, who'd become a statue during the conversation.

Catherine reached for a tray with creamer, sugar, and Santa-shaped coffee mugs. "I'll take this out to the men. Is the pie ready?" she said to Trudy.

"I'll bring it along in a minute."

Mae's gaze shifted to the arched entry to the living room once Catherine was out of sight. "How do you do that?"

"Do what?"

"Calm her down like that."

"She's a kitten."

"No, I'm serious," Mae protested.

"I don't know. I don't really think about it. I guess I don't let her control me. If I don't like what she says, I dish some of her words back at her."

Mae pulled down the plates and put a thick slice of pumpkin pie on each with a big dollop of whipped cream. "You can get her to agree to anything. If I so much as look at Mom the wrong way, she criticizes me."

"You're too sensitive, Maeflower, and you don't give Mom enough credit," Trudy said. "She was always there for us when we were kids. Mom wasn't the one who deserted us."

Mae glanced toward the door again. Her voice rose in pitch. "I'm supposed to take whatever she says, even if it's hurtful?"

"I didn't say that." Trudy raised a scolding finger. "But the truth is, you can't let what she says decide your future. You can't make Mom happy, so live your life and do what you know is right. Whether she likes it or not."

Mae turned her back to Trudy as she placed the last slice of pie on a plate.

"It's called 'growing up,'" Trudy said. "You know? It's time to grow up."

Mae didn't reply.

"Hey, are you mad at me?"

"I'm fine," Mae said, yet her stiff stance betrayed her.

"I know better," Trudy said. "You're mad, aren't you?"

Mae faced her. Sadness flecked her dark eyes. "I guess the truth hurts," she said with a shrug.

Trudy wished the truth could be kind every once in a while, or at least that she didn't feel the need to be its banner bearer.

By evening the storm had slackened to a flurry of flakes that danced and flirted under the lights on the porch. Pine branches drooped low under the burden of the heavy snow. Drifts curled across the ditch in front of the farmhouse, creating a high wave.

"Well, that wasn't bad," Peter said as he and Mae stood at the kitchen sink, his hands and forearms buried in suds. He set a plate in the rinse water.

Mae didn't reply. She lifted the plate and let it drip

for a few seconds before drying it.

"What's wrong?" Peter said. "Everything went well with your mom, didn't it?"

"Not exactly." She paused, then said, "I had my hopes so high. I guess I'd expected after everything that's happened things would somehow be better between us. But she kept making the same old comments, her digs about living on the farm." She took a breath. "I'm mad at Trudy."

"What did Trudy do?" He dried his hands and touched her back.

"Sometimes she's not very sensitive. It gets old."

"Now what did she say?"

Mae shrugged. "I want to forget about it. She was right. I hate it when she's right."

fourteen

The Chuckwagon buzzed with the happy sounds of diners enjoying a midweek break. The lunch crowd filled every seat. Ladies chatted about the latest happenings in town—who was visiting whom, what new items they'd purchased on sale—while the men talked about the weather and crops and sports. Several waitresses scurried among the tables. The cook rang his bell, signaling that someone's meal was up.

Peter and David stood in the lobby, searching for a place to sit. "Looks like we don't have a lot of choice," David said, nodding toward the counter with its red vinyl and chrome seats, still the same as the day the place had been built in 1952.

A waitress flew past, a thin woman in her midfifties with blond hair and dark roots. "Be right with you, kids," she said over her shoulder as David and Peter took their seats.

David smiled at Peter. "Some things never change," David said.

"David Morgan!" she said when she returned with menus in hand. "I haven't seen you in a coon's age, you sly one." The waitress winked at Peter. "Your dad has been dying to go out with me since we were in high school. I'm still available, honey." She patted David on the shoulder. David blushed with embarrassment.

Peter raised his eyebrows at his dad, who shook his head. "She's kidding," he reassured Peter. "Tell him you're kidding, Jody."

"I'm dead serious. Vernon won't go out with me. Will you, Vernon?" she said to an elderly man as he passed with a bin of dirty dishes on his way toward the kitchen's swinging doors.

"If you don't mind me bringing Adeline along, we could go on a date tomorrow. She tends to get jealous if I go on dates without her." Jody laughed.

"So, Jody, what are the specials?" David asked.

"Sure—change the subject," Jody said with another wink to Peter. "Special today is pork dinner, mashed potatoes and gravy, stuffing. The soup is Cowboy's Surprise."

"Cowboy's Surprise?" Peter said. "What's that?"

"Don't ask, but it tastes okay. Want a few minutes to decide?" She stepped away before they could answer

128

and began joking with the people at the table behind them. Peter gazed down at the menu.

Peter was sure he had memorized the thing over the past year. He had yet to see a change in the selection. He usually got the same thing—Reuben on rye with Thousand Island dressing and a dinner salad on the side.

"I have some news," David said. "I saw the doctor a couple of weeks ago—"

"Doctor?" Peter set his menu on the table.

David lifted a hand, then placed it palm down on the table. "It's nothing life threatening. It's my hands. Seems I have arthritis."

"Arthritis," Peter said, trying to wrap his mind around the word. "That's an old person's disease."

"Thanks for the vote of confidence," David said. "Actually, arthritis can strike at any age. Some children even have it. Unfortunately the kind I have can be quite degenerative."

"Meaning?"

"Meaning—"

Jody reappeared for their orders, and David stopped talking. Peter ordered his usual. "I'll have the pork dinner," David said. He shifted in his seat and cleared his throat once she was gone. "My violin-playing days are over. I resigned from the symphony yesterday."

"Yesterday? That's awfully fast."

"I've been in denial for a while." He laughed humorlessly. "The orchestra deserved to find someone who could keep up. I can't anymore."

"Oh, Dad," Peter said, wishing he could relieve the

anguish in his father's eyes. Peter lowered his voice. "What are you going to do?"

David shrugged. "I don't know. Music has been my life for so long. I don't know." His voice caught, and Peter felt his heart twist with the pain. What would Peter do if someone told him he could no longer farm? It'd been less than a year, and already he couldn't imagine the sadness of that loss. He peered into the older man's clouded eyes. "I'm not ready to retire," David went on. "I suppose I'll need to find a way to pay for that expensive apartment in St. Paul."

"You could come live with us." It was out before Peter thought it through, but as he said it he realized that this was not something to be thought through. This was family.

"I couldn't impose on you and Mae like—"

"I mean it," Peter interrupted.

David said, "I'll think about it. I guess it would save me some rent money. Not that I'd expect to freeload off you."

"I want to do this for you, Dad," Peter said. "That's all. Let me help you for once."

David placed a hand on his son's and said, "Thanks."

As Peter drove home and the January sun reflected off the fields in a blinding, crisp whiteness, he pondered his father's news. It was devastating, and yet deep down he couldn't help but think that now he'd have more time with his dad, unhindered by busy schedules and distance. He knew it was selfish of him, to be hopeful when the news so crushed his father. But it was there, in his heart, as it had been when he was a boy. He pictured him and his father spending long afternoons together, laughing, talking, being father and son as never before. Who knew? Maybe Peter could get his dad to take up farming with him.

ROSEMARY JOHNSON

Ten-year-old Rosemary Johnson stared out the window as the lights of the ambulance turned the corner and hurried out of sight. She strained to see where it went, but it disappeared into the murky day. She felt her father's hand on her shoulder as a tear slipped down her cheek, matching the raindrops on the window.

"Why did Mama act that way?" Rosemary said. Her father was silent, his gaze also trained on the street. "Did those men hurt her when they put that jacket on her? It looked like it hurt, the way they tied it around her back."

"Mama will be okay," her father said. He left. Rosemary could hear his shoes clicking on the kitchen linoleum.

"What happened to Mama?" Rosemary whispered to herself. "What made her act so strange?" Rosemary had come home from school and found her mother sitting on the living room floor, family pictures scattered around her. Mama rocked back and forth like a baby, muttering something Rosemary couldn't decipher. She held a long pair of scissors and was cutting out her own face from each of the photographs.

Then she cut the likenesses into tiny pieces. Her cheeks were red, and her eyes—Rosemary had never seen eyes like that. It was as if she stared right through Rosemary and what she saw on the other side made her angry. That was when she came at Rosemary with those scissors. Why would Mama do that? Rosemary had been so stunned that she just stood there, as if it were happening to someone else and she was a mere spectator. Daddy had come in then and wrestled away the scissors before Mama could hurt her.

Rosemary hugged her arms tightly around herself as she stood in the living room, staring at lonely raindrops that inched their way down the glass. She desperately needed someone to hold her and tell her everything would be all right.

Henry cried from his crib in the back of the house. Rosemary had forgotten about him. She'd laid him down before Mama "went insane." That was what she heard Daddy say to Father O'Connell.

Could that be true? Could Mama be insane?

Rosemary held three-year-old Henry's hand as they followed Daddy through the white halls of the hospital the next day. Henry was always frightened of hospitals. They smelled funny, and the people were scary. Rosemary gripped Henry's hand tighter. People in gray-and-white uniforms marched past, paying them no nevermind as they searched for Mama's room.

Rosemary had never seen Daddy so stern, so sad. She knew how he felt—betrayed. She felt the same way.

They stopped at a big metal door, and Daddy entered with the children trailing behind. The hinges creaked. Rosemary could see Father O'Connell next to Mama's bed with a black Bible in his hands. Mama seemed so small. Her frail body barely disturbed the blanket. She was sleeping. Daddy spoke with Father O'Connell in hushed tones, then he reached out and touched Mama's face with his fingers.

Her eyes opened, and she looked at Daddy, then at Henry and Rosemary at the foot of the bed. When Mama's eyes landed on Rosemary, she started crying big tears that rolled down her hollow cheeks. She murmured, "I'm sorry, baby." Rosemary's feet were frozen in place, the longing to be held unable to overcome the fear that made her heart pump so hard she thought she would faint.

Daddy sat on the edge of the bed and held Mama's hand. He pulled a handkerchief from his suit pocket and wiped her tears, gently, tenderly. Rosemary watched. Henry ran from Rosemary's grasp and squirmed to be held. Daddy lifted him up. Rosemary noticed that her mama's arms were tied to the bed.

Henry patted Mama's shoulder and said, "Don't cry, Mama. Don't cry."

Rosemary didn't move. She was immobile. An outsider.

"Rosemary," Daddy said. He reached a hand toward her. "Come say hello to Mama."

Rosemary hesitantly edged up to the bed and touched the blanket over her mother's legs. "Hi, Mama," she said in a shaky voice.

"Hi, sweetheart," her mama whispered. *Her tears renewed their strength. Rosemary wanted to cover her ears, to drown them out. Daddy leaned to Mama and held her. Rosemary had never seen him hold her like that before. Rosemary took a step back. Mama's shoulders shook. Daddy patted her back and said, "It's going to be okay. It's going to be okay, baby." Over and over again. But nothing would ever be okay, and Rosemary knew it.*

Finally Daddy turned to Rosemary and said, "Rosemary, why don't you take Henry down to that sunroom we passed. I think I saw a piano in there. You can play it while you wait for me. Father O'Connell and I need to have a talk." He looked toward the priest.

Rosemary glanced one more time at her mother's tear-filled eyes, then reached for Henry's hand after Daddy set him on the floor.

Their shoes sounded loud in the too-quiet corridor. People came in and out of the rooms. Some wore long robes and stared at them oddly. Rosemary quickened her pace, eager to leave.

No one else was in the bright sunroom. Rosemary set Henry on the floor beside the piano bench and gave him a picture book from the low coffee table. She touched the black and white keys. She began with the lilting sounds of "Für Elise"—the song she'd played at her last recital. The music took her far away from the sadness. She played and played, trying to keep it all hidden away—if only she could forget.

"Time to go," Daddy said when he finally came to get them. He stooped to pick up Henry, who had fallen

asleep in the sunshine. Daddy's eyes were red. Rose-
mary reached for her daddy's embrace, expecting him
to push her away and tell her she was a big girl. But
this time he held her, and Rosemary cried in his arms.

fifteen

If the elementary school was full of bright, chirping parakeets, the high school was a gaggle of lurking turkey vultures. Trudy spent Tuesdays, Thursdays, and every other Friday at the high school. While she had an easy enjoyment of the younger crowd, the teen set was a challenge, but when she did break through, the satisfaction was that much deeper.

She turned on the lights in the big art room and poked around, opening closets and cupboards, trying to remember where the watercolor supplies were kept. She'd discovered that art supplies were much harder to come by than they had been in St. Paul. There she'd had an endless supply of paints, brushes, paper, clay . . . In the weeks she'd been in Lake Emily she'd already had to put in two purchase requests, and even then she'd been warned to keep a tight rein on her budget.

Trudy closed the cupboard door and began walking toward the office to fill out yet another request when the strains of "Für Elise" met her in the music hallway.

"Excuse me," she said with a knock on the door-frame. A petite woman with gray hair pulled into a round bun stopped playing the piano and lifted her head.

"Oh, you're the new art teacher," she said. Her eyes were a vibrant blue, and her face was unlined and smooth despite her hair color. A pencil was tucked into the base of her bun.

"Uh-huh. I'm Trudy, Trudy Ploog. I'm sorry. I heard beautiful music, and it drew me in," Trudy said, stepping forward to shake her hand.

"I'm Rosemary Johnson, the music teacher. I teach at the elementary too, so we have something in common."

"How do you get used to the schedule?" Trudy said. "I'm exhausted already!"

Rosemary smiled. "It's pretty new to me, too, actually. I'm not sure you get used to it; it's more like you learn to make the best of it." Trudy noticed a deep dimple below Rosemary's right eye and her high cheekbones, and her mouth was a thin line when she wasn't smiling.

"How are you adjusting to small-town life?" Rosemary asked.

"Great. I spent last summer at my sister's farm, so it isn't totally weird."

"No doubt people have told you about the budget cuts and all."

"I was at the last school board meeting," Trudy confessed. "It made me wonder if I made a mistake accepting the job."

"You're secure; don't worry. Every school needs an art teacher." She echoed Trudy's words to Bob Ott. "And since you're willing to switch-hit at both schools, you're set. I'm not always so sure about some of the music programs though. They already cut the orchestra." She pursed her lips. "But that's something I wanted to talk to you about." She paused and turned sideways on the black piano bench so she was facing Trudy straight on. "I know you're still getting used to everything, and I don't want you to feel obligated, but I have a favor to ask of you."

"It doesn't hurt to ask," Trudy said.

Rosemary wove her fingers together. "Every spring our senior high puts on a musical. With budget issues it's getting harder and harder to do that. The school board has dropped all funding for it, even though we always played to packed houses. Well, anyway, I hate to see the kids miss out." She smiled, and the dimple reappeared. "I can handle the music and acting end of things, but we need help with costume and set design. Believe me, it doesn't have to be anything fancy. It's an after-school volunteer thing. You could get some budding artists to help out." She paused. "Give it some thought?"

For some reason her request reminded Trudy of something Mrs. Zernickel would have said, and she smiled. "What show are you putting on?" Trudy said.

"*Oklahoma!* We have some really talented singers. If you get to hear Lydia Lindstrom—she's amazing. I'm afraid the children who aren't into sports don't have the same level of opportunities that the athletes get. The musical gives them something creative and constructive to do through the winter months. Well, I am going on." The first-period bell sounded.

"Saved by the bell," Trudy said as she edged toward the door.

"Let me know what you think about the play. We won't start rehearsals for another month or so. I like the cast to have some time to memorize their lines before we get going."

"Okay," Trudy said. "I'm a pushover—I'd love to help."

Rosemary smiled. "Oh, good! I'll get you a script this week so you can start designing sets."

"Okay," Trudy said. She left as students began filing in for first-hour class.

This was going to be good. She would get to know the music students, and she felt good about contributing. Besides, Bert was busy with hockey and the farm work, so this would be an ideal way to fill her empty hours and to find her own way in Lake Emily.

Hockey blades *swoosh, swooshed* from side to side as the skaters moved along the rink. Sticks slapped against the puck. Air whistled as the black disk catapulted toward the net. To Bert these were nostalgic sounds that brought back a flood of glory days. State championships three years running. Weekends on the road with his best friends as they traveled from town to town. Chill air that turned his cheeks red yet left him warm and exhilarated.

Bert clapped his hands and whistled for the guys to gather around. The Lake Emily Bulldogs in their gold-and-blue uniforms huddled, some bent over at the waist to catch their breath. Coach Miller had gone to answer the phone while Bert ran drills.

"You guys need to hustle it up," Bert said. "Stick close to your man on defense. The other team shouldn't even have a chance to get the puck near the goal. It's the reason you guys keep losing—you give them too much room. So let's pair up. See if you can keep the puck away from your partner." He pointed to a short, blond ninth grader. "Kevin, take a turn at goalie."

Kevin's face lit with a smile. "Really?"

"Hurry up before I change my mind." Bert nodded. "Eric will let you use his gear." The senior nodded and relinquished the protective gear. Bert grabbed the bag of pucks, and soon the teens were skating back and forth across the ice, trying to steal the puck from their partners.

"You're going to have to skate faster than that," Bert said as two players glided past. "Keep your partner off your back."

Coach Miller came up. He wore a gold-and-blue Lake Emily hockey jacket over a red hooded sweatshirt. A worn chrome whistle hung from a lanyard around his neck.

"Thanks, Bert," he said. His gaze was on the team. "Looks like we'll have the JV boys whipped into shape in no time."

"We really need to beef up defense," Bert said. "They're slow."

Glen Miller nodded. "We never had that problem in your day, did we?" the coach said. "Not with Bert Biddle on goal." Bert turned red at the compliment. "You ever regret not taking your hockey further?"

Bert shook his head. "Nobody offered any scholarships, so I took that as a sign."

"Well, I sure appreciate your helping with the JV coaching. It's been hard since the state started cutting budgets. I had to let two of my staff go." He sighed. "It's a shame, because the kids are the ones who end up losing out." The big man lifted his face to the caged clock far above the indoor rink's white-painted boards.

"So tell me about this girl who moved all the way from the city for you. I heard she made quite an impression at the school board meeting, telling them how she'll reform the art department."

Bert laughed, then said, "She has a good heart. She reminds me a lot of you, actually."

The coach lifted an eyebrow. "How's that?"

"She cares about the kids."

Snow wandered like desert nomad caravans across white dunes until it came to an oasis of trees, where it piled in towering waves so high that they would eventually collapse in miniature avalanches.

Mae gazed out the kitchen window at the storm. "I am so glad it's Saturday and I don't have to go to work in this," she said to Peter, who reclined at the kitchen table with a mug of steaming cider.

"Good for you," he said teasingly. "I still have to go out."

"At least you don't have to drive anywhere. It's a few minutes in the cold, and you're in the shelter of the barn."

"The barn is heated?"

"Oh, stop complaining. It's plenty warm in there, and you know it."

Peter took a sip, and Mae came to sit beside him. "You have six hours until you milk again. What would you like to do with our day?" She was beautiful. Her dark hair was straight and shiny; her brown eyes sparkled.

Peter raised his eyebrows and said, "I could think of a few things to do on a cold, blustery day while we're stranded in the house." He moved closer and kissed her neck below the ear.

"Peter, knock it off." She swatted his hand. "I'm serious."

"So am I." He kissed her again.

She withdrew a few inches, and Peter saw pain in her eyes.

"What's wrong?" He touched her hair and swept it behind her shoulder. "You still mad at Trudy?"

"No." She sighed. "It's nothing."

"No, there's something. I know that sigh." Then he paused, wondering if he should risk what he wanted to say. Finally he began, "We've hardly been intimate these past two months. We need to talk about what's going on. I feel like we aren't close, and I'm worried . . . Should we get some counseling?"

"No," Mae said. She faced him and reached for his hands. As he gazed into her eyes, it struck him how deeply he loved her. That was what caused the worry and fear to edge in.

"We're okay," she insisted.

He searched her eyes but saw only his own reflection.

"Peter, I love you. I really love you. I'm sorry."

"Don't be sorry," he said calmly. Inside he wanted to shout, shake loose whatever it was that kept her distant. "You can talk to me. Tell me what it is."

"Trust me—it's nothing. Really." She gazed into his eyes, then leaned in to him and kissed him, a long, honeyed reminder of kisses past. Peter wanted to believe her. He pushed his doubts aside. "Let's go upstairs," she said, standing and pulling him along with her. "I think I have some chores for you to do."

sixteen

The broken speaker on the radio in the Biddles' milking parlor rattled with sounds of Olivia Newton-John's "Have You Never Been Mellow." Bert swatted cows' rumps to let them know they were excused from their duties. The next round of big black-and-white prisoners ambled into the parlor for their turn to be milked. Usually they were eager for their milking, but one cow dug her hooves into the dirt, refusing to cooperate. Bert swatted her harder, and she jolted forward.

"It's okay, girl," he murmured. "No different than any other day." She finally moved into position. The heavy bars clanged against her leathery neck.

Fred had lined up the five-gallon buckets of disinfectant in which the suction cups soaked between the stanchions. He took the curled blue hose to spray udders. Soon Bert was there too. They worked with silent precision that came from a lifetime of routine. The phone rang in the milk-tank room off the back as Bert headed out for another group of cows. "You wanna get that?" he called to Fred.

"Let Ma get it in the house," Fred said. He pushed the button that released the line holding the black spider and bent down to attach it to the cow's teats.

A few minutes later, Lillian came charging through the parlor's inner gate. "Bert," she screeched. The cows stamped their feet and strained to look at the loud woman. "Didn't you hear the phone ring? Why you make me trounce all the way out here I'll never know. This is the very reason we have a phone in the barn. Do you know how cold it is outside? I almost froze my butt off so you can talk to that Ploog girl. Doesn't she know what time you milk? Maybe you should write it down for her."

Bert walked over to the phone and picked it up, letting his mother's tirade fade into background noise. "Hey," he said.

"Hey, yourself," Trudy said. "I know you're milking. I wanted to hear your voice and see if you'd like to do anything tonight. Your mom didn't seem too happy about my calling."

"And I'm not so sure you don't call just to bug her," Bert said.

"Who, me?"

Bert glanced at his mother as she said, "I was right in the middle of *Wheel of Fortune*. Now I'll never know if Queensland was the right answer." Fred rolled his eyes and went back to milking.

Lillian wrapped her scarf tight around her neck and tugged her knit cap down on her head, then turned to go back to the house. She stepped forward, and the instant she'd disappeared from Bert's view he heard a shriek of pain.

Bert dropped the phone and ran to see what was wrong. "I broke my ankle!" Lillian shrieked through clenched teeth. The cows pushed against their restraints, eager to be as far from her as possible. "Who left this manure here?" Lillian ground out.

"Are you okay, Ma?" Bert said.

"Am I okay? Do I *look* okay?" She pointed at her foot. Her right ankle was twisted at an odd angle, and she was covered from rump to stern in chunky brown.

Fred stood next to Bert and said, "Nasty. You think we should hose her off?"

"You do and it'll be the last breath you take!" Lillian said. "Get me to the hospital."

"But you're all covered, and you smell," Fred said. He pointed over his shoulder at the cows. "Besides, we aren't done milking."

"Now!" Lillian said.

"We already started," Fred complained. "Someone has to finish—"

"I'll take her to the hospital," Bert said, giving his twin a withering scowl. He reached his arms under his mother's armpits and gently lifted her upright. "Can you stand on your other leg?"

"Ouch, ouch, ouch," Lillian sobbed. "I stink! Get me into the house. I can strip down in the mud room.

Get your father," she said to Fred. When he didn't move she said, "The cows can wait a couple of minutes!" Finally he left.

Bert helped his mother hobble on her good foot to the coat hooks by the door. He quickly slipped on his jacket while his mother balanced on her good leg.

"This is what I get for coming out to tell you that you had a phone call. I should've told that Ploog girl you'd call her back. Now I'll miss *Jeopardy!* too. Ouch!"

"Oh, I forgot about Trudy," Bert said. Lillian squeezed his arm, daring him to leave her. She lifted her bad leg higher and winced. The smell of ripe manure wafted up. Bert tried to ignore it.

They began struggling through the snow toward the house. Lillian wasn't a small woman, and Bert was glad he'd had years of haying and hard labor to prepare him for hoisting her along.

Winter winds pushed against them. "Ouch, ouch, ouch," Lillian said with each hop. "Where is Willie?" she complained. A few minutes later her husband was on the other side of her with his arm around her back.

"What happened?" Willie said, looking across his wife to Bert.

"There was manure on that step down to the parlor," Lillian said. "I've told you before that the step was dangerous. You don't even realize it's there, and—*wham!*—you break your ankle. Bert, you run up and get a new outfit for me—those exercise pants that zip up the side. Dad can help get this manure off me."

Willie gave his son an expression that said, *Oh, lucky me!*

Trudy had no idea what had happened. One minute she was talking to Bert, the next there was a scream and crashing sound as the phone dropped. Someone seemed angry. After waiting for Bert to come back on the line for what seemed an eternity a voice said, "Hello? Is someone there?" It was Fred.

"Yeah, it's Trudy. What happened to Bert?"

Fred cleared his throat. "Oh. Mom broke her ankle, so he took her to town."

"Is it bad?"

"Don't know. She wasn't happy when she left here. I gotta go milk."

"Thanks, Fred," Trudy said. He muttered something and then hung up.

The bell tinkled. Bert walked into the cluttered living room to see what his mother wanted this time. She lay in a heap of pillows, her cast-encased foot pointed skyward. A knit afghan covered her lap and quilted housedress. The television blared from the corner, another game show.

"Can you refill my water?" She handed him the insulated pitcher from the metal TV tray beside her. "And make it colder." Bert took the pitcher into the kitchen where Fred was putting a frozen lasagna into the oven. He was clearing the dirty dishes from the sink when the bell sounded again. Bert's and Fred's eyes met.

"Your turn," Bert said. Fred turned and stomped up the stairs. Bert heard the door to Fred's room slam. He sighed and muttered, "Thanks!" under his breath.

"Bert!" Lillian called. Bert came around the corner. "Can you bring the Tylenol 3 also, when you come? This pain is getting worse." She lay back and readjusted the mound behind her back. "Do we have any cross-word puzzle books down here?" Lillian said.

Bert shrugged.

"Would you look in the pile of magazines by my bed?" She pointed upstairs. "I think I put a couple new ones there."

Bert returned to the kitchen, where he filled the pitcher with ice water and placed it on a tray with a glass, Tylenol 3, and a plate of Chips Ahoy cookies. He climbed the stairs, found the desired magazines and some sharp pencils, and returned to his mother with everything in hand. Lillian smiled. "Do you know where some erasers are? I like to have an eraser handy in case I need to change an answer."

Bert dug through the junk drawer in the kitchen. Willie came in the back door carrying two bags of groceries filled with ready-made foods.

"Is that you, Willie?" Lillian's voice sounded. Willie glanced at his son.

"When's the last time she took some of that medicine?" Willie asked.

"I took one to her a few minutes ago," Bert said.

"Give her two next time."

M ae stared at the blue test strip. She wiped her brow with her sleeve. It was taking forever. She stared at the bathroom door, wondering if Peter had come in from milking yet. She unfolded the directions for the pregnancy test once again and reread them. She'd done everything right. She ran a hand through her long hair. It fell in a cascade down her back.

Why hadn't she gone on the pill after the miscarriage? Then she wouldn't have this problem, this fear. What if she was pregnant? The fear of losing another baby was almost overwhelming.

The mirror wasn't kind today. Her eyes peered out from dark circles. Ever since she'd missed her last period, she'd barely slept. She'd felt every shift of her stomach and wondered if it could be so. It wasn't logical; she hadn't felt Laura's movements until she was past the twenty-week mark. But she had to know. The not knowing was driving her insane.

She scrutinized the strip again. There it was—a faint minus sign. Within a minute it grew darker until the result was no longer in doubt.

The tears came. She sat on the toilet lid and wept. Relief and sadness swept through her at the same time. There was no baby.

Ding, ding, ding. Lillian's bell sounded from the living room. It had been three days since she'd broken her ankle, three days of her lying on the couch and ringing that stupid bell, then hollering if no one answered. Bert's dad had escaped to his workshop after lunch. Fred had gone back to bed after milking and was now in the kitchen making cinnamon toast.

Bert walked into the living room. "What's up, Ma?"

"I've got to go to the bathroom. Clear a path through this mess for me? You'd think you men didn't know how to pick up a pair of socks." Lillian eased onto her crutches and hobbled toward the bathroom off the kitchen. Passing the kitchen doorway, she said, "Fred, clean up that mess you made!" Fred buttered his toast, his back turned toward his mother. "Fred!" she barked.

"What!" Fred wheeled. "Go to the bathroom!" He slammed the knife into the sink and stomped up to his room with his breakfast in hand. Bert watched him go. He understood Fred's frustration, yet Fred was acting like a child.

"What's got into him?" Lillian said, staring after Fred.

"He'll be fine," Bert said. "He's just being Fred."

Lillian huffed. "Never did understand all that moodiness."

Once his mother was safely back on the couch, Bert dutifully cleaned the kitchen counters and started the Hamburger Helper for supper. The phone rang.

"Hey." It was Trudy. "You want to come over tonight? I'll make us supper. We could watch a movie."

Bert peeked through the dining-room door to his ma as she shouted, "The Big Easy Chair" at *Wheel of Fortune*.

"I'm on supper duty here tonight," he said with a sigh.

"I could come help," Trudy said. "I'm sure your mom could use some company. I could bring my world-famous Greek salad. It's really yummy."

"You've convinced me," Bert said. "Does Greek salad go with Hamburger Helper?"

"Doesn't everything go with Hamburger Helper?" she said. "I'll be there in half an hour."

"Hey," Trudy said as she let herself in the mud-room door. A hand-knit scarf covered the lower half of her face while a matching hat rode low, leaving only her eyes, nose, and the tops of her rosy cheeks exposed. "It's pretty out, but *brr*—it's cold!" she said. Bert took the grocery bag from her, then showed her where to hang her coat.

"Someone here?" Lillian called from the living room.

"It's me, Mrs. Biddle. Trudy Ploog. I came to help with supper."

"Trudy Ploog?"

Bert could hear the strain in her voice.

Then, "Well, at least *someone's* helping around here."

Trudy's eyes widened. "Has she been like that all day?" she said.

"Three days." Bert shrugged and set the bag on the counter. "Thank you for this. You're a lifesaver," he whispered and leaned close for a quick kiss.

"I have just the thing for your mother." Trudy pulled

150

a Mason jar filled with M&M's from the sack.

"What's that?" Bert said.

"Grouch pills, guaranteed to brighten any day." She shook the bottle and waggled her eyebrows.

Bert smiled. "Looks like you're about set here," Trudy said, looking at the stove where the Hamburger Helper bubbled and steamed beneath its lid. "Smells good." She pulled out tomatoes, fresh romaine lettuce and spinach, organic carrots, mushrooms, feta cheese, cracked Greek olives, croutons, and a bottle of Ranch dressing. "You'll like it." She began chopping, slicing, shredding, and crumbling until she had a huge bowl of salad. "I could live on these," she said, popping an olive into her mouth.

"Bert!" It was Lillian again. "I'm starving. Is supper almost ready?"

Trudy lifted a finger before Bert had a chance to respond. "Allow me," she said. She fixed a tray including a plate of Hamburger Helper, a bowl of Greek salad, and the jar of M&M's and carried it out to Lillian. Bert watched from the arched doorway.

"How's that ankle today, Mrs. Biddle?" Trudy said pleasantly as she set the food down on the metal TV tray.

"Lillian," she corrected. "Mrs. Biddle was my mother-in-law. And this ankle feels worse than the day I broke it. Not that anyone around here appreciates the pain I'm in."

"I'm sure they care more than you know," Trudy said nicely.

"They sure choose a funny way to show it. They

151

grumble and whine about helping me. The house is a pigsty." She waved her hand to the room. "No one comes when I ring the bell."

"Maybe if you rang it less often they'd be more apt to come."

"It doesn't matter how many times I ring it; these men are deaf."

"You're not exactly the most gracious sick person," Trudy said truthfully.

Bert flinched, though he knew Trudy was right.

"I'm in pain." Lillian pointed to her ankle.

"That doesn't give you a right to be snooty. How much do you think a person can take?"

Lillian's mouth dropped open.

"Bert has been waiting on you hand and foot, but are you grateful?" Trudy said. "No. No matter what he does, you want more."

"Trudy," Bert finally said. Trudy turned her head to him as he opened his eyes wide and said, "We'd better get the rest of supper on for everyone else. Okay?" He nodded toward the kitchen. Trudy came into the kitchen, leaving Lillian to mutter to herself.

"Why did you do that?" Bert whispered.

"I know how hard you've been working to take care of your mother, and I got mad!"

"I don't need you defending me." He scooped the remaining Hamburger Helper into a serving dish.

She gently turned Bert toward her. "I'm sorry," she said. Her voice was smaller, apologetic.

He gazed into her luminous eyes and felt his frustration settle. "She's in a lot of pain. Aggravating her

152

will only make things worse."

"Have I ruined everything?" Trudy said.

"No." He shrugged.

"Maybe I should take a grouch pill, huh?" Trudy said.

Bert smiled. "You haven't ruined anything." He paused. "I love you."

The *Jeopardy!* theme echoed from the television as Bert and Trudy stood side by side washing and drying dishes. Willie was watching the game show with Lillian. Fred was out milking. Bert had promised he'd be out soon.

Trudy wiped a dish and set it on the counter. She glanced at his strong profile. The light above the kitchen sink added golden highlights to his dishwater blond curls.

"Hey," he said when their eyes met.

"Hey, yourself."

His words echoed in her mind: *I love you . . . love you . . . love you.* Was that the first time he'd uttered those words to her? She inhaled happily.

"What?" he said.

"Just happy."

He raised a brow.

"You said you love me."

"I did?" His brow puckered.

She poked his stomach with a finger. "You did, and you know it, Mr. Biddle." His face flamed red. She loved embarrassing him. She gazed deeply into his blue eyes. Their gazes held, and she whispered, "I love you too, Bert Biddle."

She leaned in to him, and their lips touched, sending sparklers of warmth throughout her body. He pulled back quickly as if afraid his parents would catch them.

"You're going to have to get used to it, Mr. Biddle," Trudy said. "When we get married, they're all going to see us kiss."

David Morgan wandered through his stylish St. Paul apartment overlooking downtown. The clock in the hall ticked loudly, which he usually found comforting, but today it was irritating. Time was floating past like dandelion fluff on a windless summer evening. There was nothing to do, no one to see. He stood at the big window and stared unseeing at the expansive night-time view of the city lights to the south. The capitol's white dome glowed, awash in light, and the sleep-walking Mississippi River reflected flecks of amber as it wound behind the building.

David had thought of Peter's invitation countless times in the past few days. *Let me help you for once.*

He knew moving back home would be hard in some ways. Long-forgotten memories of Laura still haunted his visits. Yet he was tired of lonely hotels and an empty apartment. He yearned for the companionship of family, to be surrounded by those who knew him best and loved him most. He needed his mother's admonitions to remember the good things right now.

In his younger years it had been so difficult to accept charity. Pride. Laura's illness taught him the foolishness of that. God intended people to help each other, to allow one to be another's strength in difficult days.

He rubbed his hands. The ache seemed worse today. Maybe because today he was finally beaten. Everything he'd worked for was gone. God had given, and God had taken away.

But what would take its place? He had no idea. He only knew he'd lost something that had sustained him through his hardest days, something that had given him worth, something he'd taken for granted. He thought about Peter out in the barn, milking his grandpa's cows. Maybe David had taken him for granted too.

"Peter," he said into the silence, "maybe I will take you up on that offer. At least until I find my way."

JANELLE FOSTER

What was taking so long? Janelle Foster watched from her parked car as December dealt its cold hand to the landscape. Snow blew in shifting currents. The frigid air bit into her soul, into her very heart. She desperately wanted to get this over with.

The helpless baby girl in the backseat let out a tiny mew. Her newborn's cry seemed so weak that Janelle wondered if something was wrong, if maybe she had endangered her when she had left the hospital an hour after the baby was born.

She was doing the right thing now, what was best for her daughter and for herself. Janelle was only sixteen, living in her car, not old enough to be a mother, at least not a mother who could provide a decent home.

What kind of life would that be? Living off the government dole, chasing after a kid, always worrying, wondering what could've been if only she hadn't been so stupid.

A woman in a black coat walked briskly down the sidewalk, her head bent against the wind as she unlocked the squat gray building. Janelle looked back at her baby, who was sucking on a tiny fist. This was it. Janelle took a deep breath and closed her eyes. She needed to be strong. She needed to do this, regardless of the hollow place in her stomach. It wasn't about her; it was about what was best for the baby.

Janelle pulled her shoulders back and got out of the car. She held the tiny girl close. Her heart seized with grief. She was careful to keep the child's tender face sheltered until they were inside.

"May I help you?" the woman said. She sat behind a large desk and a sign that read Social Services. She gazed kindly at Janelle.

Janelle bit her lip then said, "I want to give my baby up for adoption." The words cut like shards of glass. They accused her, ridiculed her poor choices.

The woman glanced at the baby, and Janelle lowered her slightly so the woman could see her better. "Isn't she cute?" the woman said. Janelle said nothing.

"Are you sure you want to do this?"

Janelle nodded. "Yes ma'am."

"You'll need to talk to a counselor. I'll take you down to the office." She stood, and Janelle followed obediently beside her. Janelle felt suddenly very

young. She hastened her step to get this done as quickly as possible. When they reached the office door, the woman turned to Janelle and said, "Adoption is an unselfish choice. Someone who's been praying for a baby will love her. I know because I adopted a baby, and not a day goes by that I'm not grateful to my son's birth mother for allowing me to be his mother."

Janelle swallowed hard. A tear flowed down her cheek. "Do you mind holding her for me? I don't think I should hold her anymore." She handed the baby to the woman.

When Janelle left, her heart was a rock sinking into deep waters. The wind buffeted her bare face. She closed her eyes, vowing never to make the same mistake again.

eighteen

Mae sat at her desk in the county courthouse. The reception area adjoined the county recorder's offices, giving Mae an open view of the offices. Tan cubicles filled the interior of the century-old building, its grandeur downplayed like Audrey Hepburn dressed in rags.

"Mae, you can send in my ten o'clock appointment as soon as he arrives," Mr. Cleworth said as he came around the corner.

"Sure thing, Mr. Cleworth," Mae said. He ducked into his office. Along with answering phones and directing lost people, Mae had become everyone's secretary, typing letters for the inspectors, photo-copying, filing, doing whatever was needed. She took a long drink of her coffee from a tall stainless insulated mug.

Cindy Phelps, one of the clerks, stopped by. She was a short, petite woman with curly dark hair and a hearty laugh. Mae had liked her instantly. "Thanks for your help on that report yesterday. You saved my neck," Cindy said.

"Glad to do it. I like research." The phone rang, and Mae waved to Cindy as she scooted to her desk. "Le Sueur County. May I help you?"

"It's me." Peter's voice sounded lonely. "How's your day going?"

"Good. Real good, actually."

"Good."

"Is that all?"

"I wanted to hear your voice."

"That's sweet."

There was silence on the line.

"Sure there wasn't something else?" Mae said.

"No. I love you."

"I love you, Peter."

"Okay," Peter sighed. "Bye."

Poor Peter. The house had been immaculate when she'd first started work, but Peter had found more worthy tasks to fill his time in the barn and shop. Still, his woeful calls had become more frequent. Mae knew his loneliness was her fault. At least his dad was coming to live with them. His company was just what Peter needed. And Peter would have his father to help around the farm when planting began in April. That helped ease Mae's guilt just a little.

"Janelle!" Cindy's voice carried from beyond the partitions. A skinny woman who appeared to be in her midthirties came in wrangling an infant carrier. Cindy and the other ladies from the office gathered around to ogle the child.

"He's beautiful," one voice cooed. A chorus of similar praises arose.

Mr. Cleworth emerged from his office. "What's the commotion?"

"I'm not sure," Mae said.

"Ah," Mr. Cleworth said. "It's Janelle. The woman you replaced." He lowered his voice so only Mae could hear. "She's had a rough go of it. Gave her first baby up for adoption, and then this baby was in the hospital for weeks after he was born." His eyes crinkled at the clucking hens. "There's something about a baby, isn't there? You want to go see?"

"No thank you, sir," Mae said. "I don't know her." That familiar ache returned, and Mae pressed a hand to her stomach.

A pudgy man in overalls came up to the desk and said, "I'm looking for Mr. Cleworth."

August raised his hand. "That would be me. You must be Otto Schleeve." The tall stranger nodded, and the two men disappeared into Mr. Cleworth's office.

The cluster around the infant slowly thinned. Mae spied pale blond hair peeking from beneath a blue padded snowsuit. He yawned with that tiny mouth and then stretched out his little fists before jerking them back in newborn fashion. Cindy and Janelle eased toward the entry.

"How are you doing?" Cindy said to Janelle.

Janelle turned her head and spoke in low tones. Mae saw her swipe a tear from her eye. Cindy gave Janelle a hug.

It's time. You need a baby to love, a voice said in Mae's heart as she spied.

I don't even think I can have a baby, Mae argued. *What if I lost another? Peter's mother was never able to have another baby after Peter. Maybe I'm not meant to be a mother.*

She turned her back to the memories and tried to block out the sounds of the baby's cooing.

Sunday dawned crystalline and crisp. A storm had left behind a calm ocean of snow waves frozen in place. Fields lost their sense of distance in the sameness—one swatch of brightness led to the next in a damask quilt of white.

Mae and Peter, Virginia and Trudy sat together in church and then gathered at the farm for dinner afterward. The savory aromas of pot roast along with carrots, potatoes, onions, and fresh-baked bread lent their comfort to the after-church family tradition.

Peter leaned back in his chair and patted his stomach. "That was awesome."

"I spent the whole day slaving over the Crockpot and bread machine." Mae chuckled and cocked a brow toward Virginia.

"Well, it was still good, dear, even if it was easy,"

Virginia said. "It puts me in a mind to take a Sunday afternoon nap." She stretched and yawned.

"I like the way you think, Grandma," Peter said. "Unfortunately I have a cow about to drop a calf. I should really go check."

"Oh, poor farmer boy," Trudy said, pushing away from the table. "I'll do dishes. Payment for an excellent meal."

After the china was put away and the kitchen counters wiped, Trudy and Mae relaxed in the sunny living room. Mae knitted a long multicolored scarf in her big stuffed chair while Trudy lay on the couch and glanced through a decorating magazine.

"What did you think of Pastor Hickey's sermon?" Trudy said.

Mae looked up. "Remind me what it was about."

"Did you even listen?"

"Not really. I've been distracted."

"What's going on?" Trudy sat up.

Mae looked over her shoulder as if to be sure no one was nearby. "I haven't wanted to say anything to Peter." Her voice was low. "Although he probably suspects something. I've been thinking about having another baby."

"I knew it!" Trudy grinned.

"How did you know?" Mae laid her knitting in her lap.

"Honey, I'd be blind not to notice."

"I get so . . . afraid," Mae confessed. "Every time I think about being pregnant I get panicky. I don't know."

"Have you talked to Peter?"

"No, not really."

"You need to," Trudy admonished.

"I know, but I keep wondering, what if there was a reason I lost Laura?"

"Meaning?"

Mae twisted the strand of yarn in her hand. "Meaning maybe there's something wrong with me. Some women spend their whole lives trying to get pregnant and have one miscarriage after another . . . like Vivian Leigh and Marilyn Monroe. I can't handle the heartbreak of losing another baby."

"Mae." Trudy reached across the span between the couch and the rocker and placed a hand on her sister's knee. "You need to relax. God has a way of working things out. You'll see."

But the pain in Mae's face remained.

"I guess I hoped that once I started working away from home I'd feel better, that maybe then I could move on. But every time I see a baby . . . my heart falls apart, and I'm back holding Laura—so cold and blue." The tears came then, a silent flow.

"It's going to take time. Give yourself some grace, Mae. Eventually you'll let her go."

"I think maybe I was wrong to take this job. I feel so bad about leaving Peter to manage the farm alone."

"You are helping. Peter's managing okay, isn't he?"

"I guess," Mae said. "Although he really has abandoned the housekeeping."

"Too bad. I was ready to kidnap him to come scrub my bathroom," Trudy said.

Mae laughed and smiled. "Thank you. It's like old times, having you near."

"Oh, it won't be long and I'll wear out my welcome, don't worry."

"That's not going to happen," Mae patted her hand. "So now that you're settled, how are things with Mr. Biddle?"

"Bert? Oh, Bert is . . ." His handsome image rose in her mind, and she felt her face grow warm. "Bert is yummy. Is this how you felt with Peter?"

"I don't know. How do you feel?"

"When I'm away from him, I can't stop thinking about him. He makes me smile, and I haven't managed to scare him off yet. I do miss him when he's at hockey practice so much of the time."

Mae grinned and said, "Sounds to me like you're a goner."

"Who would've thought, huh? Big-city girl smitten by quiet, unassuming farm boy. It's *Green Acres* all over again." She raised her eyes to Mae's. "You know, Bert and I are so different. Mom said that would come back to bite us."

"Oh, I don't know," Mae said. "Don't opposites attract?"

"Aren't you Miss Cliché?"

"If the cliché fits . . ."

Lillian had borrowed her late uncle's wheelchair from her Aunt Agnes. Bert had volunteered to take her shopping at the River Hills Mall in Mankato. Virgil had died fifteen years earlier, but Agnes held on to the wheelchair like everything else in that cluttered house of hers. At the mall, Bert pulled the van into the handicapped parking spot and hung the sign from the rearview mirror so he wouldn't get a ticket.

"I've been dying to get out of the house," Lillian said.

"I need to tell you something," Bert said. Lillian turned toward him in the driver's seat. He killed the motor.

"So, what is it?" Lillian said.

Bert wiped his hands on his jeans, searching for the right way to phrase this. "I'm going to propose to Trudy. I was hoping you could help me pick out a ring."

"That girl? Are you nuts?" Lillian said. "She's nothing like you."

"You and Dad aren't exactly the same."

"But at least we both come from farm families. Trudy couldn't be more—" Her words dropped away, and her eyes searched his. "Is she pregnant?"

He felt his face warm. "No! I love her," Bert said.

Lillian stared at him. "Okay, I guess I can't argue with that." Lillian placed a hand on his. "But she does have a big mouth." Bert chuckled and got out of the van. He pulled the wheelchair out through the side door, unfolded and latched it into place, then helped his mother down. She settled her big bottom into the chair.

Bert smiled. "Trudy reminds me of someone else I know," he said.

Lillian placed her fingers on her neck and said, "Are

you calling me a big mouth?"

"All I'm saying is there's a reason I love her. She's a lot like you."

She blushed and reached up to pull her son close for a kiss on the cheek. "That's the nicest thing anyone's ever said to me." She paused. "So, what was the deal with the M&M's?" Bert pushed her through the lot.

"She was trying to cheer you up," Bert said.

"Well." She considered that. "I suppose it was a thoughtful thing to do. And it's about time you got to the altar. God only knows what miracle it will take to get Fred married. Maybe a tornado depositing a girl on our front lawn!" Bert laughed as he pushed his mother through the main entrance by the old carousel that enchanted children in the food court.

"What sort of ring do you think she wants?" Lillian asked.

"I have no idea," Bert admitted.

"You men are all the same."

Bert sat in his truck and stared at the delicate ring in the burgundy box. He touched the diamond that shimmered in the January sunlight. It didn't seem real that he was about to propose, yet inside he knew she was "the one" as surely as he knew that he was breathing. This was right.

"Classic elegance" was what the clerk had called the round diamond with a small sapphire on each side. He couldn't wait to see the expression on Trudy's face when he gave it to her.

Now, how exactly to propose, that was a different

question. He would plan something romantic, something Trudy would remember for the rest of her life.

He set the box in the glove compartment to await the perfect opportunity.

Trudy and Bert sat at the soda fountain in Ott's Drugstore. The black-and-white checked tile floor gave the place a classic 1950s feel, and the matching black vinyl stools added the finishing touch. Janey, Mr. Ott's teenage soda jerk, complete with a white paper envelope hat, was scooping an ice-cream cone for a tow-headed boy at the end of the counter.

Trudy enjoyed a chocolate malt while Bert sipped a vanilla shake. She moved the long spoon up and down and glanced expectantly at Bert's profile, searching for clues. He had a smirk on his face. If she didn't know better, she'd guess he was hiding something.

"So," Trudy said, "your mom finally let you out."

Bert smiled. "She's up and around."

He took a drink of his shake.

"Okay. I can't stand this anymore." Trudy twisted on her vinyl stool to face him. "What's going on, Bert Biddle?"

"What do you mean?" Bert shrugged and lifted his hands in an act of innocence.

"All right, tell me what you're hiding, or you'll get the torture treatment."

Bert's eyes twinkled. "I might like that."

"Oh no you won't!"

He smiled. "Can you hang on for a minute?" He stood and disappeared out the front door of the store.

"What does that mean?" Trudy said to no one. She took another long sip of her malt until her straw made that slurping, sucking noise that told her she was all out. She lifted the stainless-steel tumbler, poured the rest into the tall glass, and studied her own reflection in the wall-length mirror opposite her. Bert came back in and took his seat at the counter. Trudy gave him a long, scrutinizing stare, but he just took another drink of his shake.

"Janey," he called to the freckle-faced girl behind the counter, "do you have any pie?"

"Pie?" Trudy said. "Bert, you're driving me nuts. I can see why your mom is such a nag! It's the only way to get anything out of you."

Bert's face grew sober.

"What's wrong now?" Trudy said.

When he faced her, she could see the hurt in his eyes.

"Don't call my mom a nag," he said quietly, patiently.

"Are you blind? When Solomon wrote about dripping faucets, I'm pretty sure he had your mother in mind." She laughed.

"Trudy." He seemed at a loss for words. Finally he said, "It's easy to judge her when you don't know her." He reached for his coat. "Maybe I should go."

"Bert, I'm sorry. Okay? Can we go back and start all over?" But the twinkle had left his eyes.

Bert watched from the front seat of his pickup as Trudy disappeared inside the door that led to her apartment stairs. He pulled the ring box from his pocket and gazed down at it. He'd so wanted to give it to her today, but then everything had gone awry.

Why did it seem every time things were moving in the right direction, something would start an argument?

He placed the burgundy box back in the glove compartment, unsure now if the right time would ever come.

Trudy sat alone in the darkened apartment. She didn't bother to turn the light on; she moved to the window and gazed out at Bert's truck still parked alongside the pharmacy. Her stomach knotted. Why did she always manage to botch everything with her big mouth? She plopped into the chair by the kitchen table and put her head in her hands.

"You don't know her," Bert had said. Maybe she didn't know Lillian, but he didn't know the Trudy that she kept hidden from the world either. The Trudy he knew talked about everything except the things that she held sacred—her past, the hurts in her life, her father. Those she entrusted to no one. She thought about her father's letters tucked in the closet in her bedroom. Why couldn't she talk to Bert about those?

Bert's truck started, and he drove out of sight. She wondered if this was the end. Would he give up on her the way all the other men in her life had? She sighed and stood up, flicking on the kitchen light above the white porcelain sink. She wanted to cry, but she couldn't. What was the point of crying anyway? It wouldn't solve her problem.

She filled the sink with sudsy water and washed the dishes she'd left there from breakfast. As she was putting the last dish in the cupboard, the phone rang.

"Hey." It was Bert.

Trudy's heart quickened. "Hey, yourself," she said.

"I'm sorry," Bert said.

"I guess that was our first real fight, huh?"

"Can we forget it ever happened?" he said.

"Gladly."

n i n e t e e n

A re you sure you're okay with this?" David said to Peter, who stood alongside his car and small U-Haul trailer next to the barn. David turned off the motor. It was a lovely early February day, a precursor of days to come. The snow held a bluish tinge as late afternoon shadows fell across the yard and pasture. A pair of black-capped chickadees flitted between the bare gravel driveway and telephone wires that swooped low.

Peter stooped to talk through the car window. "Of course we're okay with it. Is this all your stuff?" He tilted his head toward the trailer.

"I put the rest in storage," David explained. "I figured there was no point in tripping over all my junk until I decide where I'm going to end up."

"Let's get you moved in," Peter said.

David rolled up the window and got out. "Mae's okay with her father-in-law living here?"

"Would you knock it off? I told you, we're glad to have you." He looked his dad in the eyes. "More than glad."

David wrapped an arm around his son's shoulders. "Let's get unloaded."

Mae came out from the house dressed in a thick padded winter coat, boots, and scarf. The three soon had the U-Haul emptied and one of the upstairs bedrooms filled with boxes and suitcases.

David gazed at the pile after Peter and Mae had gone downstairs.

"Here I am, back where I started," David said to no one. It felt good to be here with family. He was still a father if no longer a musician. At least he could still be that. He smiled to himself. This was going to be a good thing, he decided.

"I'll take my time unpacking," David said as he came downstairs. Mae was in the kitchen making a pot of coffee. Peter was nowhere in sight.

Mae turned toward him and smiled. "Coffee?" She nodded toward the coffee maker.

"Sounds good."

She pulled two mugs down from the cupboard. "Peter's finishing milking," she answered his unasked question. She bent to check something in the oven. "Do you like Irish stew?"

"Now that sounds wonderful and smells even better." He inhaled deeply.

"Oh, good. I wanted to make a good first impression." She poured the coffee and handed him a steaming cup.

"You've always made a good impression."

"I want you to make yourself at home."

He glanced around the old house. "That's one thing I've always felt here—at home. It's different to be here without Ma and Dad though. There are a lot of reminders."

"I know this isn't an easy time for you," she said, then straightened back up and smiled at her father-in-law. "But we're glad to have you. I think Peter has plans to turn you into a farmer again."

"I don't know about that." He smiled.

"He's happy you're here," she assured him.

"I have to admit, I have no idea what I'm going to do. And I don't want to be a burden. I know you have busy lives."

"You're welcome here for however long you need. That's what family does. If there's one thing I've learned since moving to Lake Emily, I've learned about the importance of family."

"I appreciate it," he said. "More than I can say." He paused and took a deep breath. "I don't know what God's trying to teach me in all of this."

"Maybe that he loves you even with your limitations, or *especially* because of your limitations?"

"That's something some of us never learn. To accept our own shortcomings, let alone God's unconditional love."

The pale sun struggled to awaken. It lifted its round head from behind a cloudy pillow of fluff, then disappeared again to snooze a little longer. David awakened feeling refreshed, hopeful for this new day. "Can I help with breakfast?" he asked Mae when he came downstairs.

"You're up early. I figured you'd sleep in," she said as the toast popped up from the toaster.

"I'm pretty much an early bird—it was bred into me. You think Peter would mind if I gave him a hand milking this morning?"

"Are you kidding?" she said. "He'd be thrilled."

"I'd be thrilled with what?" Peter said, coming down the stairs, sleep-rumpled.

"I thought I'd do some farming," David said.

Peter smiled. "Have at it. I'm glad for any help I can get."

"I might need a refresher," David said.

"It's like riding a bike."

After breakfast, father and son made their way to the snug barn. Peter flipped on the lights while David meandered into the open section of the barn to greet the cows. The girls eyed David suspiciously and kept their distance, mooing at Peter through the parlor door for their morning milking and some breakfast.

"Dad," Peter called. David joined him in the milking parlor. "You want to wear these?" He handed his father Grandpa Roy's old coveralls, which were much too short for Peter. They fit David perfectly.

"Now I'm a farmer!" he said with a grin. Peter could see his grandfather smiling down at the sight.

Peter left to open the gate for the first set of cows. The girls ambled to the cement steps, then hopped up into position, the clang of the bars signaling they were in place.

David came out from behind the door to the parlor and patted a cow's thick flank. "You remembered how skittish cows can be of strangers," Peter commented.

"Some things you don't forget. Your grandpa always had a radio on to keep the cows used to new voices."

"That's a good idea," Peter said.

Soon the milk machine's steady hum filled the room. Together they sprayed and wiped udders, attached suction cups, and let the cows go before the roundup would begin all over again.

They had a natural rhythm together that felt comfortable, right.

Trudy wiped the deep paint-splattered sink with a sponge and then dried her hands on a paper towel as her third graders came in for the last-hour class. They were jabbering and laughing in a loud roar. Except Jessie Wise, who took her seat on one of the tall stools at the table and set a thick art pad on the nicked-up surface.

"Jessie, you brought your drawings?" Trudy said. "May I see?"

Jessie nodded and pushed the pad toward Trudy. Trudy opened the first page. It was a drawing of a girl with a teddy bear. It was definitely a child's drawing, but it had a distinctive, whimsical quality that spoke of potential. The girl in the picture had bright orange pigtails that stuck off the side of her head, and she had an impish smile as she held the bear by one forepaw.

The bear's foot was blue, and beneath it sat a paint can with drips down its side in the same powdery color.

Trudy glanced up at Jessie, who was watching her face intently. "This is wonderful, Jessie," she said. "You have real talent."

Jessie beamed.

Trudy turned to the next page, which held a field of black-eyed Susans. "Beautiful," Trudy said, her gaze trained on the drawing.

"You think I could enter one of them for 4-H next summer?" The girl's eyes glowed.

"Definitely. You could do a whole bunch of pictures between now and then, and pick your favorite. You know," Trudy said, realizing she needed to get her class started as the second bell rang, "I'm in charge of making the sets for the high school musical. I could use an assistant."

"For the high school?" Jessie's mouth seemed frozen in awe. "But I'm—"

"That's okay," Trudy said. "There will be students from the high school helping too, but it'd give you a chance to see how older kids paint. If you're not interested—"

"No," Jessie said, "I'd love it. I'd have to talk to my dad and Virginia. I usually go to her house after school."

"We can work around your schedule."

Jessie grinned, and at that moment Trudy felt truly glad to be a teacher.

After milking, Peter and David headed over to the Farmers' Elevator. Peter needed to replace the failing tank heater. A thin layer of ice had capped the water that morning, and it was no good for the cows not to have access to their water supply.

"It's been years since the last time I was at the Elevator," David said as they climbed into Peter's old green Chevy pickup. "I doubt anyone remembers me."

"Are you kidding? People call me 'David Morgan's boy' all the time or 'the son of that violinist.' " Peter laughed and started the engine, then patted the side of the truck to let Scout know he could ride in the back. The yellow Lab jumped in, a huge smile on his face, and started smearing the back window with his nose.

"He doesn't get out much," Peter said. The February fields sparkled, blinding the eyes with glistening glitter. The woods in the distance were dark and bare except for traces of snow along branches, like highlights from a painter's brush. Tall golden grasses, survivors from the previous fall, poked up from deep azure ditches. Farms sat as lonely islands. Silver and blue silos glinted in the winter sun.

David stared at the scenery. "It's good to be home," he said. "Before you know it, we'll be planting peas."

"Hard to believe this year has passed so quickly," Peter said. "I hope we'll earn more from the pea crop than we did last year."

"You optimist you," David teased. "Any regrets? Now that you're in it for the long haul?"

"No. I really can't imagine living any other life," Peter said. He lifted two fingers atop the steering wheel in a wave as they met another pickup. "I'm lucky to have found something to do that I love. It's as if I was born for this." Peter glanced at his dad, who nodded reflectively.

They reached the petite town of Lake Emily. Snow-packed streets bustled with activity as folks visited and ran errands. The lake was a frozen lunar land-scape—ice houses like a village of Martian cottages dotted the surface. Some were mere plywood boxes or canvas shelters, while others were elaborate domains complete with satellite dishes and long silver propane tanks.

The Farmers' Elevator dominated the end of Main Street. Peter pulled into the gravel lot, tires crunching as they came to a stop. Peter told Scout to stay, and the dog sat obediently in the truck's bed and watched them walk into the building.

"He's a good dog," David commented. "Have you been working with him?"

Peter shook his head no and said simply, "Grandpa."

Flannel-clad patrons at the counter turned to look as they entered. A familiar voice said, "David Morgan!" Jerry Shrupp limped over. He was a tall, gangly man with a shock of red hair that was graying at the temples.

"J. D., how's it going, buddy?" David held out a hand, and the two old friends shook.

"I was wondering when you'd make it into town. When does Lake Emily's favorite son head back on the road this time?"

David placed a hand across the back of his collar and glanced at Peter. "He's helping out on the farm—," Peter injected.

"I've moved back to Lake Emily," David finished. "At least for the time being."

"Early retirement?" Jerry said. "What are you going to do? Take up farming?"

David shrugged. "You never can tell," he said.

twenty

Mae dipped the brush into the paint can. "What did Mom say?" She carefully painted along the ceiling line.

All the furniture was pushed to the center of Trudy's cozy apartment living room. Drop cloths covered the carpeted floor. Trudy and Mae had been painting all day, first the front room of her apartment in a coffee-with-cream color, and then the living room in the back, where they were now, in a rich avocado. Darkness edged in through the windows.

"Same old, same old. Wanted to know when I'm moving back to St. Paul. Yada-yada-yada!" Trudy was rolling the avocado onto the broad expanse of the living-room wall. Mae finished the trim and stood back to gaze at their hard work. A moment later Trudy joined her.

"We done good," Trudy said, with a grin at her sister. "Let's clean up." She gathered brushes and rollers and walked past Mae to the galley-kitchen sink. Mae followed and fingered the airy yellow-and-white gingham curtains at the window over the two-person table.

"Did you make these?"

Trudy nodded. "I know they're subdued for me, but that dark Bohemian theme wasn't cutting it anymore."

The apartment had been transformed into a bright welcoming place with a mere change of curtains and a layer of fresh paint. Earlier in the week Trudy had sanded the kitchen cupboards and painted them pale aqua that complemented the salmon tile counters. Trudy had tossed some red-and-white floral throw pillows and a matching quilt over the couch in the living room and bought a pair of fringed shades for the tall floor lamps at either side of the couch.

"This is going to be nice," Mae said, sitting on one of the kitchen chairs. "It's so bright and cheery in here."

"I think I'll paint some farm animals along the top of the wall." She pointed to the wall overlooking the street. "That will give the kitchen a good ol' countrified feel." She smiled at her sister. "Hey, I'm fitting into Lake Emily already. I'm dating a farmer, sewing gingham . . ."

Mae lifted an eyebrow. "Yeah, you fit right in. How's it on the Lillian front?"

"Lillian? Oh, she's a pussycat." She put the roller under the warm running water and dribbled dish soap on it. "She might hiss and claw on occasion, but basically a pussycat. Want some coffee?"

"Sure." Mae nodded. Trudy got down the filters and a big can of Folgers. When the coffee was beginning to drip, she said, "Come out to the living room. I want to enjoy my new ambience."

They sat on the chenille slipcovered couch with its red-and-white quilt.

"Thanks for your help with this project," Trudy said. "I know you don't have the kind of time with Peter you used to, so it means a lot to me."

"I enjoyed it. Your place looks great."

"I hope Mr. Ott will think so."

"What's he like?" Mae rested a hand along the back of the sofa and pulled her leg up under her.

Trudy said, "I think there's more to him than mild-mannered pharmacist. He's never been married. Did I tell you he has a tattoo on his arm? Kind of makes you wonder, doesn't it? He's really a nice guy. He mentioned a girl, but he didn't go into details. Maybe he needs a push."

"Trudy, don't go butting in."

Trudy scooted off the couch, picked up a hammer, and pounded the lid back onto the paint can that was sitting on the drop cloth.

"Me butt in? No thank you. I have enough on my plate," Trudy admitted when she returned to the couch. She was looking forward to the play, especially now that Bert was so consumed with hockey. The same jealousy rose up, and she punched it down. "We start work on the sets next week. I've been sketching ideas for how to pull the *Oklahoma!* theme off. I've drawn up rough ideas for each set, and I have a crew of high school students helping me. Oh, and Jessie Wise is going to come help paint too. You've should've seen her face when I asked her."

"Isn't Jessie kind of young to be working on the

high school play?" Mae picked at the tufts of chenille.

"She can do some of the easy stuff. She brought some drawings to school on Monday—she has real talent. I thought the play would be a good experience."

"You sound like Mrs. Zernickel." Mae smiled.

"Thanks. She was a great teacher," Trudy said, remembering. "I'd like to be like her, you know? She always knew how to draw kids out."

"You're a good teacher, Trudy. Any teacher who's in it for the kids is a good teacher."

Mae's words felt like warm bread pudding and a cup of steaming hot chocolate—they comforted a place deep in her soul.

David heard Peter shut the door as he went out to the machine shed to finish work on the tractor in preparation for plowing and planting come April. A warm March breeze beckoned him as it floated through the slightly opened window of his bedroom. A symphony of birds chirped and twittered in the windbreak. A flock of blackbirds in formal attire covered the front lawn, a sea of spectators. He gazed at the dark shapes, a reminder of his view from the stage. Turning, he clicked the On button of the CD player, and the sounds of an orchestra—his orchestra—filled the room with a Strauss waltz. His body swayed in time to the music as it carried him to another time, another place. He was simply David Morgan playing in three-four time. He unconsciously lifted his hands in the motions of playing. And then stopped and gazed at his fingers. They were hurting again.

So much hurt.

Through the kitchen window, Bert watched his brother and mother drive up in the big old tan Ford Fairlane. Even from this distance he could tell that Fred was a boiler about to blow. Lillian's mouth moved while Fred kept time with each nod of his head, a glazed expression on his red face.

When they came in the back door, Bert had to ask, "How'd it go?"

"That big-shot doctor says my ankle isn't healing right," Lillian said. "I have to wear this stupid thing for six more weeks. Help me get this coat off, Fred."

Fred gave Bert the get-me-away-from-her-before-I-kill-her look as he moved behind his mother and held one crutch, then the other, as Lillian slipped her arms out of the long quilted coat. She held it out to Fred and gestured for him to hang it on one of the hooks in the mud room. Fred's nostrils flared.

"Mom, do you want me to help you to your La-Z-Boy?" Bert asked.

Lillian shook her head. "Leave me alone. I can manage." It was almost a shout. She hoisted her heavy frame across the kitchen floor, pivoting on the crutches at every step.

Fred stomped up the stairs. Bert heard the door to his room slam a moment later and then blaring country music.

"So did the doctor say why it isn't healing?" Bert followed behind as his mother settled on the couch.

"I saw that x-ray. You ask me, it was the same x-ray from when I first broke it. Doctors! He said that older people's bones take longer to heal. My ankle is killing me. Hand me that knitting needle." She pointed to a basket on the floor with balls of yarn and an assortment of knitting accouterment.

"Which one?"

"It doesn't matter." Bert reached for one. "No," Lillian said, "the plastic one."

He handed her the long stick, and she pushed it into the top of her cast and moved it up and down. "I've been dying to do that," Lillian said. She handed the needle back to Bert. He shoved it back into a ball of yarn.

"You need anything else, Mom?" Bert asked. She shook her head and picked up the TV remote. The music of *Wheel of Fortune* filled the living room.

Bert left her and went up to Fred's room. He knocked on the door and heard a faint grunt despite the loud music. "Yeah," Fred said.

Bert eased the door open. "Fred, are you—?" Bert stopped speaking. On Fred's quilted bedspread was an open suitcase and a pile of folded socks and underwear. "What's going on?"

"I can't take another minute of her," Fred hissed and pointed toward the stairs. "If she's going to be in that cast for six more weeks, I'm . . . leaving."

"You can't go."

"Why not?" He turned toward his brother. "It's okay for you; you have Trudy. But what do I have?"

Bert sat on the bed. "Are you still mad that Trudy

and I are together?"

"No." Fred threw a pair of jeans into the suitcase, then returned to rummage through his dresser. "Marry whoever you want," he said. "I really don't care."

"Aren't you too old to be running away from home?"

"Maybe it's about time I ran away. I'm thirty-four years old, Bert. When was the last time I took a vacation? I've never gone anywhere that Mom didn't arrange for me. I'm tired of it. Tell everyone I took a vacation. A nice long break to someplace warm."

"So where's that?" Fred closed the suitcase and brushed past Bert.

"I don't know."

"You can't leave without at least telling us where you're going," Bert insisted.

Fred glanced around the room. "Disney World. Tell them I went to Disney World."

With Fred's absence came longer hours for Bert and his father. They were gearing up for spring planting so they'd be on that "start" line when April 10 hit. Trudy missed Bert stopping by school during her lunch breaks, and after school he was still busy with hockey. She often reminded herself when her patience wore thin that his loyalty was one of the things she admired about him. So she filled the long winter days with set preparations for *Oklahoma!* She'd drawn sketches of Laurey's farmhouse, the smokehouse where "Pore Jud Fry" lived, the grove where Laurey and Curly would sing "People Will Say We're in Love," and the Skidmore ranch and porch. She'd never dreamed there was so much work to do to prepare for such a production.

Trudy left the costume-and-prop room at the high school and headed down the long corridor. When she'd seen the disarray of the room, she knew she needed to put in a few days organizing costumes and determining what they'd need to scavenge. Her first order of business though was getting the shop class to fabricate the bare bones of the sets. Once that was done, her students would take on painting and decorating.

Most of the scenes were fairly straightforward—a farmhouse porch or a barn and pasture scene. The last musical the school had performed had been *Fiddler on the Roof*. With some creative work, Trudy decided, they could transform the barren Russian landscape into open fields where the wind came sweeping down the plain. But they would need to find a creative way to make an "orchard" for Curly and Laurey to stroll through and pick apples from. Chuck Wilbee, a lummox of a kid who could usually be found in the wood shop, had offered to help.

"Hey, Miss Ploog," Chuck said as Trudy entered the high-ceilinged room.

"Hey, Chuck," Trudy said. "Thanks so much for agreeing to do this."

Chuck shrugged. He bashfully handed Trudy a pair of goggles. "You need to wear these. You've only got one set of eyes." He wore thick glasses, and a thin scar ran from his upper lip into his left nostril. He bent over one of the drawings of the sets Trudy had given him.

"We can use two-by-fours for the skeleton of the trees and cover them with quarter-inch plywood. Your sketches are pretty . . . but they don't really show how to make it," he said apologetically.

"That's why I'm glad I have you." She patted him on the back.

"We'll need to make a good base so the trees aren't top heavy." Chuck pointed to a drawing on the drafting table of a tree skeleton. "I've kind of figured it out here." He handed Trudy a list of needed supplies. "I know where I can get some old skids for free. And the shop teacher said we can have whatever scraps we can find in here, but I'm not sure what to do about all the plywood or the leaves."

"We'll give it some thought," Trudy said. "If worst comes to worst, we can always make the leaves from green construction paper and glue them on. We'll worry about that later. For now, let's get started."

Chuck deftly set a two-by-four on the table saw, measured and marked the wood, then guided it toward the spinning blade.

"Looks like you know your stuff, Chuck," Trudy said once the screaming saw completed its task.

He gave her a grin. "I'm not real good at much else, but my dad and me work in the shop a lot. I've been handling drills and saws and routers since I was little."

"Do you play any sports?" Trudy asked. "A big guy like you would make a good candidate for the football team."

Chuck smiled a lazy smile. "Naw. The other kids . . . well . . . it's not my thing." He gazed back at the drawings. "We need to add supports to the bottom, I think. Also, my dad salvaged some old doors from a house he demolished. He's a contractor. I'm sure we could get one or two for the scene at Laurie's farm."

She smiled. "That would be great, Chuck. With you on the job I won't have to worry about a thing."

twenty-one

The first postcard from Fred arrived after a week. It was a picture of Mickey and Minnie waving at the camera. The back read, "Having a great time. Made some friends and am considering a job. More later, Fred."

A job? What did he mean by that? Bert turned on the auger that filled the big feeding trough along the outside wall of the Biddle barn. The cows knew the sound of their dinner bell and ambled over, some moving slowly like daydreaming kindergartners on their way to school, busily enjoying the sights along the way. Bert watched the silage roll out of the big corkscrew. It would smell more pungent come summer, but even in the cool March air its too-sweet molasses smell was strong.

Bert had been working like a dog since Fred left— his father helping where he could—milking a hundred head twice a day, getting the tractor and planter tuned up for pea planting, and then going to hockey practice from three to five. He enjoyed the solitude of farming as well as the camaraderie of being with the team. What he didn't enjoy was the longer hours away from

Trudy. They'd mended fences, for which he was grateful. But he still was unable to propose. Why he was procrastinating he didn't know. But when the right moment came, he would seize it. For now, Trudy seemed to be happy and busy at school.

Until today Bert hadn't considered what would happen if Fred did indeed stay in Florida. He thought he knew his twin brother, but then Fred had up and driven off without any sort of plan. Who knew what the man was capable of? Bert lifted his green sweat-stained seed cap and ran a hand through his curly hair.

When they were young, they'd been close. But somewhere in their teens they'd lost touch, and that bond had never really been restored. Bert often missed the closeness they had shared.

With the trough filled, he flipped the feeder power off. March winds blew hard against the barn, and the thick beams creaked and moaned in response. Bert turned out the light and stepped out into the sunshine. Temperatures were in the low forties, although it felt colder. Water dripped off the eaves in tiny streams.

What had happened to Fred that had caused him to change like that? What if Fred didn't return? Bert shook off the thought.

April was a whirl of activity. With rehearsals each evening, Trudy was hard at work assessing the costuming needs for each actor. The boys were easy to outfit since most could wear jeans, flannel shirts, and bandannas, but the girls presented a challenge, especially the characters of Laurey and Ado Annie, who

187

required multiple outfits. The Mankato Salvation Army had proven an excellent source for costumes, and a couple of girls who were home-ec whizzes volunteered their sewing skills for alterations.

Chuck had built four "apple trees" that could be easily rolled onto the stage during scene changes. His father had donated the needed plywood for the project. He had yet to add bark and leaves. Through resourceful investigation he had discovered that the local electric company would gladly supply the school with all the mulch they needed for free, making perfect tree bark. He would hot melt that onto the plywood trees in the coming week. Chuck had even purchased some wax apples that would add a realistic touch.

Next to come was construction of the big backdrops and larger props. Trudy formed a committee of students to collect the smaller props for the show. Many items were found in the school's collection; the rest became objects of a huge scavenger hunt. The hardest to find would be a wagon for Ali Hakim, the peddlerman. She put the word out in hopes some farmer had a small old wagon they could modify and paint with the perfect Persian feel. Mae's old collectible was much too big to wrestle into the school's hallways. Trudy had called Swap Shop on the radio, but still no wagon.

Jessie and Virginia came in the door as she set up the first plywood backdrop in the art room. It would be for the opening scene in which Curly would sing "There's a bright, golden haze on the meadow" as he ambled through the cornfields toward Laurey's farm.

"Hi, guys," Trudy said. "Come on in."

"I can't stay long," Jessie said. "I have homework, and Virginia and I are going to see some baby lambs."

"Ooh," Trudy said.

"For 4-H," Virginia explained.

"That's fine," Trudy said. "Beggars can't be choosers, right? Besides we have lots of help." She pointed to several high school volunteers who were already painting tall cornstalks on the panel. "This is the first scene of the play. We have to paint corn and make it seem happy." She smiled at Jessie. Then she pointed to a tall stalk that leaned against the wall. "Someone brought this in so we can study it as we paint. I've already outlined where the field ends and the pasture to the farm starts. You ready?" She handed a brush to Virginia, who attempted to hand it back. "Sorry, Grandma," Trudy said. "You're here. You get to help. We'll start with grass over here. Anyone can do grass, right, Jessie?"

"You can do grass, Virginia," Jessie said with a grin.

Soon they were all engrossed. "I didn't know I'd like this so well," Virginia admitted.

"Maybe you'll be the next Grandma Moses," Trudy said.

"Moses' grandma was a painter?" Jessie said. "Oh, Miss Ploog."

"Yes," Trudy said.

"How do these flowers look?"

A colorful array of daisies and wildflowers covered the foreground of the fifteen-foot board.

Trudy gazed at the black-eyed Susans Jessie was pointing to. "Those are great," she said. She picked up a brush and dipped it into the yellow paint. "I like to do mine like this, see?" She deftly added some more blooms to the bouquet. "But I wouldn't change a single petal on yours." She lifted her head toward Virginia. "How's the grass coming over there, Virginia?"

The old woman gave her a wry expression.

"You make great grass, Virginia," Jessie said, then turned back to her flower bed. Her tongue poked out as she painted. "These remind me of the bouquets I used to bring my mom," Jessie said. "Only my bouquets were dandelions. They were weeds."

"I bet your mom didn't see weeds," Virginia said.

Jessie's face held a question in her brow.

"I bet she saw a beautiful bouquet because it came from you. Weeds are whatever people don't want, but if you want it, anything can make a beautiful bouquet, even dandelions."

Jessie thought about that and smiled. "Maybe you're right. She'd put them in a jelly jar and leave them on the window sill by the kitchen sink. She always said she could enjoy them while she did the dishes." Her smile faded. "I can't remember what she looked like sometimes." She pulled a chain from around her neck and lifted a small locket. Opening it, she held the tiny image of her mother for Virginia and Trudy to see. "This helps me remember."

"It's good that you remind yourself of things your mother did—like the dandelions—so you won't forget," Virginia said.

"Yeah," Jessie said, slipping the locket back inside the neck of her blouse. "So I don't forget."

"Oh my." Virginia glanced up at the round clock on the wall. "We need to go see those lambs."

David sat in a rocker in his room. Hazy daylight filtered through the lace curtains. The house was still; the only sound was that of a small flock of swallows darting here and there outside.

Mae was working. Peter was in the barn doing something or other. Aside from helping with milking most mornings, David had wandered around the house aimlessly. Nothing piqued his interest.

His hands had ached too much to help with milking this morning, reminding him of his deficiency.

The familiar room with faded forget-me-nots on the wallpaper was the same as when he was a boy. Even the furniture remained unchanged. David remembered his sister, Sarah, under her white coverlet pretending to be sick so she wouldn't have to go to school. It hadn't worked. He smiled at the memory; he missed his sister. This was still her room, even if she was all grown and living in California.

He stepped into his slippers and padded toward the bathroom. When he reached Mae and Peter's room, he stopped in the open door. Laura's touch was still evident. This room had been their bedroom. He fingered the flowered wallpaper. He could see his new bride. She stood by the window, her long blond hair pulled into a ponytail as she labored to paste that paper up, determination etched on her face. She was so beautiful.

"You're going to need a taller ladder," his voice echoed across the years. He pointed to the short stepladder she had propped in the corner of the room.

"No I won't," she'd said coyly. "I have a tall, handsome husband who can reach the top."

David laughed and took her into his arms.

She rested her head against his chest. "Husband," she said. "That word sounds so good."

The memory faded as David wiped his eyes. He touched the old dresser and tried to open the top drawer, but it was locked. He bent down and reached underneath, to the very back of the dresser. The key was still there. He retrieved it and unlocked the drawer.

Inside, everything was the same—Laura's jewelry box with the class ring he'd given her in high school, the pearls, the necklace with Peter's birthstone . . . and her journal. He pulled the leather-bound volume out and wiped the dust from its cover with his sleeve. He closed and locked the drawer and returned the key to its hiding place. David sank slowly into the stuffed chair by the window and opened the cover.

Laura's handwriting. He hadn't seen it in a long time, and now the ache it brought to his heart almost choked him. There was something intimate about seeing the perfectly formed letters in her hand. He'd always teased her that she wrote like a second-grade teacher. He touched the script tenderly and then began reading.

January 3, 1987

I have not told David this, but I think I might be pregnant again. We have tried for so long since having Peter that I dare not believe it. Sometimes I feel sick to my stomach and I know it's real. I have prayed so long and hard for this. I think I will wait until I'm certain to tell David. But I can barely keep the news to myself. Oh, could this be true? I hope so. I pray so. I can't wait to see the joy on Peter's face when he has his own brother or sister. He's been praying for it since he was five. I know God will work things out. He always does . . .

David set the journal down in his lap. Laura had died of cancer that next year. No baby. No hopes fulfilled. No answered prayers. She'd left him and Peter while she was still so young. It had been so unfair. He squeezed his eyes shut to force away the tears and gazed at the ceiling. Was all of life to be this way? Full of heartaches that piled higher and higher until his time on earth was done? Would he end up a bitter old man who waited for nothing more than death to ease his pain?

"Dad." Peter's voice cut through the silence. David turned his eyes to his son's in the doorway. "You okay?"

David lifted the journal for him to see.

"Need some company?" Peter said.

David nodded. Peter sat on the foot of the bed. "You're thinking about Mom."

"And life in general. You know, when your mom died, I didn't know how in the world I'd keep on living. But I had you"—he patted his son's knee—

"and I had music. Somehow life went on without her. I wasn't always sure that it would. I threw myself into music, and eventually a year passed, then two. Next thing I knew you were grown and gone . . ."

"And now your music's gone too," Peter finished for him.

"Something like that." He stood and stared out the window. "I know that God cares, but knowing it and feeling it aren't the same." He came to sit next to Peter on the bed.

"I might be grown, Dad, but I'm not gone," Peter said. "I'm right here. Always will be."

Vernon Elwood

Vernon Elwood stood in the Piggly Wiggly aisle watching Adeline Wenzel from behind the canned goods. He'd been spying on her for ten minutes, but he hadn't found the courage to talk to her. It was silly; he'd known Adeline for years. But it was as if she had been transformed into someone altogether different. Or maybe it was he who had changed since the fire that had claimed his wife and children. He had committed himself to living again. And part of living was learning to love.

He gazed at Adeline's petite, trim figure. She moved with a grace that mesmerized. Her long salt-and-pepper hair was pulled back into a tidy bun.

A shadow passed as someone walked by. Vernon quickly turned to face the shelf. When the shopper disappeared around the corner, Vernon turned back to

Adeline. She was kneeling before a low shelf, putting price stickers on cans of Green Giant corn. The blue "gun" sounded ka-chun, ka-chun *with each label.*

Vernon's palms grew sweaty, and he wiped them on his overalls. He hadn't asked a woman out in decades. It almost felt inappropriate. Taking a deep breath, he moved slowly forward. Adeline glanced up, her pale gray eyes curious.

"Can I help you, Vernon?"

He took off his red-and-white Kent cap and ran a hand through his hair. Then he twisted the cap slowly in his hands. "Um . . . Adeline . . ."

"Yes?" She looked at him innocently.

"I was wonderin' . . . if you were planning on eating supper tonight." He swallowed hard.

"Well, of course, silly. I eat supper most nights." She quirked a brow.

Vernon cleared his throat. "What I mean is, I'd like to invite you to come to supper at my house." He couldn't bear to meet her eyes once the question was out.

"Are you asking me on a date, Mr. Elwood?"

Vernon blushed crimson. "Well, yes. I am." He risked a glance.

She was smiling. She sat back on her haunches and said, "Vernon, we've known each other a lot of years. Why on earth—?"

"Well, I've been thinking. I've been alone a long time. Now that your youngest has graduated, I was hoping you might be—I'd understand if you—I mean, I could never replace Harold. I wouldn't be offended

or anything." He shrugged. "It's supper, Adeline. Between friends."

She stood and reached for his hand. "What time will you pick me up?"

twenty-two

Aged machinery lay here and there in the wind-break and across the pasture like carcasses of extinct animals. The once-proud century-old farm-house had lost much of its paint. The front porch sagged in shame. Steers and sheep grazed in rich alfalfa fields, oblivious to the decaying bones and tired architecture.

Vernon and his wife, Adeline, emerged from the two-story structure as Mae pulled her Jeep into the gravel driveway and parked next to Virginia's white Oldsmobile and got out. Adeline gave a wave from the porch while Vernon lumbered toward Mae, Virginia, and Jessie with a wide gait. Mae noticed a rough, wide scar across the back of his forearm.

"Howdy," he said. He tipped his white-and-red seed cap and smiled with pale blue eyes that creased in well-worn lines. "Here for a lamb?"

Jessie was grinning with such excitement, Mae was certain she would jump out of her skin.

"Is this your first lamb?" Vernon asked the girl.

"Uh-huh," Jessie said. "It's for 4-H."

"Well, come on then. The newborns are in the barn." He tilted his head toward the massive white building. The four of them walked to it and entered; after a few moments their eyes adjusted to the darkness inside. Thick, dark rafters reached to the high expanse like a cathedral. Late-afternoon sunlight filtered through spaces between the weathered board slats, creating faint shafts of yellow with flecks of dust hanging in suspension.

Mae could hear the tiny bleats of newborn lambs from stalls in the back.

Vernon opened a gate to reveal a ewe with two newborns, white creatures with nubby wool and knobby knees. "Oh, look," Jessie said as she bent down and gazed at the lamb twins. "They're so cute!" She held out a hand and bent close, trying to pet their coats. The mother ewe pushed between her and the babies and lowered her head. She kept her eyes on Jessie.

"Miss," Vernon instructed a bit gruffly. "Better come back here. She's liable to get personal."

Jessie withdrew her hand and took a step back.

Seizing the opportunity, the lambs folded their hooves under and knelt facing their mother's udder. They punched their noses into the ewe's bag as their long necks bent down, then up, to reach the teats. After a long drink, they plopped onto their rear ends in the soft hay. Jessie reached to touch one of them on the nose. The lamb's mother stepped away and jerked her head up and down in irritation.

Jessie leaned back on her heels. The ewe watched Jessie intently, not moving. Then, once she was assured that Jessie meant no harm, she lay down in the same fashion her lambs had, knees first, then a *thunk* as her rump settled onto the hay. One of the twins climbed awkwardly onto her back and then nestled into the deep wool.

Vernon ran a hand along his wrinkled brow. "It'll be a couple of months before they're ready to leave their mama. But I'd be happy to hold one for you." He pursed his lips, then said, "Come here; I've something else to show you."

He opened the next stall, where a lone lamb lay in a circle of light. Seeing them, he bleated to be fed.

"What's wrong with him?" Jessie said, climbing up onto the gate's boards.

"He's a bummer. The runt of triplets. His mother won't feed him, so we've got to bottle-feed him."

"So he's like an orphan?" she said. Vernon nodded his gray head. "That's so sad! Can I hold him?"

Vernon gave another nod, and Jessie slipped into the stall to sit next to the tiny creature. The lamb lifted his back legs up and scooted on his elbows toward Jessie, punching her in the arm with his nose. "What's he doing?" she asked Vernon.

"He thinks you're going to feed him."

"Could I?" she asked Virginia.

"I guess it is about that time," Vernon said. "I'll go get a bottle." He disappeared into a side room. Virginia and Mae joined Jessie in the cozy stall.

"Isn't he cute, Virginia?" Jessie whispered.

"Yes he is," Virginia replied.

"Adorable," Mae agreed. The lamb bumped into Jessie's arm again, and she laughed. "He's funny, too, isn't he? Could we take this one?" Jessie's hopeful eyes searched Virginia's face. "He doesn't have a mama anyway." She reached to pat the lamb on the head.

"He will take a lot more care," Virginia started. "He'll need to be bottle-fed around the clock, and you're at school all day."

Jessie's face fell, and she lifted the lamb's small face. "I'm sorry," she said.

"I could . . . I mean we could take care of him," Mae said, instantly wondering if she'd regret the offer. "Peter's home all day anyway. I'm sure he wouldn't mind a couple of feedings during the day. He has to bottle-feed calves anyway. And I can get up to feed him at night."

"Really?" That smile was back.

"I'd be happy to," Mae said.

Vernon returned with a warm bottle of lamb's milk replacer and handed it to Jessie. The lamb sucked eagerly, almost punching the bottle out of Jessie's hand. Jessie laughed and smiled up at Mae.

"Is this one for sale?" Mae asked the farmer.

"This one's a lot of work. I'm not sure you want . . ." His voice trailed off as his gaze returned to Jessie. "Sure he's for sale. Pretty cheap too." His smiling eyes met Mae's.

"We'll have to get a stall ready for him over at your place, Mae," Virginia said. "We weren't planning on bringing a lamb home so soon."

"We could keep him in the basement where it's warm," Mae said. "That way I won't have to hobble to the barn in the cold during the middle of the night."

"Are you sure you want to do this?" Virginia whispered to Mae.

"For Jessie, sure."

Her gaze landed on the newborns with their mother in the other stall. Their white fleece was short, and their sides shivered in the cool air. They nursed on either side of their mother, punching their noses in alternate rhythm, almost knocking the ewe off balance.

"It's okay, baby," Jessie cooed. "I'm going to be your mama now." The little orphan answered with a mewling bleat, revealing small baby teeth and a pink tongue.

As they drove back to the Morgan farm, Jessie held the orphan wrapped in an old towel. She gingerly petted his small head. Her gaze never left his tiny face. Vernon had given them enough milk replacer to last for a few days, as well as an oversize bottle with a nipple and instructions to call him if anything seemed out of sorts.

"Why did the mother sheep reject her baby?" Jessie asked absently.

"Because she didn't know this one was hers. A weak lamb can't nurse, and nursing is what bonds the lamb to its mother," Virginia answered. "Doesn't seem right, does it?"

Jessie shook her head. "Doesn't seem like a very good mother to me. If I had a baby, I wouldn't forget it."

Her words thudded in Mae's ears.

· · ·

The alarm on the stove sounded. Mae could hear it faintly from her bedroom upstairs. She turned over in bed. Peter mumbled something incomprehensible. Then Mae remembered what the alarm was for. With a groan she got up, wiped some drool from her cheek, and stumbled down the stairs to turn it off.

Two in the morning. "Agh!" she moaned. The lamb was bleating loudly from the basement. "Why did I do this?" she said to herself. She slapped her own cheeks twice in an attempt to wake up. Turning on the tap water until it ran lukewarm, she measured two cups and added another cup of the powdery white milk from the bag of milk replacer. Then she stirred it until all the lumps melted and poured it into the oversize bottle.

The lamb's crying increased as Mae stumbled down the basement steps. "Hold your horses," she said. The lamb circled his box in excitement. "You already know what's coming, don't you?" She lifted the fluffy baby from his straw bed and sat on the cold basement step in her pajamas while the lamb bent his head to suck noisily. He turned his rear end toward her and sat down on her lap, the whole time never letting loose of the bottle. Mae petted his woolly coat.

There was something intimate about the whole thing, something the two of them shared. A 2:00 AM feeding. She wondered if this was what it would be like to get up with her own baby in the middle of the night.

The orphan lifted his head and pushed at the bottle

to drain the last drops. Within two minutes he had finished the entire bottle.

"You were hungry!" she said. The lamb punched at her arm. "Sorry, buddy, that's all you get."

She set him in the box. He circled the cozy home and nestled down for a nap.

"See you in two hours," Mae said, and she turned out the light.

Amused, Bert watched his mother as she hopped between the counters in her kitchen. She muttered something under her breath, then when she saw Bert, she gasped. "Why don't you tell a person you're there?" she scolded.

"Sorry, Ma," Bert said. "What are you doing?"

"Getting supper started. I'm so tired of being in this cast I could hit somebody!"

Bert raised his hands in surrender, and Lillian smiled.

"You're a good son. But I tell you that brother of yours has shown his true colors. I'm so angry with him. What does he think he's doing, taking off right now? He knows the peas have to be planted in a couple of weeks."

"He needed a break," Bert said, although he'd thought he was the one who deserved the break. "Fred's never had a vacation by himself." His ma measured and dumped flour into her trusty bread machine. "I thought it might have something to do with me and Trudy," Bert confessed. "He did like her an awful lot."

Lillian stopped and gazed at Bert as if considering. "Well, if he did, he's going to have to get over it," she said finally. "Have you given her that ring yet?"

Bert shook his head. "I'm waiting for the right moment. But now that hockey season is almost over, she's busy with that play."

"Well, hurry up and *find* the perfect moment. You bought that ring weeks ago; no sense letting it sit and rot."

Bert saluted. "Yes ma'am." That brought on another smile from his mother.

"How does Fred think he'll cope when you two are married and living under his nose?"

"Living out here?" The words struck Bert like an airbag in a crash. He'd never really considered where he and Trudy would live once they were married. All that had mattered was that he wanted to be with her. Had they even talked about where they would live?

"Of course you'd live on the farm. You're a dairy farmer, Bert," Lillian said. "How many times have you spent the night in the barn during calving? Who wants to drive back and forth to town all the time?"

Bert knew she was right, but he couldn't seem to shake the worry. Why hadn't he and Trudy discussed it? He knew why—because he still had to propose. The image of Trudy and his mother butting heads at the breakfast table rose up and along with it a nagging uneasiness. He needed to talk to Trudy.

"Hello-o," Trudy singsonged into the phone in the noisy art room. A few high school students, along with

Virginia and Jessie, were painting the porch of Laurey's farmhouse amid bouts of laughter.

"Hey," Bert said.

"Hey yourself, lover boy," Trudy said low enough so the others in the room wouldn't hear.

"Are you busy?" Bert said.

"Swamped. We're almost done here for today, but then I have a meeting with Rosemary. I'll be done around five."

"I'll be milking—"

"I know, until eight or eight thirty. It seems we never see each other anymore."

There was an awkward silence.

Trudy twirled the cord around her finger.

"Could I come by tomorrow after school?" Bert said. "No more hockey. I could help out. We could talk."

"That'd be great." She breathed deeply. "I've missed you."

"I've missed you, too."

Bert's uneasiness lingered. He kept thinking about Trudy living on the farm, and he couldn't seem to reconcile the image. He was being ridiculous, he told himself. He needed to talk to Trudy and get this settled; then everything would be fine.

"Hey," he said from the art-room door. Trudy's back was to him. Her long curly red hair was wild and exciting on her tall, thin frame. She turned, and a smile meant just for him lit her face.

"Hey, yourself. Come on in." She had a stack of

watercolor paintings on her desk. Others were propped here and there as if she were admiring them.

"What you up to?" he asked.

"Art contest—I'm picking finalists. What do you think of this one?" She held up a bright painting of orange tiger lilies. They filled the whole page with their bursts of brightness.

"It's good," Bert said.

Trudy set the drawing down and raised her face to Bert. She motioned for him to take a seat on one of the tall stools.

Bert lifted his green seed cap and ran a hand through his curly hair. "Yeah," he said, struggling with how to phrase what was coming. "I . . . um . . . I was talking to Ma the other day, and . . ." Trudy moved to a stool next to his and climbed up onto it. "I . . . guess I realized we've never talked about where we'd live if we got married."

"Is this a proposal?" Her face took on a grin.

"Well, um . . ."

"Yes?" she said expectantly. She moved closer, and his face warmed.

"There's nothing more that I would like"—he licked his lips—"than for you to be my wife." Despite his pounding heart, the words felt right.

"Really?" Trudy said. She reached for him and kissed him softly. "Yes," she whispered into his ear. "I'll marry you, Bert Biddle."

Bert's head swam, and when he gazed into her eyes, he'd forgotten what he'd been saying. He felt as though fireworks were exploding in his heart.

"Really?" he echoed.

"I said yes!" Trudy nodded her head up and down. "You have made me the happiest woman alive, Mr. Biddle."

Bert reached for her hand and wove their fingers together. "I love you, Trudy."

"I love you."

"I left the ring out in the truck." He pointed over his shoulder, then a cloud crossed his face as he remembered the reason he'd wanted to see her in the first place.

"Was there something else?" Trudy said.

"Well . . . yeah." He studied his own hands. "Where do you want to live? I mean, you know, after we're married."

"You had me worried," Trudy said. She kissed the tip of his nose. "I don't expect a big house, if that's what you're worried about. If you wanted to move into the pharmacy with me until we can save up for a down payment on a place. I don't know. What were you thinking?"

"I . . . well. I figured we'd live at the farm."

"Where would your folks and Fred live? It doesn't seem very kind to kick them out of their own home."

"They wouldn't move . . . We'd . . . It's not as if there isn't plenty of room. My parents lived with my Grandma and Grandpa Biddle."

"I'll bet that was great," Trudy said sarcastically.

"What is that supposed to mean?" He pulled his hand away.

"How can you even suggest living with your parents?" Her voice rose. "Honestly, Bert, I know your mother, and she bugs you, too. We don't want to start our married life constantly at her beck and call."

"She's my mother." Bert couldn't think of anything else to say.

"Our marriage will be doomed from the start if you can't cut those apron strings."

Bert's ears burned. If she loved him, how could she say such cruel things about him? Trudy must have read his expression, because her voice softened, and she said, "Hey, I'm not trying to hurt you." She reached for him again, but he pulled away.

"You know, I guess I knew this. You want your own way, no matter how I feel. You might think I'm not man enough . . . ," he sputtered. "You spend all your time on this play, it's no wonder we can't—"

"I spend all *my* time?" Trudy's voice rose by a decibel. "You're the one who's at stupid hockey all the time! You were in a hurry to fill up your spare time as soon as I moved to town—"

"I've got to go," he said. His gaze was on the floor. He couldn't look her in the eyes.

"Bert."

"No," he said. He stood to leave.

"Bert," she called to his back.

"I'll talk to you later," he said without turning to face her.

WILL BIDDLE

Winter was always so cold in their drafty farmhouse. The bedroom window was covered in snowflake designs where the frost had etched its signature. Six-year-old Will Biddle climbed under the thick hand-made quilts on his bed and moved his legs back and forth to warm the frigid sheets.

"We need a fireplace up here, Ma," he said as his mother came in to kiss him good night. He wasn't only thinking of the cold. She laughed, and Will watched her round belly bounce up and down with each chuckle. "Is the baby laughing too, Ma?"

"Yes, sweetheart. He's laughing at his funny big brother."

"If I had my own fireplace, would Santa come right to my room?" he asked, his eyes alight with Christmas Eve sparkle. His mother sat on the edge of his bed and brushed his bangs out of his eyes.

"We've talked about this before, Will. With Daddy away in the war, we don't have money for presents this year. Do you understand?"

Will nodded his head. "But couldn't Santa—?"

She put a finger to his lips. "I don't want you getting your hopes up, okay? What matters is we'll be together for Christmas. I'll make a nice dinner for us tomorrow, and Grandma and Grandpa will come over." A tear glistened on her lower lid, and Will brushed it away. "We'll pray that Daddy comes home real soon."

Will put his small hand in his mother's. "It'll be okay, Ma."

"I love you," she whispered. She kissed him on the forehead and dimmed the kerosene lamp. Will listened to her steps fade as she returned downstairs. The kitchen was directly beneath his room. The sound of his mother humming Christmas carols floated up as Will started to doze. Sleigh bells awoke him. His eyes opened wide in an instant. He ran to the window to peer outside. There beside the tall martin house covered in snow was an honest-to-goodness sleigh. Instead of reindeer, a horse pranced in front, and a man in a red-and-white suit called, "Whoa!"

The door of the kitchen creaked open, and then his mother came into view on the back stoop, standing with a sweater on, her arms folded against the cold. Santa hoisted a large bag onto his shoulders and walked into the house.

Will was down the stairs before Santa even made it past the kitchen door. The six-year-old stood at the bottom of the stairs and gaped in awe.

"What do we have here? Are you Will Biddle?"

Will nodded.

"I heard you've been pretty good this year," Santa said. "Let's see what I have in here for you."

Will looked to his mother, who nodded, then he ran to Santa. He had never seen so many toys in one place before, except at the store. There were toy trucks and fire engines, a blackboard that transformed into a writing desk, a coaster wagon, toy tractors, Chinese checkers, a bag full of clothes—a

*wool coat, pants, shirts—and best of all an electric
train. Will played until his eyes drooped. Santa carried him upstairs to his bed. Will heard the stairs
creak as he snuggled deep under the covers, contented.*

*"Thank you so much, Mr. Morgan. This meant so
much to him and to me." Ma's muffled voice carried
up through the vent.*

*"Don't mention it. With Roy married and gone to
war, we thought Will would enjoy his old toys. Girls
don't exactly want their brother's hand-me-down tractors. I'm glad to see Will put them to good use."*

*"Tell Mrs. Morgan thank you from the bottom of my
heart." Will could hear the crack in his mother's voice
that always meant tears weren't far behind.*

*"You take care of yourself. We're praying that your
young man comes home soon," Gus Morgan said.
"Merry Christmas."*

*Will's eyes drifted shut with dreams that Santa
would bring his daddy home in his big bag of toys.*

twenty-three

Willie Biddle bent over the 1925 Alpha DeLaval
milking machine engine as he wrenched a bolt
snug.

"Son," he said, acknowledging Bert's entrance into
the cavernous shop.

Bert waited for him to finish and gazed at the hit-
and-miss vacuum pump as his father bent to check
something. Ever since Bert was a boy his father had

collected and worked on the antique motors that he faithfully displayed at the annual Pioneer Power threshing show. They were lined up along the walls of the shop from smallest to largest, each mounted on a wooden wagon and all labeled with an engraved plaque indicating the manufacturer, model, and year.

Like his sons, Willie had deep dimples in his cheeks. His eyes were a pale blue. He had gray brows and a full head of thick white hair.

Willie handed Bert a postcard without saying a word. The front carried a picture of the Magic Kingdom. On the back Fred's sloppy handwriting: "I met this guy, Bob. He offered me a job as a ride mechanic, so I guess I'll be staying here for a while. The weather's great. Fred."

Bert sighed and set the postcard on the chipped and dented wooden counter.

"Leaves us in a spot, doesn't it?" Willie said.

"That's Fred," Bert said. "Thinking of number one."

"You sure don't seem grateful for all the years he put in around here."

"I'm still mad." Bert ran his hand along the worktable. "Dad." Bert rested his backside against the bench as he faced his father. Willie lifted his pale eyes. "When you and Ma got married, how did you know she was the one?"

"I didn't know. Why? You and Trudy having troubles?"

"I tried to propose to her, but we ended up in an argument." He stared vacantly at the wall of collectibles. "We've been arguing a lot lately."

"A little tiff now and then isn't the end of the world," Willie said. He finished tightening the bolt and placed the wrench back on its hook on the workbench wall.

"We're very different—Trudy and me. She's all artsy and sophisticated, and I'm some hayseed farmer."

"And you're wondering if that will cause problems down the road?" Willie leaned against the bench and crossed his arms.

"Her mother seems to think so," Bert said.

"Do you love her?"

"Yes, but is that enough?"

"I won't lie to you, Son," Willie said. "It hasn't always been easy with your mother. She's a difficult woman, but we find ways to . . . adjust."

Bert was all too familiar with his father's *adjustments*. Half the time he was hiding out here, especially since he'd retired. Was he willing to risk his heart to that fate?

A week after bringing the lamb home to the farm, Jessie and Mae made a pen for him in a stall at the rear of the barn, secluded from the other animals. They scattered straw in a thick blanket and hung a heat lamp from the rafters. A round black rubber feed tray and a five-gallon bucket of water made baby's warm nook complete.

And yet even a week after moving to his new home, he cried constantly. When anyone came near, he would cry. When he was all alone, he would cry. Peter had told Virginia he was always hearing him cry from the milking parlor.

"What's wrong with him, Virginia?" Jessie gazed at the lamb, and he tilted his head and bounded over to her, hopping sideways. He bleated and punched his nose into her thigh. She petted his head. "Is he sick?"

"I don't think so," Virginia said from her post by the gate. "No signs of bloat or scours. I think he's lonely."

"Do sheep *get* lonely?" Jessie said. She sat on a bale of hay and took the lamb's face in her hands, gazing into his eyes.

"Sure they do. They need companionship like we do."

"What can we do?" Jessie lifted her gaze to Virginia.

"We could put him with Mae's calf."

"That big steer? Wouldn't he hurt him?" Jessie said.

"We could get another lamb to keep him company."

"Really?" Jessie said hopefully. Virginia knew she was a lost cause whenever she saw that expression; the hardest of hearts couldn't turn Jessie down when she made that face.

"At least he wouldn't make such a racket," Virginia said.

All Trudy wanted to do was get home and soak in a hot tub and forget the fight with Bert. She'd been thinking about it all week. She'd managed to get engaged and then break up all in the space of a few minutes; even for her it was some kind of record. And yet she was right, wasn't she? Starting a marriage under Lillian Biddle's watchful eye would be disastrous. Why couldn't Bert see that?

She had climbed the stairs to her darkened apartment, kicked off her shoes, and begun filling the tub when the doorbell rang. She turned off the water and went to answer it.

Bert stood there with a picnic hamper in one hand and a large plastic shopping bag in the other. His green seed cap was gone, and his curly dishwater blond hair had a part that seemed ready to break ranks at any moment.

"I'm sorry," he said, looking like a repentant seven-year-old. Trudy swallowed the lump in her throat. "I've come with a peace offering."

"I didn't even hear you out," Trudy said. "I totally ruined your proposal."

"Maybe this will help." He reached into the hamper and pulled out a small burgundy ring box. "I've been keeping it in the glove compartment for the perfect time."

Tears flooded Trudy's eyes so she couldn't see. She opened the box and touched the exquisite setting. "It's beautiful." She gazed up at him. "Are you sure about this?"

Bert dropped to one knee, setting his bags down as he did. "You're right about living with my mother. It's a bad idea. I don't know how we'll manage the farm." When he said it, Trudy felt very small. He could find it in his heart to compromise, to risk the farm for her, but what compromising had she done?

Bert paused as if trying to decide something, then went on. "I want to be with you. You're worth more to me than the farm. I love you. Please say you'll marry me."

"Yes," Trudy said. "I'll marry you, Bert Biddle."

He placed the ring on her finger, then stood and pulled her within the circle of his arms. "Are we okay?"

Trudy nodded mutely, feeling loved, elated . . . humbled.

Finally she sniffled and pulled back. She pointed toward the basket. "So, what is all this?" She tried to peek into the bag.

"No, no, no," he scolded teasingly and pulled the bag away. "It's a surprise. Come with me." Trudy followed him down the stairs and into the darkened pharmacy. "I called Bob Ott—he said this was okay," Bert said.

Trudy lifted a pale brow as Bert opened the basket and withdrew a red-and-white checkered tablecloth that he spread across the soda fountain's stainless-steel counter. Next came crystal candleholders and two long tapers, which he set in place and lit. His face glowed in the candlelight, and the boyish delight she saw there made her long to kiss him again. He pulled out China plates and silverware, goblets and cloth napkins. Appetizers came first—tiny smoky Joe wieners in barbecue sauce. Then came a thick T-bone steak and baked potato with white rolls and coleslaw for the main course.

"Mmm," Trudy said, rolling her eyes back in ecstasy. "This is the best food. Where did you learn to cook like this?"

"It's all in the Betty Crocker cookbook; it's a matter of keeping it all hot." He blushed.

Trudy sighed happily. "I was a brat," she said, taking his hands in hers. "Forgive me? I promise I'll try harder with your mother. I know she's important to you." Their eyes held, and Trudy could see tenderness in his gaze. She placed her hand on the curve of his neck, and their lips met. When they moved apart, Trudy was weak. She placed a hand on her chest and inhaled. "Why, Mr. Biddle," she said. "You've never kissed me like that before."

Bert turned three shades of red. "I . . . I've never felt like this before."

She laced her fingers into his and rested her head on his chest, happy to simply "be."

"So . . . what's in the bag?" Trudy asked after a few moments. Bert laughed.

"I knew your curiosity was eating at you." He grabbed the sack and held it closed so she couldn't sneak a peek.

"Come on!" Trudy whined. "Show me."

Bert pulled out two thin, long sticks, flat, about an inch wide, one about two feet long and the other about four feet long. Next came a big sheet of paper, paints and brushes, pencils, string, an old sheet and glue. Puzzled, Trudy lifted an eyebrow at him. "We're making a kite," he explained.

"Fun! So how should we decorate it?" Trudy placed her forefinger on her chin. "H'm. How about a big diamond ring?"

"Okay, Miss Artist." He grinned at her, and they fell

to decorating their creation. Trudy stuck out her tongue like a six-year-old as she drew. Her pencil moved in smooth, flowing lines. Soon both were painting, their heads almost touching as they concentrated. Bert's arm brushed Trudy's, and she felt a surge of energy pulse through her body.

She had never met a man who intrigued her more, who constantly surprised her. Who forgave so willingly. She eyed him covertly as he painted. His brow was knit in concentration, and the sparkle that lit his eyes seemed to dance. Trudy vowed she would never cause that expression to leave his face again.

Adeline Elwood came onto the sloping porch as Virginia, Peter, and Jessie pulled up in Peter's green truck. A petite woman with silver hair, Adeline pulled on a bulky coat with a fur-trimmed hood as she came toward the car. "Hello, Virginia, what can I do for you?"

"Good afternoon, Adeline. I called Vernon about a lamb."

"Oh, that's right. He mentioned something about it. Why don't you come on in? He's taking a nap." She led the way into the house. Despite its crumbling facade, the interior of the house was an antique dealer's dream. Every available spot was taken up with curios, old picnic baskets, and aged knickknacks of all manner and make. In the corner of the living room stood a Hoosier cabinet with even more collectibles. Jessie touched a frail-looking porcelain doll in a 1950s-era buggy. Virginia shook her head no, and

Jessie pulled her hand back and stood next to Virginia inside the door. Peter winked at her.

Adeline climbed the creaking stairs to awaken her husband. A few minutes later a rumpled-looking Vernon Elwood came down to greet them.

"Afternoon," he said. "Sorry you caught me napping. I think I pushed it a bit hard at the diner today."

Adeline gave him a scolding expression and said, "I tell him to take it easy, but he never listens." Vernon waved the comment aside and put his jacket on to lead them to the barn.

It was a warm day, in the high forties. Melted snow ran in rivulets across the driveway. The pasture was a mudhole. Bachelor steers stood in the muck gazing at them with curious eyes.

"The lambs have grown a bit since the last time you were here," Vernon said, holding the door for the visitors to enter the dark barn. "If you want to pick one out, I'll try to catch it."

The frightened sheep surged from corner to corner of the large pen where they all now congregated. Finally Jessie pointed to a medium-sized young ram with a gray spot on its muzzle. Vernon opened the gate and slowly edged toward the group. Each time he drew near, the sheep ran in a panicked cluster around the stall.

"Looks like they're pretty sheepish," Peter joked. Virginia shook her head at him, and Jessie returned the wink he'd given her before.

The old man circled the sheep, his arms spread wide. The creatures moved in a perfect dance out of his reach. "Let me help, Vernon," Peter finally said. Vernon gratefully stepped aside as Peter took the ring. He stood in the center, his eyes locked on the lamb Jessie had chosen, trying to find an opportune moment to pounce. The lamb moved behind his mother, who stared back at Peter with threatening eyes. Peter tried to draw closer; the lamb's mother backed up and lowered her head.

Finally Peter had the ewe and lamb cornered. The other dozen or so sheep stood in a tight clump, making it impossible to tell one animal from the next, and watched in fright from the opposite side of the pen. Peter took a step toward the lamb. Its mother moved forward, then back, keeping her body between him and her baby. Then Peter faked left and ran right. The ewe opted for flight rather than fight and took off like a shot counterclockwise in the stall, leaving her youngster exposed. Peter grabbed his wool in an instant. He threw his arms around his midsection as he bleated loudly and struggled against Peter's embrace.

"Flip him on his rump," Vernon instructed.

As soon as Peter had the lamb sitting on his rump, he ceased fighting. He merely sat like a giant cotton ball on a La-Z-Boy and gazed subdued at his surroundings. His complaining mother joined the cluster of onlookers and called out to him. The lamb answered, but his fight was gone.

"That's it?" Jessie asked.

"Yep," Vernon said. "Don't ever expect sheep to be smart or amiable."

Vernon helped Peter pick the lamb up by its four

hooves and carry it to the livestock trailer Peter had hooked behind the pickup.

Vernon's words proved true. Back at the Morgans', the new lamb wouldn't let Jessie touch him even though she sat patiently for hours on a bale of hay with her hand extended. He stared blankly at her and kept to the far wall.

Jessie contentedly watched the lambs getting acquainted, sniffing each other. The smaller of the two bunted at the larger as if testing to see if he was Mama. Jessie laughed at his silliness.

By the end of the day the two had become fast friends. They frolicked and played, twisting, hopping, and chasing each other.

Jessie and Virginia settled into the routine of driving to the farm each afternoon. Jessie fed the lambs and talked to them, telling them what had happened at school or at home. She had a natural way with animals, never pushing or babying them. She simply sat.

Virginia spied her one day before Jessie knew she'd come inside. The nine-year-old was talking quietly. "Daddy got a job yesterday, guys! He says it's a dumb job at a gas station, but I think things are going to be much better. Maybe now he'll be happy instead of sad all the time."

It was another quiet, lonely morning. David rinsed his coffee cup and set it in the drainer. He gazed out the window above the sink. Thick, heavy clouds rode low in a muted gray sky. He could use some sunshine today. He slipped into his chore coat and walked outside.

Peter was long gone, puttering around at odd chores. David strolled to the Quonset shed. Opening the door, he switched on the lineup of bare bulbs marching lengthwise down the top of the arch. He stood gazing at the long, hollow room. A workbench ran half the length of one wall. It was nicked and stained from decades of his father's use, and a pegboard held the Craftsman tools over it. So many memories at that workbench—his father fixing tractors, putting Peter's bike together for Christmas, making 4-H birdhouses, and working on other projects together. The back of the round-roofed metal building was dark. The combine slumbered next to the Oliver tractor and Roy's first tractor, a Minneapolis Moline, his father's pride and joy. He touched the plaque that read "Minneapolis Moline, 1947, owned by Roy and Virginia Morgan." So many Fourth of July parades this tractor had ridden in while he and his father waved from the top.

"I don't know what to do, Dad," he said to the empty seat. "You told me to reach for my dreams. What happens when your dream times out?" He stood in the empty silence for a long while. "God," he prayed, "I'm a man. I know you love me, but I don't understand why this had to happen. You have always walked with me, even in my darkest times. And I've had darker times than this, but I need to know what to do. Where to go. I'm tired of feeling sorry for myself. It gets me nowhere but deeper in self-pity. I trust you, Lord, even if I don't know the outcome, because I know you love me without fail. I need your help. Start me dreaming again."

Trudy had been singing all day—tunes by the Beatles, Lovin' Spoonful, the Mamas and the Papas. It didn't matter what the song—today every song was a love song. Every five minutes she lifted her hand and gazed in amazement at the sparkling engagement ring.

"Trudy," Rosemary called above the din in the crowded prop room. Trudy was digging for various "doodadles" that the peddler-man would sell from the wagon Chuck Wilbee had magically secured for the play. Trudy lifted her head from the box that she was interrogating. "I had to come by and tell you how wonderful the sets look. I can't remember when we've had a more becoming stage. The kids are thrilled."

Trudy smiled. "I'm glad you like them. We have some very talented art students to thank."

"But you've gone above and beyond." Then Rosemary grew quiet and sighed.

"What is it?"

"I got a call from Don Lind."

"The school board president?"

Rosemary nodded. "There have been rumors that we've been spending a lot on the sets."

"Are you kidding? I haven't spent a penny! I even paid for the hot melt out of my own pocket!"

Rosemary lifted a hand, ending Trudy's building tirade. "I thought so, but I had to check it out. I hope when people see how dedicated our young people are to the play, they'll stop all this. I'm sorry, sometimes people in small towns have small minds. Not always, but sometimes." She gazed out the window. "These kids need to explore their abilities as much or even more than the kids in the sports program. I wish . . ." Her words faded.

"What do you wish?" Trudy said.

"When they cut the orchestra, some really gifted children lost out. I've tried to find time in my schedule, but it's not there. Private lessons are tricky; most parents can't spend the extra money. It would be wonderful to have some strings in our performance . . ."

"Hey," Trudy said, an idea dawning, "I know a concert violinist who'd make a great tutor."

Rosemary gave her a puzzled expression.

"David Morgan."

"You mean David Morgan of the St. Paul Chamber Orchestra? He wouldn't have time to—"

"I'm pretty sure he would," Trudy said. "He's a family member." She grinned. "Let me ask him."

Trudy couldn't remember a more wonderful day. After her talk with Rosemary, she called David and asked him to help with the orchestra. He seemed almost grateful for the request and said he'd set things up with Rosemary right away. She couldn't wait to see the excitement on Rosemary's face when she heard the news.

Everything was falling into place—at school and with Bert. She sighed contentedly as she made her way up the steps to her apartment. She could hear Bob Ott singing through the door of the adjoining apartment. She stood listening, eavesdropping.

"If I were a rich man . . ." He drew the words out dramatically in a rich baritone voice, full throated and perfectly on key. "All day long I'd biddy biddy bum, if I were a wealthy man . . ." Trudy chuckled. He was indeed a very rich man.

For no reason an image popped into her head like a slide on a View-Master. Bob Ott and Rosemary. Together. Neither had ever married. Both had an obvious love of music. They were close to the same age. H'm.

twenty-four

Spring had its own scent, especially when the dew was heavy in the mornings as it was today. Peter breathed in the earth-tinged air. He lowered the plow for the first pass. The soil tilth was perfect this year— the right amount of moisture, easy access to get the machinery in and out of the fields. Peter drove the John Deere in a slow, straight path. The claws of the plow left deep furrows of rich black earth like breaking ocean waves. When he glanced back he saw that hundreds of sea gulls had appeared as if from nowhere to feast on the insects the plow unearthed.

Peter was relieved to be back doing what he loved best, although it was different now, no longer a novelty or a passing fad. He was a real farmer, seasoned by the experiences of the past year. Some of the nostalgia had worn off, yet when he lifted his eyes to the horizon he longed for this moment to last. He hoped that in ten, twenty years he would still be glad he'd made the decision to commit to the farm.

His thoughts shifted to his father. David had withdrawn since coming to the farm. He'd tried to hide it. But to Peter it was becoming obvious that his father felt he did not belong here. He had seen that expression in his eyes too many times, the same expression he'd had when Peter had found him crying over his mother's journal.

At lunchtime, Peter parked the tractor and planter alongside the ditch and climbed into the pickup to head home. Lake Emily's silver tower bloomed proudly in the morning mist of the valley. Dust followed his path, a persistent suitor that smothered every farm along the way with its unwanted attentions. By the driveway, Grandma's crocuses and daffodils were poking their pale heads from the still-cool soil. Peter left the keys in the ignition and set the brake.

The screen door's spring squeaked in protest as it stretched, then slammed shut behind Peter. "It's looking great out there," Peter said to Mae. "Do you think the asparagus is up yet?"

Mae gave David a blank shrug. "I have no idea. What does asparagus look like?"

"Like asparagus," David said. "Been a long time since I did any asparagus hunting, back then it was forced labor. Dad absolutely loved the stuff. We'd watch the ditches every trip into town." His eyes bent into a smile. "I don't know how, but he would always spot a patch before anyone else. As I recall, it would be in late May, maybe mid-May." A wistful expression crossed his face, then he said, "Shouldn't be long now. I can show you the patch in the grove."

"What's for lunch?" Peter said. "It smells heavenly."

"Don't commend me," Mae said. "Your dad was the chef today."

David lifted his eyebrows. "A treat," he said.

Mae brought a stack of plates and silverware and cups to the table. David pulled a steaming dish of red cabbage and polska kielbasa from the oven.

They took their seats around the long table, and David said grace.

"You always were a great cook, Dad," Peter said when they lifted their heads.

"Not always, Peter, but after your mother died, I had lots of practice. You don't remember all the burned meals." There was a smile on his dad's face he hadn't seen in a while.

"You seem happy today," Peter said.

"Trudy called and asked if I would volunteer to tutor a few orchestra students at the high school. I'm kind of looking forward to it," David said. "I'm headed to the Music Mart in Mankato tonight to pick up a few lesson books."

"That's great, Dad," Peter said.

"Well, it remains to be seen how good a teacher I'll be." He winked at Mae and handed her plate back. "Back to the fields tonight, Peter?"

"In a bit. Actually, I was thinking of letting Jessie's lambs into the big pasture. It's such a nice, warm day. They're so cramped in that tiny yard."

"Do you think the steer will mind sharing his space?" Mae said.

"You're going to put sheep and a steer together?" David said.

"Is that a problem?" Peter asked.

David shrugged. "Don't know. I never raised sheep."

"I'll give Jessie a call and see if she wants to come watch," Mae said. "It might be fun."

Jessie had named her lambs Thing One and Thing Two after the rascally Dr. Seuss characters. They had each grown a thick coat that had mutated from nursery-rhyme white to dirty gray in the weeks since their arrival. Now instead of "cute" they were in that awkward stage of early teenhood. "Baa" was far too dainty an utterance for these gross-out boys. When they bleated, it was more of a low barfing sound.

The bottle-fed lamb known as Thing One ran to Peter like a pup in search of a doggy biscuit. As for his cohort, he still had attachment issues. When anyone came near, the wide-eyed creature ran headlong into the boards of his pen.

Peter stood just inside the gate and held out a calming hand. Thing Two backed away, shifting left to right, then pushing his fleece against the barn wall, as far away as he could possibly get from Peter. Thing One paid his buddy no mind. He stayed at Peter's knees, bumping into him, begging for a handout even if it meant Peter stepped on him a time or two. Peter took a step, and the rear boy ran at the wall like a kamikaze. Then, rebounding off the boards, he paced between the back sides of the pen. Peter stepped back and scratched his head.

Mae, David, and Jessie came in the side door. The light from the pasture shone through. "How's it going?" Mae said.

"This isn't going to be easy. This poor guy is afraid of his own shadow." Peter glanced around. "You want to open that door?"

Mae walked to the gate. Her steer gazed at the scene from the outside and then ambled to within a few inches of Mae and lifted his wet nose to sniff her hand for food. His long sandpaper tongue extended to clean each of his big nostrils, then swiped at Mae.

"Ewww!" She leaned back. "Keep your tongue to yourself!"

She reached up and scratched him behind the ridge at the top of his head. The big calf lowered his head and stretched out his thick neck in a brazen request for more.

"He's not shy." Peter laughed.

"He's my baby," Mae said. The steer's liquid eyes confirmed the statement. "Aren't you, sweetheart?" She gave his neck a final pat.

"Okay," Peter said. "What we need to do is get Thing One and Thing Two to come out of their stall, go down the aisle, and then through the door to the pasture without killing anyone."

"Piece of cake," Mae said.

Peter opened the gate to their stall. Thing One ambled easily out and hopped sideways down the aisle to Mae. Thing Two stared on in shock and horror, still glued to the back wall. Thing One touched noses with Mae's calf in a formal livestock introduction.

"Stand over there." Peter pointed to the right of the gate. "Then this one won't have to go past you to get to the door." Jessie, David, and Mae moved to the spot. He eased himself into the left side of the stall, and the sheep jumped headfirst at the wall. As Peter moved to the back of its home, Thing Two edged first into the back right-hand corner and then up the side. Once he was out of his stall he froze and looked first at Peter, then the trio.

"Move forward," Peter whispered calmly. "We can pressure him to the door." With every step they took, the lamb cautiously kept its distance until he was on the threshold of freedom. When he saw his cellmate in the green pasture, he darted forward, startling the steer. The fifteen-hundred-pound animal turned his rump to the newcomer and gave a couple of swift kicks. While the kicks didn't connect full force, they did send Thing Two running.

Right through the boards of the old wooden gate and through the electric fence.

Jessie's lamb followed closely. They paused and gazed back toward the barn as if to make sure their plan had succeeded. Then they nodded at each other, lowered their heads, and charged into the bare field beyond.

Peter dropped his jaw.

"That electric fence didn't stop them at all," Mae said. "Is wool an insulator? Did you read up on what kind of fencing sheep need?"

Peter gave her "the look," and she clamped her mouth shut.

"Shouldn't we try to get them?" Jessie said in a panicked voice, her eyes following the animals that were sprinting like paired sleds across the field.

Peter said to his father, "Dad?"

David turned to Jessie. "Call your lamb, Jessie," he said.

Jessie ran to the middle of the pasture and began calling. Thing One slowed, then stopped and turned toward her. He bleated and bounded back with twisting hops along the way.

Thing Two didn't even notice. The lamb was almost to the woods at the north end of the pasture, now a good fifty yards from the farm. He ran full tilt, his head down, a defensive lineman ready to tackle anyone who got in his way. Then he stopped at the edge of the woods, inches from freedom but afraid.

Mae and Peter both took off at a run. Mae closed in from the left and cut toward the lamb. Instead of risking the woods or turning around and going back to the barn, the animal darted right past Mae. She lunged in a full-body assault, her arms wide as she grabbed for the lamb, but the animal was too quick. Mae lay spread-eagle in the spring earth. She lifted a blackened face to Peter.

"Are you okay?" he said.

"Do I *look* okay?"

Peter grimaced, then took off running again. "Mae, come on. He's getting away!" he shouted back, then to

Jessie, "Put Thing One in his regular pasture." Jessie quickly led him to his cramped but secure quarters.

"Keep him off the road!" David shouted as he pointed toward the highway as the lamb emerged onto the dirt road and accelerated toward the distant ribbon.

Peter scrambled to his truck. His dad was at his side.

"Get in," Peter said. He started the engine and peeled out of the driveway after the unrepentant sinner. Dust swarmed behind them as they gave chase. Peter's eyes fixed on the animal, which showed no signs of tiring. "Get out when I stop up here, and herd him back toward home," Peter instructed. He was parallel with, then past the lamb. Peter steered hard left, cutting off the creature's path and raising gravel in a spray. David jumped out and began the chase. Peter returned home as his dad outmaneuvered the beast. Mae stood bent over by the driveway with her hands on her thighs, gasping for breath.

Peter joined her. Sweat beaded on her forehead and nose, and she panted for air. "The lamb . . . doesn't do what . . . you want him to." She stood up and took a deep breath. "You saw him dart right past me . . . How do sheepdogs do it?"

Sheepdogs, Peter thought. "That just might be the ticket." He ran to get Scout from his kennel.

"Peter, Scout isn't a sheepdog. He's a Labrador," Mae said, following him. "It won't work."

"How do you know?"

"Peter." It was her turn to give him "the look."

"Fine." He raised his hands. "Help me come up with a better idea." By now David had managed to get the

231

escapee to the outside perimeter of the pasture. The chase had slowed to a walk. The creature was panting heavily. "Dad seems to have a knack," Peter said. David caught his breath. The lamb lowered his head and ate grass from the fence line. Taking a step forward, the lamb simply slipped back inside the electric wires.

"He's back in," David shouted as Peter reached him.

"The way he meanders through the wires we may as well have no fence at all. We have to get him in the barn till we come up with a better solution, or at least in his old pasture."

Peter glanced toward Jessie and saw she was coming their way. He held up a hand to her and said, "Stay there in case he makes a move, Jessie." He turned to his dad. "Any brilliant ideas?"

David thought, then said, "He's tired, so if you're going to get him, it better be now. Do you have any rope? We could lasso him."

"When's the last time you threw a lasso?" Peter said with a raised eyebrow.

"It's worth a try," David said.

Peter went into the shop in search of a rope. He had lead ropes, but none were long enough to tie into a lasso. He had baling twine, but that was too thin— he'd never be able to toss it far enough. He gazed around. A long orange extension cord caught his eye. He pulled it down and took it outside. He tied it into a decent lasso.

"What are you doing?" Mae said when she returned from putting her steer in the barn.

"We thought we'd lasso it."

She placed a hand on her hip.

"It might work!"

"With an extension cord?" Mae said.

He gave it a toss, and it untied itself. "Okay, it won't work." Peter dropped the cord onto the driveway.

"He's still in the same spot," Mae said, plotting. "Maybe you could slowly crawl up on him."

"You stay there," Peter said. "If he runs toward you, chase him back toward the barn." Peter crept inside the pasture near where the animal munched contentedly on grass. He lay flat on the ground and began inching forward through the tall grass. When he was almost to the fence, he realized that the electricity was still on. He caught his father's eye and pointed at the wire. David nodded and left to turn it off. When he gave the thumbs-up, Peter moved forward again. The lamb didn't seem to even notice him, merely chewed and grazed. Peter got within a yard of the lamb and carefully pulled his legs up under himself into the pounce position. With all his might he sprang up, arms ready for the catch. For a moment he was airborne, flying toward the woolly backside, arms stretched. The next moment he was on the ground with a mouthful of grass as his only prize. The lamb was sprinting again, this time toward Jessie.

"Wave your hands and arms around," Peter shouted to the girl.

She did, and a car on the dirt road honked at her. But the lamb stopped where he was and leered at her suspiciously. Then he dropped his head and ate. Peter put his hands over his face.

Peter sat up and watched the lamb as he contentedly nibbled and meandered with impunity in and out of the electric wires meant to contain him. Finally Peter returned to Mae. "If we don't figure out what to do, I'll have to put him down."

"Peter! You are not killing Jessie's 4-H project!" Mae whispered to him.

"It'll get killed on the road if we can't get it into the barn, or someone in a car could be killed."

"I've been thinking about sheepdogs," Mae said. "When Jessie held out her hands and arms, he stopped. I wonder if we could kind of steer him that way, at more of a distance though, like the dogs do. Maybe then he wouldn't bolt right past us."

"You might have something. When we get too close, he panics. I'll go tell Dad. Then we can pretend we are all sheepdogs." He smiled at her. "Pray that this works. I do not want to break a little girl's heart today."

He told David the plan, then gave the signal to Mae. She stood fifty feet back and raised her left hand only. The animal stared at her fearfully and moved away to the right. Then Mae threw out her right hand and the animal moved to the left. She stayed within his sight, and with every change in movement, he shifted.

"It's working!" she shouted. Then David took over, managing to get him within twenty feet of the barn, but the animal darted around him toward Peter. Peter threw out a left hand, and the creature moved right. Then Peter stopped, and so did the sheep.

"Move in but not too much," Peter said to Mae. He glanced over at his dad as he came from the west. David stood a few feet back, arms spread wide. The door was open before the lamb; he only had to go inside. Gradually the foursome applied more pressure, but Thing Two seemed nervous. Peter was afraid he'd bolt past them again. But then Thing One bleated, and the lamb meandered calmly inside to find his old buddy.

A cheer of joy rose up as Peter quickly slammed the barn door, then went in the side door. The lamb had gone back to his cell where his accomplice waited. He panted and drank deeply from the five-gallon water bucket. Peter shut them in, then joined the celebrants outside.

"That was a lot of fun!" Jessie said with a grin. "You and Mae got really dirty."

Peter looked down at their dirt-covered duds. "Matching mud!" he said.

"I'm relieved," Mae said, looking seriously at Jessie. "Very relieved."

twenty-five

Costumes lined two walls of the prop room like a parade of historic ghosts. Shelves along the left wall held boxes that reached to the ceiling. They harbored aged feather boas, shoes of all sizes and styles, all the accouterment of great high school drama. A mirror filled the narrow end. A makeup table waited before it with a row of white globe lights down either side, lending it Liza Minnelli glamour. A tall folding screen offered a bit of privacy for the actresses and actors who needed to make costume changes.

Lydia Lindstrom stood before Trudy in a hoop skirt and ribbed camisole, her arms wide as Trudy pinned and measured.

"This is going to be awesome, Miss Ploog." Lydia was a senior with long blond hair and a voice to die for. She would be a perfect Laurey—coy yet beautiful. Trudy tugged the frilled yellow dress over the girl's head, then stood back to admire. Lydia placed her hands on her rib cage.

"Stunning," Trudy said. Lydia blushed. Trudy tugged on one poofy sleeve and then the other.

"Miss Ploog?" Lydia said. "Where did you learn to do so many things? You paint, sew, do pottery . . ."

"I don't believe anyone should ever stop learning. There's too much great stuff to know," Trudy said.

"So you taught yourself?"

"Sometimes," Trudy said. "Or I found people who could show me. Trust me, there's a lot I'm not so good at. You don't want to hear me sing." She smiled at the seventeen-year-old.

"Do you think I could be a professional singer?"

"You, my dear, could be anything you set your sights on. You have a great voice." She bent down to tug on the hem of the dress.

"There are a ton of people with great voices."

"Sure," Trudy said. "But there are all kinds of tastes too. It isn't always about having the best possible voice. Ever hear of Neil Young or Bob Dylan?"

Lydia nodded.

"Those two guys can't carry a tune in a handbag," Trudy said, "but they've done all right for themselves."

Lydia smiled.

"Sometimes it's about persistence," Trudy said, "and finding your place."

"Have you found your place?" Lydia said. "I mean, are you happy with being an art teacher in Lake Emily?"

Trudy sat back in thought. Bert's face flickered. "Yeah, I've found my place. I love teaching and Lake Emily."

Rosemary came into the tiny room. She had a grin on her face. "Bob Dylan can't carry a tune, huh?" She raised a brow and gave Lydia a smirk. "He's a nice Minnesota boy, ya know."

"That doesn't make him a singer," Trudy said. They laughed.

"Are we done now?" Lydia asked. "I have a ton of homework."

"Go ahead," Rosemary said. Lydia slipped behind the screen and pulled off the dress and petticoats and got dressed to go. Then with a quick wave she was out the door.

"She's a good kid," Rosemary said. "Straight-A student, even with all her extra activities."

"I like her. She's talented yet humble." Trudy put away her sewing supplies, then gathered the dress onto a hanger to take it home to alter.

"I have to thank you," Rosemary said. "David

Morgan started tutoring the orchestra. He's amazing."

Trudy shrugged, feeling a glow of pride. "I knew he would be."

"He's a godsend." Rosemary touched the bun at the nape of her neck.

"Are you doing anything tonight, Rosemary?" Trudy changed topics.

"Not much really. There's the school board meeting. Maybe watch some *Jeopardy!* before that." Trudy thought of Lillian. "What did you have in mind?" Rosemary said.

"Thought I'd treat you to a malt over at the pharmacy," Trudy said.

"I haven't sat at that soda fountain since I was eighteen years old."

"It's about time, don't you think?"

The bell above the door tinkled as Trudy and Rosemary entered the aged Rexall. They picked their way through the crowded aisles to the soda fountain along the far side of the building and sat on the black vinyl stools. Foreign medicinal scents aimlessly wandered the aisles. Bob Ott came over, wiping his hands on a towel. A burgundy cardigan hung from his stooped shoulders.

"Afternoon, ladies. Janey's home sick today, so I get the honor. What would you like?"

"Chocolate malt for me," Trudy said.

Bob turned toward Rosemary. Light reflected off his bald head. "Banana split for you, Rosemary?"

"How did you know?" Rosemary asked.

"Lucky guess." He shrugged and bent his head as he began scooping ice cream. Trudy noticed the scars again inside his hairline.

"Are you coming to the school board meeting?" Rosemary asked. "They're dealing with budget cuts again."

"Sounds delightful," Trudy said. "After the last meeting how could I miss it? Actually, Bert and I have a date to attend the school board meeting—how romantic is that?"

"How long will it take to get all the costumes done?" Rosemary asked, changing subjects. Trudy saw Bob raise his eyes to watch Rosemary as she spoke.

"Oh, I don't know," Trudy said. "It depends on how much help we have and how many problems we bump into. A few weeks at least."

Bob placed the banana split in front of Rosemary, then began scooping the ice cream for Trudy's malt. "We're working on the school musical together," Trudy told the druggist.

"Is that a fact?" he said with an interested smile. He placed the stainless-steel tumbler onto the blender.

"Mr. Ott's quite a singer," Trudy informed Rosemary. "I heard him singing 'If I Were a Rich Man' from *Fiddler on the Roof* last night. He could've sold tickets."

Bob cleared his throat. "You'll have to warn me when you're eavesdropping," he said without seeming offended. "I like to know when I have an audience so I can really ham it up." He turned back to finish Trudy's malt, then handed her the tall glass along with the stainless-steel tumbler, which was still half-full.

"If you'll excuse me, ladies, I have some prescriptions to fill," he said. He disappeared to the back of the store. Trudy didn't miss his backward glance at Rosemary.

The idea that had been on simmer began to bubble again. After all, love is a many-splendored thing.

Candles flickered on the glass shelf alongside the mirrored medicine cabinet in Trudy's tiny bathroom. Their coconut scent put her in the mood to hula. She gazed at her reflection, adding a bright red lipstick to her lips and then scenting her wrists, neck, and the backs of her knees with Clinique's Happy Heart. She knew she was overdressed for a school board meeting, but she was still going to be with Bert. Their time together was precious; she wanted every minute to be memorable. She twisted the cap back on the perfume bottle.

The phone jangled, and Trudy ran to answer it.

"Hi-dee-ho," Trudy said.

"Hey." It was Bert.

"Where are you? You're supposed to be here in fifteen minutes."

"I know. I'm sorry," Bert said. Trudy's joy clicked down a notch. "I'm still in Mankato with Mom. She's got her cast off, but the doctor was running behind all day. We're heading home now." *Lillian,* Trudy sighed inwardly, then reprimanded herself for begrudging the woman a ride to the doctor's office.

"I'll save you a seat in the back."

Bert paused. "There was another reason I called."

"Oh?"

"Glen Miller, you remember the athletic director at the school? Well, he invited me last-minute to a Timberwolves game."

"Basketball? Tonight?" Since when did Bert like basketball? Was she going to end up a sports widow? She shuddered.

"With hockey season over, he thought it would be nice to take me out. Kind of a thank-you. I can't remember the last time I went to a pro game. I'll make it up to you."

"Sure," she said, even though her head was screaming, *Foul play!* "You go ahead and have some fun."

"Really?"

"Yeah, really." She bit her lip. She could've taken a role in the play, her acting was so good.

"I'll call you when I get home, okay?" Bert said.

"Sure. Call me." He hung up, and she stared at the phone. She was suddenly numb, cold. Old insecurities rose like specters from the dead. He was already making excuses to spend time away from her, and they weren't even married yet!

twenty-six

T rudy fidgeted with a sheet of paper, tearing pieces off and letting them fall to the floor. Her gaze was fixed on the front of the high school lunchroom, where the school board meeting was in full swing. Her anger grew by the moment, compounded by the event in this room and her frustration with Bert. She squeezed her eyes down to slits, determined to forget Bert's rejection and concentrate on the discussion. She glanced at Rosemary beside her. Rosemary twisted her hands into a knot. Trudy wondered which of them would lose it first.

"I'm not saying that we *want* to cut anything," Don Lind, the school board president, was saying. He was a white-haired man with perfectly straight teeth. His eyes and eyebrows were so dark they seemed unnatural. Trudy studied his body language, trying to get a read on where he leaned, but he was an enigma. "We don't have a choice—the voters of Lake Emily made our choices for us when they voted down the referendum." He glanced around the room. "We've put this off long enough. What are our options? That's what we need to know. And we need to decide rationally and dispassionately what is essential and what is not, for the sake of the children."

"Mr. Lind, I agree with you that these are hard choices." This from the heavyset woman Trudy had seen Mr. Lind talking to after the last meeting. She went on, "Surely there are other options. Can't we cut back on hours without totally cutting one program over another?"

"So the children can learn a little of everything without learning anything well? We won't pass our Iowa Basics with that tack," Mr. Lind said. He turned his attention to the room that was filled to capacity. "If parents and concerned citizens volunteer, we can fill in these gaps. Community Education offers many music and art classes."

Trudy felt her neck grow red at that comment.

"There are many volunteers who teach Junior Great Books, math . . . No one wants our children to suffer—"

"We can't force anyone to volunteer, Mr. Lind," the woman cut in. "Sending kids to additional after-school classes will only add to their stress and sched-ules. We have enough of that already with sports and other extracurricular activities. Unfortunately the children who need those opportunities the most are the ones whose parents don't give a whit about them, or they're already working too hard and can't make the time. Those children will fall through the cracks."

"We're here to discuss the Gifted and Talented pro-gram," Don Lind said, turning away from her. "That's the simplest to eliminate."

A general murmur filled the lunchroom as a woman near the back stood and raised her hand to speak. Mr. Lind called on her. Everyone shifted to see Annette Pulaski move to the microphone. She was petite with streaks of gray in her brown hair. Trudy had met her at Mae's Extension group last summer; she was the woman with nine children.

"Why should the brightest and best students be held back? Aren't they the ones who make our school dis-trict look good on the state's tests? If my son were in special ed, you'd provide for him, so why wouldn't you offer the same additional opportunities to the advanced students? Is average what this school board aims for?"

"You raise a lot of good questions," Mr. Lind said. "And in a perfect world everyone's needs would be met. Like I said, we're not here to single out one group as more or less worthy than another. These are the cold, hard facts: We have to choose, and in that choosing someone's going to be offended. Unfortunately, that's part of the job."

In the end, the Gifted and Talented program was scrapped, and talks of further cuts were tabled until the next meeting. The phone rang as Trudy walked in the door. She knew it was Bert, and she dreaded talking to him. It would only stir up the cauldron in her gut. It rang a second time. She picked it up.

"Hey," she said.

"Hey." His voice was low. She wondered if he had any clue how horrible he'd made her feel tonight. She bit her lip. "Thanks for letting me go tonight. I had a great time."

"H'm," was all Trudy could get out.

"I forgot what a good friend Glen used to be, you know? He even asked if I'd be willing to help with the football team in the fall."

"What did you tell him?" Trudy sat down at the kitchen table. She prayed Bert had said no.

"I told him I'd help as long as it fit in with the farming schedule. Harvest and all." Trudy couldn't speak. Had he even thought about the time he'd be away from her? She felt her cheeks flush.

Clearing her throat, she said, "It's late. I should head to bed."

"Okay," Bert whispered. "I love you."

"Bye." She hung up. Tears stung her eyes, and she brushed them away. Stupid coach and his interfering. She was losing Bert. She could see it already. He'd be gone to games every night this week. Then, as if that wasn't mistress enough, some cute soccer mom with a ponytail and a baseball cap would start flirting. How could she fight that? By taking him out for sushi?

She grabbed a Kleenex and wiped her face. She was being paranoid, and she knew it. She stood and paced the living room. Bert hadn't even asked about the school board meeting, though he knew her job might be on the line.

Don Lind's words echoed in her head, *These are the cold, hard facts*. She thought about Mrs. Zernickel and how that kind woman had encouraged her when she'd most needed it. What would've happened to her without Mrs. Zernickel? She pictured Jessie and the expressin of joy on her face as she painted sets. Lydia Lindstrom, the lead in the play. Chuck Wilbee—he hadn't been a football hero, but he'd found a place where he fit in, where his contributions mattered and he could feel good about himself.

The school board hadn't even talked about cuts to the athletic program. Obviously Glen Miller felt secure enough to be off gallivanting at a Timberwolves game. She paced to her studio filled with easels and canvases and paints, then back through her bedroom to her tiny kitchen. She sat at the table and gazed down the street.

A group of boys in gold-and-blue letter jackets sauntered into the movie theater across the street. Trudy watched as they joked with each other and disappeared into its lighted depths. Why couldn't every child experience the advantages those boys had? She placed her hands on the table and took a deep breath.

An idea began to form.

Peter stood outside the high school's practice-room door, watching through its tiny windows. His father's smile had returned. David sat in a folding chair beside a young teenage girl as she played the violin. Both teacher and student swayed slightly with the music. When she finished, David nodded his head. That was when Peter saw the smile. It turned the corners of David's eyes into deep creases. And that sparkle. Peter had wondered if he'd ever see that sparkle again, but there it was.

He was glad for his dad, and yet fear crept in at the corners of his mind. David caught sight of Peter in the window and waved him in.

"What are you doing here?" he asked when Peter opened the door.

"I'm sorry to interrupt," Peter said to the girl, who smiled bashfully back at him. "You forgot your wallet and checkbook. I know you'd said something about stopping at the bank."

"Oh, thank you. You didn't have to come all the way into town," David said as he took the items.

"I had to run to the Elevator anyway," Peter said.

"I'll let you get back to your lesson."

He gave a wave and withdrew from the little room. As he walked to his pickup, he knew he'd seen real joy in his father's eyes. Somehow that joy left Peter feeling hollow.

Peter gazed up into the blackness. Even as tired as he was, he couldn't sleep.

"Honey?" Mae said. She rolled over in bed and touched his chest. "You're awake. I can tell by the way you're breathing. What's wrong?"

"I'm thinking about Dad."

Mae nestled her head into the dip of Peter's shoulder. "What about him?"

"He's given his whole life to music . . ."

"And?" Mae said.

He paused, then admitted, "When I found out he had arthritis, I was kind of happy. Not glad that he was suffering, but I saw it as a chance to spend more time with him, to get my dad back. I know that was selfish—"

"You wanted to be close to your dad," Mae said.

Peter sighed and ran a finger along Mae's cheekbone. "But I wasn't thinking about what would be best for him."

"You're going to have to trust that God will work everything out for the best."

"But that doesn't exactly allow me to control the situation," Peter complained.

Mae reached over and kissed his cheek. "Sorry, honey, that's why it's called 'faith.'"

The heart monitor beeped in steady rhythm. The hospital room was quiet and dark except for a low light near Laura Morgan's bed. She lay sleeping. Her long blond hair spread across her pillow. David sat in the low brown vinyl chair beside her. He couldn't sleep, not with the end so near.

Laura and Peter had already said their farewells. David felt a sob rise up at the memory. Peter hadn't wanted to leave, but Laura had insisted that his last memory of her shouldn't be of watching her die. She'd held him for so long, weakly stroking the blond hair he'd inherited from her, comforting him even as cancer was destroying her body.

"I love you, Peter," Laura had said. "I will see you in heaven—I will." She'd gazed deep into his eyes. "Hold on to Jesus. Never forget that he loves you. That I love you."

Peter had nodded as tears rolled down his thirteen-year-old cheeks. Then he'd gone home with Grandma and Grandpa Morgan. David wiped the tears from his eyes. No father should ever have to watch such a scene, he thought. It wasn't fair—to Laura, to him, and most of all it wasn't fair to Peter.

Laura's breathing stopped for a moment, yanking David from his thoughts and into panic. He shook her. "Laura! Not yet, honey," he said. "I'm not ready yet." Her breathing resumed, and David sighed in relief. He stroked her cheek as her chest rose in rattling breaths.

A faint knock sounded on the door. David assumed it was the night nurse and said, "Come in." It was Jerry Shrupp, David's best friend since boyhood. "J. D."

"Hi," Jerry said as he came into the room. His gaze moved to Laura. "I called your ma. She said you were here alone." He laid a hand on David's shoulder.

"What am I going to do?" David said. "I still need her."

"I know," Jerry said. "She's a great lady."

"It's two in the morning, J. D. You should be home with Mary and that little one of yours."

"They understand," Jerry said. His voice broke. "You'd do the same, and you know it."

For the next three hours they stood vigil, pacing, sitting in the vinyl chairs, talking in low voices. Laura never woke. At almost five o'clock her breathing became worse. It was as if she were drowning, struggling to find air. Her small body writhed, lifting as it searched, each time finding less. David never left her side. He held her hand. The panic was returning, even in his weariness.

"David," Jerry said, "let's pray." David nodded his assent, and Jerry rested a hand on his shoulder. He began, "Dear Lord, please be here with us. We need you so badly. Laura is struggling in body, and David is struggling too. We love this lady. She's been a gift to us. Help us to let her go. Help David and Peter to go on living, knowing she's in heaven with you. Give them courage and strength. Never leave them, not even for a moment. Be their comfort, their resting place. In Jesus' name, amen."

When they lifted their heads, the panic had left David, replaced by a quiet calm. Everything was quiet. He gazed at Laura, and then he knew. She was with Jesus. He leaned over and kissed her still-warm cheek.

"I will see you again," he whispered in her ear.

twenty-seven

"M ary doesn't mind me stealing you on a Saturday morning?" David said as Jerry Shrupp scooted into the vinyl seat at the Chuckwagon. Tall windows, slanted outward at the top, gave a full view down both Main and Ferry Streets from the row of booths. The pharmacy and movie theater were quiet at this early hour. Occasionally a car meandered up Main.

"Are you kidding?" Jerry said. "She's happy to get me out of her hair. She sends her greetings, by the way."

"Hi," the teenaged waitress said. She set down two glasses of ice water and menus, swinging her thick, dark ponytail. Then, pulling pen and pad from her front apron pocket, she said, "Our special for today is ham and eggs—that comes with toast, hash browns, and coffee. All for $4.95."

David and Jerry looked at each other and nodded. David said, "Two ham and eggs it is." He handed the menus back to her.

"Great," she said and left to place the order.

"So tell me the truth, David," Jerry said as he leaned in. "Why the early retirement? You're still young. I know you too well. You loved playing with the orchestra."

"You don't waste any time getting to the point!" David laughed and held up his hands. "These," he said. "My hands aren't cooperating. I have arthritis."

"So that's it? You quit? That doesn't sound like the David Morgan I know, the David Morgan who raised a boy alone after his wife died. That guy would've fought."

"This isn't a battle I can win, J. D.," David said honestly. "When the hands go . . ." He shrugged.

"I'm sorry. So, what now?" Jerry asked.

"That's what I'm trying to figure out."

"I don't envy you," Jerry admitted. "If I had to give up farming . . ." He shook his head. "It's such a part of me. I think I'd have to find a way to at least be near it, teach FFA or be a consultant or something, maybe sell tractors. At least something so I wouldn't get depressed."

"Lucky for you that you don't have that problem," David said.

"But you do." Jerry paused and searched David's eyes. "It's me, you know . . . I know that expression on your face. It's the same look you had for months after Laura died. You know, David, you always talked about reaching for your dreams. Not sitting around waiting for things to come to you but seizing every opportunity. You showed this town that it could be done. We were so proud of you—still are."

"I'm sorry to disappoint everyone." David's shoulders sagged. He knew Jerry was right. He'd fought feelings of uselessness ever since coming home. It had only been in recent days, since he'd started tutoring, that he'd felt a flicker of hope.

"No one's disappointed in you," Jerry continued. "Don't you see? You gave us faith, hope. That's ours to keep. But you're letting yourself down, David. That kid who loved music is still in there—you can't let him wither because of one setback."

"It's a pretty major setback."

"Only if you let it be. Otherwise it's a hiccup, David. Just a hiccup."

Spring was when baby chicks arrived in their mail-order boxes. Because Mae was working all day and Peter had begun field work, Virginia volunteered to come out to the farm to get the birds set up in their home. The shallow, enclosed cardboard box filled with chirping yellow pompom balls sat on the front seat next to her as she pulled into the driveway at the Morgan homeplace. Scout barked a greeting and bounded over to the white Oldsmobile. Virginia grabbed the cheeping box and lifted her heavy frame from the car. A chickadee hopped across the gravel in front of her, then joined its sorority of friends on the sagging power line overhead.

The back screen door of the house slammed shut, and Virginia glanced up to see David putting on a spring jacket.

"What're you up to, Ma?" he said.

"Mae's chicks." She lifted the box.

Her son reached an arm around her shoulder and

kissed her temple. He nodded toward the chicks where a downy feather drifted to the ground. "Looks like spring is finally here."

"I get to show them their new home. Want to help?" They walked toward the coop. "I take it Peter's in the fields?"

"Plowing the pea fields so he'll be all set to plant," David said.

"He'll have a better harvest this year. That boy's learned a lot," Virginia said.

"It certainly is quiet around here now that he's started the field work," David said. "I have to get used to that." They stepped into the coop.

"Mae already has everything set up," Virginia said. Two heat lamps that Mae had plugged in the day before swung low over a blanket of wood shavings, creating connected pools of warm light. Two trays of feed, topped with a sprinkle of grit, were in place, as were the upturned Mason jar waterers. "You remember how to do this?"

"It's like riding a bike, right?"

Virginia opened the cheeping box. A hundred heads gazed up. She and David each picked up a chick and dipped the beaks first in the water and then the feed to show them where their grub was before setting them loose and moving on to the next. The fluff balls seemed amazed at their new freedom. They stood silent, stock-still for a few moments, and then began cheeping as they explored the perimeter of their cozy abode.

"You were saying that you're lonely now that

Peter's in the field," Virginia said, her gaze on the chick in her hand.

"I was?"

"In roundabout fashion." She gave him a sidelong glance and lifted another yellow babe from the box. "Have you come to any conclusions?"

David sat back on his haunches. "It's a hard one, Ma. Music was such a big part of who I was."

"It still is."

"That's what Jerry said. And I guess tutoring has shown me that. But it's different." He sighed and dipped a beak in the small red water trough. "I've been feeling sorry for myself, and while coming back here has been a comfort, it's also brought back memories I had put away."

"Memories have a way of surfacing whenever you're struggling with change. Trust me—I know a little about that one." The corners of her eyes crinkled in a smile, and she reached down for another chick. "But memories don't have to hurt. They can help you heal if you let them. They give you a perspective you would never have had without them."

She lifted her head toward the exposed rafters of the coop and then continued, "If I hadn't lost your dad and had memories of all that he gave to me and the knowledge of how very brief and precious this life is, I never would've reached outside myself to be a friend to Jessie and her dad." She gazed back at her son. "So as painful as losing him was, good came from it. It's what redemption is about—taking the bad and turning it into good."

"I'm not ready to give up music."

"Then don't," Virginia said. They'd finished placing the chicks under the warm lights. Virginia pulled the box away and stood to watch. "Just because there are obstacles doesn't mean you shouldn't try. I thought you were old enough to know that."

David smiled and reached over to touch her hand. "I guess I'd forgotten."

twenty-eight

The digital clock next to the bed provided the only light in the room. It was midnight two days after the board meeting. The phone jangled. Coach Miller fumbled to pick it up before it woke his wife.

"Yep," he said on the second ring. Glen's eyes were still closed.

"Coach Miller?" a scratchy male voice said on the other end. He spoke in a low voice, and Glen wondered if the caller was drunk.

"Who's this?"

Glen's wife moaned and turned over in the bed next to him. "What's going on?" she said.

"Shh, honey, go back to sleep," Glen said. "It's some crank call."

"This is no crank call. It's Arvin Tibbs down at the *Herald*." The coach shifted the phone to the other ear.

"I already get the paper. It's kind of late to be—" he began, but Arvin cut him off.

"No. This is nothing like that. We got a very interesting letter to the editor that I'm running next

Thursday. It's from that new art teacher up at the school. Thought you might like to write a rebuttal."

"Bert's girlfriend? What would she have to say about me? I've barely even spoken to her."

"It's not about you. Let me read it:"

Dear Editor,

After attending last night's school board meeting, I knew I had to write. I can't believe the people of Lake Emily want their children short-changed. I can't believe they want these kids to grow up to be bumbling idiots who can't put two sentences together, much less achieve anything of worth in their lives. Well, if choices such as were made at last night's school board meeting continue, I guarantee our problems have just begun.

Last night the Lake Emily school board decided that the Gifted and Talented program wasn't worth trying to keep. So now all of our brilliant and promising students can sit on their hands and let their brains rot from disuse. But this is supposed to be the lesser of two evils! Give me a break.

What was so important that the Gifted and Talented program was cut? Sports, in which our children are taught to give each other brain damage day in and day out, or worse, where they sit on a bench for a year and learn all about "teamwork"—which is basically learning that they're second-class citizens if they aren't blessed with excessive testosterone. I'll tell you why the school board didn't touch sports—cowardice. It doesn't matter to this school board whether the children benefit or are harmed. They are too busy hiding from unpopular decisions.

Our children's future is worth a lot more than this. How many Lake Emily students have grown up to be professional hockey stars? None ever! So why are they wasting our tax dollars, I ask you. They should spend our dollars where the children will actually learn and grow, where we are preparing young people to be productive and successful citizens.

Sincerely,

Trudy Ploog, Lake Emily art teacher

There was silence on the other end of the line. "Glen?" Arvin said after a moment.

Glen felt his blood boil. "What is her problem? As if she has a corner on helping kids, the sanctimonious . . . *city girl.*" The last words came out as a curse.

"I thought you might be interested," Arvin said, obvious glee in his tone. "I'd need the response by tomorrow if you want it to run in the same issue of the paper."

"I'll write a response, all right," Glen said. "And then I'll have a talk with this buttinsky art teacher."

The April breeze was cool, cleansing. The cemetery was quiet except for the trills of birds and the occasional car that drove by on the gravel road. David walked past aged headstones bleached white from the years. Tall conifers like oversize Popsicles bordered one side of the field. Thick elms and oaks shaded the rest.

David bent by Laura's headstone to place the peach-colored roses he'd brought.

"Hi, honey," he said quietly to the cold granite. "It's been a long time, hasn't it?" The wind kicked up, and he pulled his jacket tighter. He gazed at the tombstone: "Laura Morgan, 1950–1988, Beloved Mother, Wife, Friend." His own name was etched next to hers.

A tear slipped down his cheek, and he took a deep breath. "I figured it's about time. I wish you were here to see our Peter; he's quite a man. You'd be so proud . . . I've been struggling with some things, but I've come to a few conclusions," he said. "Even after all these years, I'm still missing you. Feeling sorry for myself. But I know now that I need to go on from here." He paused and tilted his face heavenward. "I need to start living again."

The peas were being planted, or "drilled" as Peter informed Mae. So that meant the men were the living dead for the next few weeks. Especially dairymen who had pea crops, like Peter. He was up at five to milk, eating lunch out of a paper sack in the cab of his tractor, then off to a quick supper with Mae and his dad, followed by the evening milking, and back in the fields until exhaustion ended his day. Every day, until all the acres were planted. It was the farmer's lot in life, and there were no choices, so Mae figured she had better get used to it.

The pale April sun was cool in the timid sky, but Mae sensed it would warm and become bolder as the day wore on. Today she would put in her garden. The ladies from Extension had told her if she wanted to get a good potato crop, she needed to plant on Good Friday. That gave her six days to prepare the soil and buy seed potatoes. Since the ground had been broken and worked the previous year, tilling the garden was much easier this time. Mae trudged back and forth, pushing the old Red Snapper tiller as it coughed, sputtered, and mixed the rich, dark earth. Her green muck boots reached to her knees, and oversize yellow-and-red felt chore gloves made her hands seem huge. Mae was at home in the garden, no longer a stranger to the soil but a friend. So different than the year before. So much had changed. Marriage had done that too, she supposed. She'd learned that Peter loved her and was willing to sacrifice his own wants and desires for her. She wanted to do as much for him.

What about the baby? She pushed the thought aside. She wished the thought would stop always shouldering its way to the front. Things were going so well. She didn't need to complicate life with baby notions again.

The Chuckwagon was usually the center of community gossip, but at times it positively throbbed with news, like after President Kennedy was shot or when Nixon resigned or when Martin Luther King marched on Washington. But the following Thursday the hot topic was more local—namely, Trudy Ploog.

Jim Miller poured the coffee for Vernon Elwood and Jake Jenkins.

"She has some nerve," Jake, the fire chief, was saying. "How long has she lived in Lake Emily—a couple of months?"

"I heard that Principal Rosen hired her so she would shake things up." This from a short, stocky man at the end of the counter.

"I know Rosen. He wouldn't do that," Officer Jason Jenkins, Jake's younger brother, put in.

"I'll admit it takes nerve," Vernon said. "And it takes courage, too, to stand up for what you believe."

Jim Miller snorted. "Come now, Vernon, you don't think this *city person* is right? Coming in here with her artsy-fartsy talk. Towns like Lake Emily need their sports. It brings communities together. You remember how hockey was for us—it gave us a lot. Self-confidence, a sense of belonging . . ."

"Sure, that was because you were good," his wife, Delores, said, setting a Reuben and fries on the lunch counter before the policeman. "But a town can get behind its speech and drama and debate teams as much as a football team."

"Who wants to go watch a debate?" Jim scoffed. "You can't cheer that."

"What I want to know is who this Ploog girl is?" Jason said.

"She's a sister of that Morgan girl," Vernon said. "You know, David Morgan's daughter-in-law. Mae and Virginia bought a couple of lambs from me. They seem like nice enough people."

"It was bound to happen," Jim said. "The father moved off to the city, and now we're being invaded by idiots who want to bring their liberal agenda to our town. They come because it's so simple and nice. They get their warm Andy Griffith feeling, and then they try to change everything into the very place they left." He laughed cynically. "I tell you, I've seen it before. First they get on the school board and finagle a fancy junior high, and the next thing they're putting in a Starbucks and a Wal-Mart. Before you know it, the bars outnumber the churches, and people will have to start locking their doors at night. We'll all go to hell in a handbasket."

The Clip 'n' Curl was an old storefront on Second Street. Outside, it was the same as any other brick building; inside, it was a tribute to Doris Day. Its salmon-colored walls and faded posters with hair-styles from the '60s and '70s gave the appearance that the owner—Darla Bueller—had time-travel capabilities.

Darla stood over Annette Pulaski, the mother who'd spoken up at the school-board meeting, rinsing her hair. Virginia read a copy of *Reader's Digest* with perm rollers in her hair. The pungent scent stung her eyes and nose. Ella Rosenberg, her oldest and dearest friend, was under the loud hair dryer beside her along the wall.

"Good for Trudy," Ella shouted. She lifted the plastic hood from her head and folded the *Herald*. She set it on the squat end table covered in magazines. "Have you read her letter to the editor? I can't tell you how many times I went to my sons' games only to watch them sit on the bench. The boys got so discouraged they finally quit the team. What kind of lesson is that?"

Virginia sat quietly, not wanting to join the debate.

"It's not as if the jocks get very far after graduation—the kids who achieve academically get the better jobs," Annette said as Darla helped her sit upright.

"I don't know about that. There's some truth to Coach Miller's words though," Darla said. She wrapped a towel around Annette's head. "Every winning team needs a support system. The kids on the field wouldn't be nearly as good if they hadn't had the kids on the bench to practice with. It's part of teamwork—sometimes you get the glory, sometimes you don't."

"That's wonderful if you're one of the kids who get to play," Annette said with perhaps more force behind her words than was warranted. "Do you think Bill Gates was a football hero? No, you can bet he was a benchwarmer or the nerd who didn't even make the team. Who's laughing now?"

"But is life all about how much money you make? I like what the coach had to say," Darla said. She lifted the paper and quoted, "Do art and music have a corner on building self-confidence? I'm sorry, Miss Ploog, but we hicks have been raising fine citizens for a long time. You might want to actually find out the facts before you go imposing your opinions on our community." She looked up. "He's right. The school board already cut two positions in the sports program last year before this referendum thing ever came up. She doesn't even have a clue what she's talking about."

twenty-nine

L illian dropped the paper in front of Bert as he ate his cornflakes. He closed his eyes and let the ball in the pit of his stomach roll around.

"Did you see this?" his mother said. Oh, he'd seen it all right. Glen had called him about it two days ago. Yet Trudy had said nothing. He'd waited for her to call, to at least warn him that her letter was going to run, but there was no call.

"Leave the boy alone," Willie said from his seat at the table.

"I will not," Lillian said. "She knows you've been coaching the hockey team, that you were Class C state hockey MVP. What's wrong with that girl?" She picked the paper back up. "Annette Pulaski called me from town. Everyone's upset about it. What's ridiculous is that she moves down from the city and thinks she has a right to stick her nose in our business. She's disrespectful of our community. She's obviously disrespectful of you." Her voice softened a bit. "I warned you that this marriage won't work." Bert looked through his mother. His face grew hotter with every syllable that came out of her mouth.

"Lillian," Willie said, "I said leave him alone!"

"You can't think this is a good thing." She faced her husband. "You drove to more hockey games than I did."

Bert tuned her out and left. The screen door slammed behind him. It was cloudy, moody like him. He tossed a stone across the furrowed fields as though he were skipping it on water. Wasn't Trudy's sassy truthfulness the very thing that had attracted him to her? Her spunk, her vivacious approach to life? Her joy? Why did everything have to be so complicated?

He loved Trudy. But he was no longer confident that she loved him. How could she write such a thing, knowing full well how he felt about it? He hated admitting his mother was right, and yet her words rang, echoing his thoughts of the past few weeks. He and Trudy were too different.

What would he say to Trudy? Bert had rehearsed since yesterday, and still he was blank. He gripped the steering wheel tightly, then drummed his fingers along the top. How could he make Trudy see what was happening when he wasn't even sure himself? His mother's warning ricocheted inside his thoughts, and he pushed the gas pedal.

Pulling the pickup into the diagonal parking spot alongside Ott's Pharmacy, Bert killed the engine. Trudy's yellow-and-white kitchen curtains were pulled shut. He should've called to see if she was home. He walked around to the back and climbed the stairs to her apartment, dread weighing down his every step. He lifted his green seed cap and readjusted it on his head, then knocked.

A moment later the door cracked open.

"Hey," he said.

Trudy's face broke into a smile. "Hey, yourself." She reached for his hand and pulled him into the apartment where the vacuum cleaner sat in the middle of the floor, its long cord a twisted snake that slithered into the kitchen. She had big yellow Playtex Living Gloves on her hands, and the pungent scent of lemon filled the room.

"I've been cleaning," Trudy explained. She seemed almost nervous. She quickly tied a bag of trash shut and tossed it into the kitchen. "It's been so crazy. Ever since the letter, people have been in a tizzy." She stopped. "What's wrong?" she said.

Bert took off his cap and turned it in his hands. "I think we need to talk."

Trudy's face flushed. "You're upset."

"How could you think I wouldn't be? You didn't even talk to me about the letter before it ran in the paper. Glen called—"

"Glen!" Trudy sputtered. "If it wasn't for him—"

"This isn't about Glen," Bert said. "Trudy." He stared at the stereo for a moment, then gazed at her earnestly. "We're a couple. Couples talk about things, consult each other."

"I was going to talk to you—"

"When? Everyone in town is talking—"

"What do you mean? Those narrow-minded people at the diner?"

"Those 'narrow-minded people' are my neighbors and friends. Maybe they know a little more than you give them credit for."

"Sure they do," Trudy scoffed.

He'd never seen this side of her, and he felt himself recoil. "I never knew you could be so . . . arrogant," he said. "Sports teaches a lot more than just the rules of a game. It teaches intangibles like determination, courage . . ." He stopped himself and tried to rein in his anger.

"You think my letter was about stupid hockey?" Her voice rose, and her eyes sparked.

Bert raised a hand and said calmly, "I don't want to argue, but . . . your letter has brought up a lot of issues."

"Issues? Give me a break—you can't think like those Neanderthals in the locker room. This is such a no-brainer, Bert," she went on. "I should've known you'd side with Coach Miller over me."

"I'm not choosing anyone over you."

"I suppose that's why you're going to coach football now too. Any excuse to—" Her voice broke off. "Or is this still about living with your mother?"

"No. It's about being a couple. It's about respect, compromise, talking about what's going on inside."

Trudy's eyes glistened as if she were about to cry, but the steely stare never dimmed.

"The truth is, Bert Biddle, that you don't love me, not as much as you love your precious sports. Hey, even your mother is more important than I am."

Trudy slowly withdrew the engagement ring from her finger. She touched the setting one last time, then held it out to Bert. "I knew it wouldn't last."

"Trudy—" His voice broke along with his heart. How could she do this? How could she give in so easily?

"We're too different, Bert." Her eyes shimmered, brimming with tears. "It's not going to work." She dropped the ring into his hand, then turned her back to him. He longed to take back every hurtful word, but instead he silently let himself out.

"Are you sure it's okay with you if I go to Extension?" Mae asked as she came down the stairs.

Peter was putting on his chore coat to head out to the fields for another night of planting. "Don't you want to go?"

"I know I'll be glad I went once I get there, but I'm tired, and it feels like I'm never home these days. I miss you." She put her arms around his neck and gave him a long, delicious kiss.

"Ahem." David's voice broke their embrace. "Do I need to go upstairs?" He had a big smile on his face and a lift to one eyebrow.

"Sorry about that, Dad. Mae's feeling guilty about leaving us to go to Extension."

"Ah, Extension," David said. "That brings back memories. Extension night was always our night with Dad. Mom said she needed a girls' night out."

"Those girls have grown up," Mae said.

"You go enjoy yourself—no guilt," Peter said. "I'll be out till all hours anyway."

"Okay, you've convinced me. But don't have too much fun without me."

When Trudy was depressed, she cleaned. She cleaned the bathroom, even that nasty spot behind the toilet. She vacuumed her couch and armchair; she vacuumed under her couch and armchair. She knocked down the cobwebs that had accumulated along the ceiling. She dusted the ceiling fan. She cleaned until there was nothing left to clean. Until she could no longer outrun the voices that taunted her. Voices that told her how pigheaded she was. Voices that accused her of ruining the good things in her life. Voices that told her to stop trying.

The phone rang. She didn't answer it.

What was wrong with her that she couldn't admit when she was wrong? It wasn't that she couldn't see Bert's perspective. She could. She knew she was dead wrong. And yet she was right, too: both sports and the gifted program deserved to exist. But something inside kept her from giving him that ground.

Ha! She mocked herself. *Chased away another one.*

If Bert loved her, if he really loved her, he'd be able to see past all this, wouldn't he?

She plopped down at the kitchen table and gazed out at the streets below. Lake Emily had gone to bed; even the movie house across the street was darkened. Tears poured down her face, and she breathed big hiccuping gulps that she couldn't control. She loved Bert, loved him more than she'd loved anyone in her life. Now who was the idiot?

She ran a finger along the rim of her cup and hugged the chenille robe around herself. She missed him already. Did he miss her too? Probably not. She went into the bedroom and gazed defiantly at the box of letters from her dad. "They're all like you, I guess," she spoke to her father. "Take off when the going gets rough."

She meandered to the tiny bathroom off the living room. She'd painted the walls an aqua blue and added a coral reef along the wall opposite the toilet. A moray eel poked its head out from behind the hamper. Starfish and angelfish swam here and there in a profusion of color. The mirrored medicine cabinet revealed that her hair was an untamed bush, and dark circles lined her eyes.

"Trudes," she said to herself, "you've screwed it up again." She sighed and sat on the wicker stool next to the hamper, her head resting on a barracuda.

"Why do I keep wrecking things, God? Me and my big mouth." She stared up at the ceiling. "I want to make things better, but they keep getting worse. I feel so alone." She scrubbed her face with one hand and then got up to splash cold water on her cheeks.

"Come on, Trudy," she told herself. "Feeling sorry for yourself won't get you anywhere. You're going to have to do it better. Get it right."

Finally at 11:45 she crawled into bed, hoping that sleep would be better than reality.

On the drive to Minnie Wilkes's house for Extension, Mae thought about Trudy. She'd overheard talk at work about the letter to the editor, and the comments were not kind. She had tried to call Trudy, but Trudy wasn't answering her phone. Mae wondered if something was wrong, then decided she was jumping to conclusions. Trudy was probably out on a date with

Bert or doing some work on the play. If something was truly wrong, Trudy would call.

Mae pulled into the long gravel drive. The cool night air stirred with a soft breeze. Blackbirds called noisily from the windbreak. A horse whinnied at her from the pasture and trotted to the tall white fence beside the drive.

She saw a circle of faces through the house's back-door window and realized that the meeting was about to begin. Minnie Wilkes, a short, round-cheeked woman, came to greet her.

"Mae, I'm so glad you could make it," she said. She smiled with her eyes and patted Mae's hand. Minnie led the way into the living room, where a chorus of hellos greeted her. Mae sat next to Virginia, who leaned to kiss her cheek. Lillian Biddle was on Mae's other side.

"Good evening, Lillian," Mae said.

"Hello." It was curt and welcomed no further conversation. That wasn't particularly unusual for Lillian, yet Mae sensed that something lurked beneath it. She turned to talk to her, but the meeting was called to order, so Mae decided it could wait.

The lesson for the evening was "Investing for Retirement." They talked about 401(k)s and 403(b)s and Roth IRAs and CDs until everyone was totally confused.

"Isn't it kind of late in life for this lesson?" Minnie joked. "Except for you, Mae, you're still young enough to earn some compound interest."

"It's a good thing we don't have any money to

invest, or I'd really be in trouble," Mae said. Everyone chuckled.

"You ask me, people today think they need a lot more *stuff* than they did in our day," Irene Jenkins, the fire chief's mother, said. "In the '50s the wife could stay home because we didn't try to afford two cars and a three-thousand-square-foot house. Children shared bedrooms, and parents didn't feel guilty about it."

"You've got that right," Ella Rosenberg said. "My grandkids have so much stuff already that I hate to spend another penny on them. Isn't that sad to say? They don't appreciate it anyway."

"Kids today aren't any better off if you ask me," Irene said. She leaned forward, blue eyes snapping. "They sit in front of the TV or some video game all day. They have no idea how to use their imaginations—they're getting fat and dull."

"Speaking of what's good for children, Trudy raised quite a stir in town," Annette Pulaski said. Her gaze was on Mae. "Everyone was talking about her letter to the editor." Mae shifted in her seat, then glanced at Lillian, who crossed her arms over her chest. "I say," Annette went on, "good for Trudy. The school board needs to decide what's good for all the children, not just the ones the state pressures them to take good care of. My three youngest were all in the Gifted and Talented program—I don't know what I'm going to do now."

Every head turned to Mae for her two cents on the issue. She lifted both hands and said as if fending off paparazzi, "I haven't read it yet!"

Minnie said, "If you don't mind my breaking up this press conference—snacks are ready. We have our priorities." She motioned toward the table. Everyone moved to the dining room, which was set for royalty—crystal goblets, china, real silver.

"Minnie, you've outdone yourself," Mae said. "Live it up, everyone, because when Extension's at my house, it'll be Chinette and Styrofoam."

"I don't get to use the good china as often as I like; Extension is a nice excuse," Minnie said. She set a dish of mints on the white linen.

Mae took a seat next to Virginia as the rest of the women settled. Everyone was still talking in little clusters in a comfortable hum. By the time Lillian got to the table only one chair remained, on the other side of Mae. She squeezed past the other chairs and into the vacant spot. Cheesecake, nuts, and mints began their appointed rounds.

"How are you today, Lillian?" Mae said.

"I suppose you heard," Lillian said in a quiet voice to Mae as she put the cloth napkin in her lap.

"Heard what?" Mae said, curiously.

"That Bert and Trudy broke up."

Lillian continued speaking, but whatever she said was lost on Mae. So that was why Trudy wasn't answering her phone.

She'd gone into hiding.

It was midnight by the time Mae managed to extricate herself from the gathering, call Peter to let him know that she was going over to Trudy's, and drive to town. She saw the kitchen light on in the apartment, so she figured Trudy was still up. She pounded on the door, banging long and loud.

Finally the door opened. "Oh, it's you," a weary Trudy said.

"Why didn't you call me?" Mae said. She wrapped her arms around her sister and pulled her to the couch. Trudy began sobbing.

"You didn't answer your phone," Mae said. "Then I find out from Lillian, of all people, that you and Bert broke up? Did you?"

Trudy nodded mutely. She choked on another sob and said, "He said I didn't respect him or compromise. What is that supposed to mean? He was upset about the letter. I'm sure the thing about living on the farm didn't help any. Why do I keep doing this?" She swiped at her tears. "I should've known this was coming. The way he acted when I said I didn't want to live with Lillian . . . She never liked me. Oh, Mae!" She cried on her sister's shoulder until her sobs became silent gasps. "What am I supposed to do now?"

"Oh, honey." Mae patted her hand. "Let me go put on a pot of hot chocolate. That'll cheer you up. We can talk." She got up to go to the kitchen.

"You know what's really sad?" Trudy raised her voice so Mae could hear her in the next room as she filled the teakettle with water. "I quit my job in St. Paul and moved ninety miles for him, and now I don't even have him! I can't wait to hear Mom's 'I told you so.'"

"I thought you moved here because of me," Mae said as she came back into the living room and sat on the couch beside her. "Besides, I know you. You never stay down for long."

"Do you know any other bachelors? And not Fred!" Trudy smiled despite herself.

"That's my girl."

Trudy's face darkened again, and she gazed dolefully at Mae. "But I love Bert. I have loused up so many things. No one in this town is even talking to me. I stopped answering the phone because I got some not-too-nice calls. Maybe I should move back to St. Paul." She pulled her chenille robe tight and tucked her feet under herself.

"The ladies at Extension were pretty supportive of your letter."

"Really?"

Mae nodded. "This will pass, Trudy. Everything does."

"You're just saying that."

"Maybe. I'm sure you'll be eighty and still crying about some letter to the editor."

Trudy wiped her cheeks with a Kleenex. "I'm glad you came." She ran her hands through her long hair and absently began twisting it. "You should have seen him, Mae. He was so angry. You know Bert—it takes a lot to make him mad. I pushed him too far this time." The tears were regrouping for another assault. "Stupid tears." She dabbed them with her tissue. "I don't know how to keep a man. I'm going to miss him, you know? I really thought he was the one."

"Give it some time. Maybe he is the one." She lifted Trudy's chin with her index finger. "You'll find the right guy, I promise you."

"Don't make promises you can't keep."

GLEN MILLER

"Spell the word 'hinterland,'" said Mr. Lewis, the bent gray-haired judge, into the microphone. The high school auditorium hushed as Glen Miller waited for the word to come to him. He couldn't believe he'd made it all the way from Lake Emily to the state spelling bee championship in St. Paul, much less emerged as one of the final two contestants.

"Hinterland," Glen repeated. His heart flopped in his chest like a landed fish. "H-I-N-T-E-R-L-A-N-D. Hinterland."

"That is correct," Mr. Lewis said with a grin for Glen. Thunderous applause filled the room, and Glen sighed in relief.

Maria Cummings, the other final sixth grader, leaned toward her microphone in anticipation. She was from Marshall, Minnesota, and she wore thick horn-rimmed glasses on her oily face. Glen saw her bite her lower lip as Mr. Lewis peered down at his paper.

"Capillarity," Mr. Lewis said.

Maria took a deep breath. "May I have a definition please?"

"Capillarity," he said. "The elevation or depression of part of a liquid surface coming in contact with a solid."

"Capillarity," Maria repeated. She lifted her face as if she could read the letters on the ceiling and began, "C-A-P-P-I-L-A-R-I-T-Y. Capillarity."

Mr. Lewis stared down at the page. "I'm sorry. That isn't correct," he said. Maria's face fell. The audience gave a sympathetic groan.

Glen's hands grew sweaty. He looked over at his dad in the crowd and got a grin and a thumbs-up. He felt bolstered and leaned forward to wait for his turn.

"Okay, it's your word, Mr. Miller. Capillarity," Mr. Lewis repeated.

Glen didn't think he'd ever heard the word before. He waited for the word to form in his mind, then he began slowly, "Capillarity. C-A-P . . ." He paused, wondering if there were two ps or two ls. Finally he went on. "I-L-L-A-R-I-T-Y. Capillarity."

Mr. Lewis turned his gaze to the audience. Glen crossed his fingers. "That is correct."

Glen breathed in relief. Just one more word.

Mr. Lewis gazed down at the card in his hand, then winked at Glen. "Ready?" he said.

Glen nodded.

"Leucine," Mr. Lewis said.

"Leucine," Glen repeated, trying to visualize the word. "L-E-U"—he paused and took a breath—"C-I-N-E. Leucine."

"Glen Miller, you are the new state champion!" Mr. Lewis beamed.

Glen couldn't believe it. His mouth dropped open. He couldn't speak. Surging to their feet, the audience erupted in cheers. Glen searched for his dad's face *again, but with all the bedlam he couldn't find him. Mr. Lewis came over, followed by a number of other adults Glen had never seen before. Mr. Lewis patted Glen on the shoulder. "Congratulations, young man. That was a fine exhibition!" His teacher, Miss Splitchucker, was there too, all smiles and congratulations.*

Then he saw Dad at the front of the crowd. "I won," Glen said.

"I couldn't be prouder, Son. Couldn't be prouder."

thirty

Trudy pulled her Pacer into the school parking lot and killed the engine. She glanced at her reflection in the rearview mirror. Dark bags underscored red-rimmed eyes, and somehow Bozo the Clown had slipped his wig onto her head. Trudy patted it down, but it popped right back up.

"Fine!" she muttered and decided to call the salon for a trim after school. She dug in her huge camel-colored purse, retrieved her sunglasses, and set them on her nose. If she couldn't do anything about her hair, at least she could camouflage her raccoon look.

She entered the dark hallway of the high school, pausing to let her eyes adjust. She realized suddenly that someone was standing directly in front of her, blocking her way. He was a big man, his arms as thick as tree branches planted on his hips. "Excuse me," Trudy said, but the man stayed put.

"I don't know what I've done to offend you," he

said, nostrils flaring. "But I do *not* give teenagers 'brain damage.'"

Trudy grimaced.

"Do you know how many upset parents have called me to pull their kids off the team since your letter? It's hard enough getting support for the sports programs without you sticking your uppity nose into it."

Trudy's face flamed. She clenched her fingers around her purse. "I didn't intend—"

"What? To make me look like an idiot? I've lived in Lake Emily all my life. What makes you think you can come to town and know anything about what our school needs?" He leaned closer, and Trudy took a step back. "You'd better learn that you are not the only teacher here who cares about our kids. Stunts like this divide communities rather than bring them together. You don't belong here if you can't be part of the team."

Then he turned and stalked away.

Trudy blew a pent-up breath, causing her long bangs to float upward. "Good morning to you, too," she said as he disappeared into the gymnasium. She wondered how many more people would confirm her failings by day's end.

"Let's start from the top." Rosemary stood before the stage to begin the after-school rehearsal. Trudy slipped into the back of the auditorium. No one seemed to notice. She took a seat on the aisle and slid the shoes off her aching feet. She had spent the day briskly moving throughout the high school, doing her best to avoid the stares that followed her everywhere.

Trudy was safe here, safe among the students and staff who agreed with her, who had felt the sting of not being in football or hockey or cheerleading—second-class citizens.

"Ken, you need to sing out, 'There's a bright, golden haze on the meadow,'" Rosemary sang the line for him in a warm alto. *With a voice like that,* Trudy thought, *Rosemary should be doing Broadway—or, better yet, duets with Bob Ott.*

Had the two ever noticed each other romantically? Rosemary didn't exactly have a come-hither way about her, with those dowdy clothes and that knot that looked like a musty hamburger bun on the back of her head.

"And be robust," Rosemary was saying to Ken. "We want everyone in the audience to hear you. This is their first impression of the performance, so make it a good one." *A good impression* . . . Trudy mused.

Ken disappeared backstage, and the pianist began the introduction. The girl who played Aunt Eller sat behind a wooden butter churn and gazed at the empty audience while Ken sang from offstage. A smile of pride tingled Trudy's lips.

Practice moved swiftly, and as Rosemary was dismissing the kids, she spotted Trudy. She walked up the aisle toward her. "I didn't see you there."

"I was enjoying the show."

"They're doing a great job, aren't they?" Rosemary turned back toward the stage.

"We're almost done with props and the set," Trudy

said. "So I'm focusing on costumes now." She glanced down at her watch. "Oops! I lost track of time. I've gotta go. Want to tag along to my hair appointment? We could talk some more, and I could really use the company."

Darla Bueller, a fifty-something woman with deep auburn hair and plucked eyebrows redrawn with a pencil, was the proprietor of the Lake Emily Clip 'n' Curl. She reminded Trudy of a Claymation figure out of an old Rankin-Bass movie. Several women sat patiently under hair dryers, magazines in hand; others chatted amiably and waited for the perm solution to set. Its industrial reek filled the air.

"Hello, Rosemary," Darla said. Her eyes moved to Trudy. "Are you Trudy?"

"Yes." Trudy held out her hand. "Trudy Ploog, your five o'clock," she said.

"Where else have I heard that name?" Darla said.

"Don't ask!" Trudy said with a smile toward Rosemary. "You can't believe everything you read."

Darla seemed confused by the comment, then her face brightened. "Oh . . . the paper. My, but you did cause quite a stir."

Trudy wondered if it was wise to trust this woman to cut her hair. Darla led her to the nearest chair, where she placed a large plastic cape around her neck.

"This is a hopping place," Trudy said, trying to change the subject. "Do you get your hair done here, Rosemary?"

Rosemary touched the bun on the back of her head.

"It's been a while since I've had my hair cut."

"You ever think about getting it trimmed and styled?" Trudy said. "I bet you'd look great in a sportier cut."

Rosemary gazed at her own reflection in the mirror. "I wore my hair in a pageboy cut when I was a young girl."

"I bet you were adorable!" Trudy said.

Rosemary blushed and waved a hand. "I'm a little too old for that."

"No way!" Trudy said.

Darla examined Rosemary like an artist scrutinizing her own painting, evaluating where the next brush stroke should go. "I don't know. A lot of older women have short hair. It's easy to care for."

Rosemary touched the side of her head. Trudy raised an encouraging eyebrow, and Rosemary broke into a smile. "Do you have an opening, before I change my mind?" Rosemary asked Darla.

"I think we can squeeze you in."

April, a short, young beautician with long blond hair in braided pigtails, beckoned Rosemary to a chair. She turned her toward the mirror and released her long locks from their bobby pins. Dull gray hair spilled in cascades over her shoulders.

"So, what will it be?" April said, fingering Rosemary's hair.

Rosemary gazed at Trudy. "Why don't we live dangerously?" she said. "Make it something fun, and get rid of the gray. I'm tired of looking like a schoolmarm."

"Me too," Trudy said.

Rosemary seemed twenty years younger in her sharp pageboy. April had managed to revive her original auburn tones, and the difference was striking.

"What do you think?" Trudy asked. Rosemary couldn't stop staring at herself in the mirror.

"Why didn't I do this a long time ago?" She glanced up at April. "You're a miracle worker!"

April pulled the cape off Rosemary. "You're going to knock 'em dead, honey."

Trudy, too, looked like a new woman—Sandy Duncan's Peter Pan. She'd never had her hair so short in her life; none of it was more than two inches long. She touched it again behind her ears. At least she wouldn't have to worry about brushing for a while.

The two of them paid, then headed out to Main Street, pausing to gaze in storefronts. Rosemary laughed, "Maybe I should get a new outfit to go with the new Rosemary."

"You look great," Trudy said.

"I feel young again. I love it. How about you?"

Trudy stared at her own reflection in the glass. "It's going to take some getting used to. My neck feels cold."

"I think you look darling," Rosemary said. "It's . . . sassy."

"Okay, that's not a good thing! I've gotten into enough trouble being sassy already." They walked another block, past Lion's Park.

"I heard you and Bert broke off your engagement."

"That news didn't take long," Trudy said, but the words stung.

The lake shimmered in neon blue as the indigo sky dipped its toes in the water. They sat on one of the wooden benches to enjoy the day's finale. "Why didn't you ever marry?" Trudy asked.

"I had my opportunities," Rosemary said. "I was engaged twice."

"And?"

"It never worked out. Seems we'd eventually stumble across some difference that we couldn't get past, and that was the end. I was stubborn and idealistic." She lifted her face to the view. Beams of sunlight shot through Swiss-cheese clouds. A gaggle of Canada geese landed on the far side of the lake. "I'm still stubborn." Rosemary laughed humorlessly. "So living alone is my cross to bear."

Bert's words echoed in Trudy's mind, and her heart spoke to her. *You are stubborn too—and idealistic.* "Do you have any regrets?" she asked.

Rosemary stared at her seriously before admitting, "I keep myself busy so I don't have time to think. But, yes, I have my regrets. That doesn't mean I can change anything. Sometimes you have to live with your mistakes."

"You're going to get yourself in trouble, playing with people's emotions like that," Mae warned as she folded and sorted. She had dropped by after work and found Trudy buried in costumes—piles of skirts, camisoles, blouses, jeans, flannel shirts, and bandannas.

283

"Rosemary and Bob Ott have a lot in common. I think they could make a go of it," Trudy insisted.

"You've got enough on your mind without playing yenta."

"If you'd heard how sad Rosemary was talking about her regrets, you'd know that I'm right."

Mae locked eyes with Trudy in an expression that always meant *Time to come clean. I'm not buying what you're selling.*

"Really," Trudy pressed on, "you should've seen the way Bob looked at Rosemary when we went for malts. He likes her. I'm just priming the pump. I'll leave it to them to take it to the next level."

"As long as no one gets hurt," Mae said. "Trudy, you always think you know what's best for other people. Don't you remember setting me up with Scott Biffwanger? He thought belching was the path to a girl's heart." Mae lined up the seams on the jeans to create a perfect crease down the front before folding them.

"You don't need to be so particular." She pointed to Mae's folding job, then continued. "So I made a few bad assumptions. I have a feeling about this one." She pulled a blouse from the heap and inspected it for mending.

"I know about those 'feelings' you get. You need to stop trusting them. Look at what your feelings did to your hair."

"Hey! That's mean!" She touched the back of her head.

"I know why you're doing this," Mae said quietly.

"Oh, you do, do you? And why is that?" She crossed her arms to wait for this brilliant insight.

"Because you're frustrated you can't make things work with Bert," Mae said. "You figure that if you can get these two together, then you weren't wrong to break up with Bert, because, after all, you are a good judge of character, and Bert comes up short in that department."

"That's ridiculous."

"Is it?" Mae's eyes searched Trudy's.

"Oh, leave me alone. I hate it when you do that sanctimonious mom thing."

"Tell me. What have you eaten today?" Mae said. Trudy tilted her head and raised an eyebrow. "I know you," Mae insisted. "When you're depressed, you eat junk food." She walked over to Trudy's trash. "Aha!" She pulled out an empty ice cream carton and bags of Fritos and Funyuns.

"That proves nothing," Trudy said.

"Tell me I'm wrong!"

"Don't be the big sister. It doesn't become you."

"Trudy, I care about you."

Trudy gave Mae a half smile. "I'm okay. Really."

It was near noon when Peter saw dust approaching on the road. He'd been in the fields since eight that morning. He flicked off the radio in the enclosed cab of the tractor. His stomach rumbled in hunger. The unappealing brown-bag lunch he'd brought along mocked him. What he wouldn't give for one of Mae's tuna melts.

The pickup drew closer, and Peter realized it was his.

He climbed to the ground as his dad turned onto the field approach and killed the engine. "What's up, Dad?" Peter said as David climbed out.

David lifted a small cooler and said, "Thought my son could use a break and some good food."

"You're reading my mind!" He leaned against the green-and-yellow tractor and watched his father withdraw a covered casserole of taco hotdish and a small thermos of coffee and place them on the tailgate of the truck. Then he reached into the cooler for a large Ziploc bag of mixed lettuce, onions, tomatoes, and olives. He sprinkled that on top of the ground beef, kidney beans, and corn-chip base.

"The king of hotdish," Peter said. "I'd forgotten about this one."

David filled two plates with food, and they leaned back to eat. The April air was warm and smelled of turned earth and rain-heavy clouds. Skeletons of corn had been plowed under so that black furrows had replaced the stubbled rows.

"Almost done with soybeans?" David asked.

"Pretty soon," Peter said. His belly warmed at the comfort food. "It's nice not to be behind everyone else like last year."

David nodded. His gaze was trained on the shimmer of the lake in the distance. "Peter," he said. "I've got something to tell you." Peter set his fork down. "You know this hasn't been an easy time for me. You and Mae have been so great." He paused. "Well, I've been thinking and talking to Mom and J. D."

Somehow Peter knew what was coming, not the specifics, but he knew the gist. He waited for the words to come from his father's lips. "I'm not ready to give music up. It's too much a part of who I am."

"I know."

He placed a hand on Peter's. "You got your hopes up that I'd be around, help with the farming, and I really wanted to."

Peter shook his head. "Dad, you've been miserable. As much as I want you with me, I don't want you to be unhappy."

David wiped his hands on his jeans and sighed. "Thank you for that. It makes my news easier."

"News?"

"I've accepted a job in Arizona, a conductorship with the Phoenix Symphony."

"Oh." Peter felt his heart sink. "Arizona?"

"I know it's far away, and I hate to leave my new students in the lurch, but I've lined up some tutors from Gustavus."

Peter saw the hopeful expression on his dad's face, yet he couldn't find any joy in the news. "When do you leave?"

"Next week."

thirty-one

T he debate over the school board's decision hit a nerve. The next week Arvin Tibbs ran even more letters regarding the issue. Some supported Trudy's stance, and others got downright nasty.

One read:

If Miss Ploog thinks she could do a better job, perhaps she should run for school board. Then she'd discover that there aren't just a few highbrow art lovers to accommodate, but a whole town of us "Neanderthals" who think there's nothing wrong with a good game of football. Miss Ploog needs to get out in the real world and stop imposing her ignorant opinions on the rest of us.

Seeing her name in print was too much for Bert. He put the paper down on the kitchen counter, then thought better of it and shoved it in the trash.

"Hey! I haven't read that yet," his mother complained. Bert grunted and reached for his truck keys that hung on a hook over the sink.

"I'm going out," Bert said.

"We got another postcard from Fred," Lillian said, holding it up.

"Great, more bad news." Bert slipped his chore coat on.

"Says he's dating Minnie Mouse," Lillian said.

Willie chuckled, coming in from the living room.

"How's Mickey feel about that?"

"Bert, what's wrong?" Lillian said.

He couldn't talk about it to anyone, least of all her. He let the screen door slam behind him, climbed into his pickup, and headed for town. Nothing had been right since Trudy had given back his ring. He'd tried to immerse himself in his work or playing his banjo, but nothing helped. She was still gone.

Fields in contrasting shades of newborn green and textured brown, like a checkerboard, whipped past the open window of the truck. The May air was warm and perfect. Farmstead lilacs bloomed. Their sweet scent rose on the wind. A tear wandered down his cheek. He didn't wipe it away. After everything, he still loved Trudy. He always would.

Mae and Peter lay in bed. Headlights from a passing car cast their silent movie across the bedroom walls. His dad was gone. They'd put him on an airplane to Arizona that afternoon. In his heart Peter knew that his hopes to farm with his father had never really had a chance. He felt angry, hurt, gypped of his father's presence one more time. His childhood pain resurfaced, but he knew this was right for his dad, regardless of how he felt. His dad was happy again.

"You awake?" Peter asked Mae. Her back was to him.

"Uh-huh," she answered, rolling toward him.

"I miss Dad."

"I know you do."

"Do you want another baby?"

He felt her body stiffen. "Why?"

"I don't know," he said. "I want more family around."

"Your grandma's here."

"I know. But I'd like the Waltons' whole big clan thing so we'd never run out of family around us."

"You're missing your dad."

"Yes, but I still mean it. I want kids, and . . . we need to talk about this. It's time to stop avoiding the question."

Mae sighed. "I'm not avoiding anything."

"We haven't exactly talked about when we want to start a family either."

"I haven't been working very long at my job," Mae said.

"We can't let a job dictate when to start a family. Besides, you told me this job was temporary. Now that Dad's gone, I'll really need your help."

"Do you want me to quit?"

He knew the answer she wanted to hear. She wasn't ready to try again. Finally he relented. "It's your decision. I don't want to push you. You know that, right?" When Mae didn't answer, he said, "It's okay to wait. We can talk about this some other time."

Trudy's kitchen table was set for two. A white votive candle in a crystal holder illuminated the lace cloth and white Ironstone plates in flickering amber. The garlicky smell of lasagna filled the apartment. Through the gingham curtains overlooking the sidewalk, she saw Rosemary parking her car, then walking around the corner of the building. Trudy met her at the back door.

Bob Ott was singing from the adjoining office, "Some enchanted evening, you will see a stranger . . ." Trudy smiled to herself. Rosemary appeared at the bottom step. Her new hair was darling. She wore a smart navy suit.

"Hi, Rosemary," Trudy called downstairs to her. "Come on up."

Rosemary waved and started up. "Who's singing? Rossano Brazzi?"

Trudy tilted her head toward the door. "He has quite a voice, doesn't he? That's Bob Ott."

Rosemary pursed her lips. "Not bad," she said. "I'll have to keep him in mind next time the community playhouse puts on *South Pacific*." Trudy led the way into her apartment.

"What smells so good?" Rosemary said.

"I made lasagna."

"Ooh, this is quaint." Rosemary motioned to the tiny but chic living room.

"Mr. Ott said I could decorate however I liked. He's a really great landlord."

"So. Where are the costumes?" Rosemary said. Trudy had sewn two dresses for Lydia Lindstrom as Laurey and one for Maggie Rinehart, the girl who played Ado Annie. "You know, you didn't have to go to so much trouble," Rosemary said. "I'm sure we could've made do from the prop room."

"I know," Trudy said. "But I wanted to do it. Besides, I suddenly have a lot of spare time on my hands." Trudy retrieved the pile of costumes—full skirts and petticoats. "I think you're going to love this one. I found this pretty pink broadcloth at Ben Franklin's in Le Center." She laid the frilled dress next to Rosemary on the couch.

A knock sounded at the door. When Trudy opened it, Bob Ott stood there with a small toolbox in hand. "Oh, good, you're home." When he saw Rosemary, he said, "I can come back later."

"Don't be silly," Trudy said as she pulled him into the living room. Rosemary was still preoccupied with the dresses. Trudy answered his puzzled look. "You know Rosemary, the music teacher from the high school."

The bald gentleman smiled broadly and dipped his head as he greeted her. "Rosemary." Then he turned to Trudy. "You said something about a leaky faucet?"

"Oh yes," Trudy said. He followed her to the galley kitchen.

"Smells heavenly," he said.

"We're having lasagna," she said. "Would you care to join us?" She glanced at Rosemary, seeking her permission. Rosemary nodded, albeit reluctantly. Trudy said, "I can add one more setting."

"That sounds nice," Bob said.

Then the phone rang. Trudy picked up the receiver. "I'm calling at 6:35 like you said." It was Mae. "What's this all about anyway?"

"Really?" Trudy said, alarm in her tone. "Are you okay?"

"Of course I'm fine. What's going on?"

"I'll be right there," Trudy said.

"Huh?" Trudy heard Mae say before she hung up.

"That was my sister, Mae," Trudy explained to Rosemary and Bob. "I am so sorry, but I need to head out to the farm." She grabbed potholders from a drawer and handed them to Bob. "I'm so sorry," Trudy said again. "You two will have to go ahead without me. I'll be back as soon as I can. I'd hate for this to go to waste." She picked up her purse and keys from the counter.

"But—," Rosemary faltered.

"I'm really sorry," Trudy said. She slipped her coat on and left Rosemary and Bob Ott to themselves.

thirty-two

The halls of Lake Emily High School were a combustion engine of activity. As students hustled from one class to the next, voices and laughter punctuated the air.

"Hey, Miss Ploog," Chuck Wilbee said as he rushed past. His "hey" reminded her of Bert, and she caught her breath. She'd seen Bert's pickup parked at the Chuckwagon yesterday when she'd left Bob and Rosemary. She'd almost given in to an inner urging and gone to find him. Instead she'd gone to the farm and sat with Jessie and her lambs. At least it had taken her mind off him.

Rosemary came down the hall. Trudy asked, "I'm so sorry about last night. How did it go?"

"What exactly happened? You never even called."

Rosemary's stare was penetrating.

"Uh-oh. Am I in the doghouse?"

"I am fifty-four years old." Rosemary's lips were a thin line, and her gaze was unyielding. "I have long since given up silly schoolgirl notions of finding Mr. Right."

"I thought since the two of you have so much in common—"

"We're grownups, Trudy. Thankfully Bob was very gracious, but I've never been more embarrassed in my life."

"I'm sorry," Trudy squeaked. "I guess I wasn't thinking."

"No, you weren't." Rosemary turned and walked back in the direction she'd come from. Trudy felt her eyes sting. She swallowed hard to hold the tears back. What a disaster. Everything was a disaster.

As she entered the school office, she recognized the back of Coach Miller at the counter.

"This is great," he said, his voice oozing sarcasm. "Another student dropped off the track team. That's three since that ridiculous—"

Margaret, the school secretary, cleared her throat and pointed with her gaze to Trudy in back of him.

"Oh, it's you," he said. "Miss Merry Sunshine."

"I'm rubber, you're glue," Trudy said, trying to lighten the mood.

"That's mature," he said. He leaned toward her, his voice low. "If I were you—which I'm glad I'm not— I'd keep my big mouth shut."

For some reason that ended Trudy's argument. How

many times had she heard those words? *You and your big mouth.* Her ears burned. She wanted to kick the man in the shins.

Instead she spoke to the secretary. "I'm heading to the elementary school to do some grading." Then she gave Glen Miller the evil eye and marched, back erect, out to the parking lot.

As if the big brute could intimidate her. Of all the nerve! She was about to climb into her Pacer when she noticed the shiny new black Ford pickup parked beside her. It sported a Minnesota Wild sticker in its back window. She'd seen Coach Miller driving that very vehicle the night before. Trudy peered around cautiously. No one was in sight. She leaned near the vehicle and slipped a fingernail beneath the sticker. It came off in one tug. Then she bent down and twisted the tiny black cap off the valve stem of the rear tire. She reached in her purse for a pen and depressed the valve. The hissing of air seemed loud as the tire slowly deflated.

"Um, Miss," a male voice said from the rear of the truck. The sun behind him cast his face in shadow, but there was no mistaking the outline of the police uniform, the shiny badge, the gun in its holster. Trudy's heart rocketed into her throat. "What do you think you're doing?" the police officer said. "That's Coach Miller's truck."

Trudy quickly stood up and put the tire cap and pen behind her back. "I was . . . um . . ." For once words failed her. She looked him in the eyes. "I'm in big trouble, aren't I?"

The officer nodded and held out his hand. Trudy deposited the tools of her crime in his hands and then held out her hands to be cuffed.

"I don't think we need to do that." The officer smiled; he looked to be in his early twenties. "Unless you plan on escaping." He raised an eyebrow.

"Could you give me a warning?" she said hopefully. She read his nametag. "I'm really sorry, Officer Jenkins. I'd give a nice big donation at the policemen's dance."

"No can do," the kiddy cop said. "Vandalism is a crime, and trying to bribe an officer—"

"I wasn't bribing anyone!" Trudy protested.

He raised a hand, which silenced her. Trudy felt hot tears threatening again.

"Please come with me." He led the way to the squad car and opened the back door. "I'll give the chief a call, see how he wants to handle this. I'd rather not cause a scene here at the school."

"How did you know whose car—" she asked from the backseat.

"Everyone knows the coach's truck."

Receiver at her ear, Trudy stared at the black pay phone in the foyer of the police station. It rang twice before Mae picked up. "Le Sueur County Courthouse. How may I help you?"

"Hey, Maeflower," Trudy said, forcing cheerfulness into her tone.

"Trudy, what's up?"

"I was wondering if you could do me a favor."

"Sure."

Trudy wrapped the black cord around her fingers. "Okay. Well, I'm in jail, and I need you to come get me. Do *not* tell Mom about this."

"You're *where?*" Trudy wondered if the police officer could hear Mae's shrill voice across the room. His head was bent over his desk, so if he could, he at least wasn't letting on.

"I was kind of . . . letting the air out of the coach's tires," Trudy said.

"Oh, Trudy!" Mae scolded. "How old are you?"

"Please don't yell at me. Are you going to come or not?"

"Yeah, I'll be there." Both sisters hung up.

Trudy turned to the officer. "For the record, I did not realize letting air out of tires was a crime. I was—"

"Tell it to the coach," the kiddy cop said, but he smiled at her.

"Is there any way we can keep this out of the paper? I've kind of had a lot of bad publicity lately, and if I can avoid it . . ."

The officer began laughing. "You should've thought of that before," he said.

Trudy put her face in her hands, and the tears came full force. "That's the problem," she squeaked. "I wasn't thinking."

This was the last straw. She'd put her job at risk, alienated Bert, embarrassed the Morgans, and divided a community. Tears grew from silent, polite Minnesota hiccups to loud gulping New York sobs.

"Now don't go and do that," the police officer said.

He brought her a box of Kleenex.

"I'm sorry," Trudy said as she pulled three tissues from the container. "But everything has gone wrong lately, and this is . . . perfect. The whole town is against me, and I have no one to blame but myself!" The sobbing took a higher pitch, and the officer reached out to awkwardly pat her shoulder.

"There, there," he crooned like an old woman despite his teenaged appearance. "It's not as bad as all that."

"Yes it is!" Trudy insisted. "If this makes the paper, I might as well die!"

Officer Jenkins said, "I know the coach pretty well. If you apologize, I doubt he'll press charges."

Trudy lifted her eyes. "You think so?"

"I'm almost positive. You didn't cause any lasting damage. Not yet anyway. I don't know about the school board, but folks in Lake Emily tend to be very forgiving."

Trudy cleared her throat and said, "You really think the coach won't press charges?"

"Sure. If you apologize."

"What about the bribe attempt?"

"Well. It wasn't really a bribe, was it?"

Trudy shook her head.

"We could forget about it."

By the time Mae arrived, Trudy and the kiddy cop were enjoying a quiet cup of coffee and a game of cards.

Mae entered the room. "Hey, Maeflower," Trudy said.

"Isn't this cozy?" Mae raised a thin eyebrow.

"You sure took your time to get here. This is Officer Jenkins," Trudy said, pointing to him.

Mae reached to shake his hand. "Any relation to Jake Jenkins the fire chief?"

"He's my big brother."

"I can come back later if this is a bad time," Mae said, her gaze sliding to the card game.

"No, no," Trudy said. "I'm glad you're here."

Officer Jenkins rose to retrieve Trudy's personal belongings, and Mae gave Trudy an expression that said, *We'll talk about this later, young lady.* Trudy thanked the officer, then began her long walk on the plank.

Once inside her Jeep, Mae let loose, "Trudy, what were you thinking?" She started the motor and backed out of the parking spot.

"I wasn't thinking."

"This is what you do, Trudy. You hold things in, and then it all comes out at once, like a volcano." Trudy knew the pattern all too well herself. She didn't need Mae to elaborate.

Mae turned and stared at her sister for a moment, then returned her gaze to the road. "You're spiraling out of control."

"I'm going to apologize to Coach Miller. Officer Jenkins says he's sure the coach won't press charges."

"That's not what I'm talking about," Mae said. "This incident is one in a whole series of incidents. You're destroying your life and hurting everyone who cares about you." Mae pulled the Jeep to the side of the road. "I want to know what's up."

Trudy kept her eyes trained forward. She didn't want to look at Mae. Mae was right, and Trudy knew it.

Mae sighed. "Do you remember when you put Jack Linder's lunchbox under the school bus tires, and it was flattened like a pancake?"

"I remember," Trudy sighed. "The principal was ready to put *me* under the bus tires."

"Do you remember why you told me you did it?"

"No."

"It was when Mom and Dad were getting divorced."

"I don't want to talk about it." Trudy folded her arms.

"You never want to talk about it." Mae's tone gentled. "You're afraid what happened between Mom and Dad will happen to you and Bert. So you pushed him away before there was a chance."

"I'm not afraid," she protested.

Those stupid tears were back. Trudy swiped at them with the back of her hand and stared hard out the window. She reached to twist her hair, then realized it, like Bert, was gone. "Why are you pushing me?"

"Trudy, I love you. I want you to be happy. But you're hurting yourself. Talk to me."

Trudy exhaled heavily. "Okay. I've ruined everything. I wanted to be important to Bert, but he won't even choose me over his mother or sports."

"Have you talked to him? Told him how you feel?"

"We've talked." She paused, then said quietly, "If he knew the *real* me—well, let's say he would've ended it much sooner than I did."

"I know the real you, and I think she's a pretty special person," Mae scolded. "Give Bert a chance to love you—he deserves to know the real you."

"It's too late for that."

Trudy lay in bed that night and stared at the ceiling. Remorse flooded through her like a drumroll of pain. *Maybe if you give Bert a chance* . . . Mae's words wouldn't go away.

Maybe if you apologize, Officer Jenkins had said.

Rosemary's voice joined the chorus: *Silly schoolgirl notions.*

Trudy had fallen into old habits she'd tried her whole life to reform. She'd been strong all right, so strong that she'd built a barricade around herself. A barricade that kept out everyone she loved.

But Mae always managed to scale the walls. She never gave up on her.

Neither have I.

She knew the speaker; he had spoken his love in the darkest hours of her life. As a child without a father, she had him as her father. He never left, never judged, always forgave, and held her close within his arms.

"Jesus." Trudy was sobbing now. "I've messed up. Again. I don't know what to do, and I feel so alone."

The next morning was warm for May. Dark clouds bubbled in a brew across the sky. Trudy pulled into the parking spot in front of the high school. Mingling students perched on the cement benches by the school's

301

front doors. Trudy checked her reflection in the rearview mirror. Even though she'd gone to bed late, her rest had been complete. It was a good thing, because today wouldn't be easy. First on her agenda was apologizing to Rosemary, then to Coach Miller. As much as she dreaded facing them both, she knew it would be a relief.

Rosemary was in the choir room, pulling files of sheet music from the tall cabinet.

Trudy cleared her throat. Rosemary glanced up.

"Hi," Trudy said with a wave.

"Hi," Rosemary said, turning back to the cabinet.

"I've come to apologize. You were right yesterday—I'm sorry I meddled. Your friendship means a lot to me. I'd hate to think I've lost it." She waited.

Finally Rosemary turned toward Trudy. "I was harsh," she said. "You had good intentions, even if they were misguided."

"Can we start over?"

"Deal." Rosemary smiled. "You're coming to dress rehearsal today?"

"I wouldn't miss it."

Rosemary pushed the file drawer in. "Did you hear that the school board has called a special session tonight?"

"No, but I just got here," Trudy said.

"Rumor is, a teacher was arrested yesterday." So it was starting.

"Yeah. That would be me," Trudy said. She raked a hand through her short hair. Yet somehow a comforting hand rested on her shoulder.

"What happened?" Rosemary said.

"Let's say my apology to you is the first of several."

thirty-three

T here's a bright, golden haze on the meadow," Ken sang in his rich baritone as he sauntered onto the stage. A girl with bent shoulders and exaggerated age lines around her eyes sat behind a butter churn and gazed out at the audience contentedly. "There's a bright, golden haze on the meadow . . . ," Ken repeated.

Everything had turned out wonderfully—the sets, the costumes. The students glowed with excitement. Lydia Lindstrom sashayed onto the front porch, echoing Curly's song. She was radiant in the frilled pink broadcloth dress Trudy had made.

"What do you think?" Rosemary sat beside her.

"They're amazing."

Rosemary smiled. "They sure are." She turned toward Trudy. "So how did it go with Coach Miller?"

"I couldn't find him. The secretary said he had a sub today."

"You'll have other opportunities," Rosemary said.

"I know, but I really wanted to get it over with before the school board meeting tonight."

"Do you want me to come for moral support?"

"I'd be honored, but you probably shouldn't. People might be packing stones."

Trudy kicked off her shoes and stretched her back as

she walked into her tiny kitchen to fix herself a cup of tea. She turned on the burner under the cobalt kettle and rubbed her arms. Despite Coach Miller's absence, the day had gone better than she'd expected. Now she only had to survive tonight's meeting. She wondered if they'd send her packing back to St. Paul, not that she had much reason to stay in Lake Emily now, except for Mae. Maybe it would be better if she moved back. There weren't any reminders of Bert there, and she was tired of being the focus of so much negativity. She could be anonymous there.

Trudy glanced out the window. The day had grown darker yet. Stifling heat pushed from all sides. The lowering clouds had a greenish color. Everything felt motionless—paused and waiting for resolution.

The teakettle began to whistle as the siren at the firehouse sounded loud and shrill. Trudy jumped. Someone pounded on her apartment door.

It was Bob Ott. "There's a tornado headed our way. Better get to the cellar." Trudy quickly turned off the burner and slipped on her clogs before following him down the stairs and into the darkened space that held the furnace and water heater. The cramped room smelled of dampness and mold. Trudy sat on a crate turned sideways while Bob paced before her.

"Are you sure it's a tornado?" Trudy said. Her eyes were trained on the tiny window on the top of the wall, the cellar's only natural light source.

Bob ran a bandanna across his bald head and pulled his mustard-colored cardigan tight around himself. His gaze too remained on the short window. Darkness deepened outside and with it the sound of plinking. Bob moved closer to the window where shadows whipped past.

"What's that?" Trudy said.

"Hail," he whispered. "Golf-ball size. Not a good sign."

"Bob," Trudy said, "I . . . need to apologize to you about the other night."

"Don't worry about it, kid." He patted her hand. "I've suffered worse things than an unexpected dinner with a beautiful woman. The lasagna was delicious, by the way."

The storm raised its voice, and Bob stared back out the window. A sound like that of a distant volcano rattled the building. The wind whistled and shrieked. Suddenly a new fear entered Trudy's thoughts: Was Bert out in this? Was he in a field with nowhere to escape? There were no fire alarms in the country. How would Bert know if a tornado was bearing down on him?

Trudy reached for her hair to twist it but had to fidget with her earring instead. She prayed for Bert's safety, that God would cover him in his own shelter. She thought of Mae and Peter and prayed for them too. Outside was a swirling gray blur. A sound like an exploding steam engine erupted before the power went out. The pharmacy quivered. It was so loud. The walls shook and rattled, and the window exploded, raining shards of sharp glass.

"Against that wall," Bob ordered sternly. Trudy obeyed, then watched in amazement as the ceiling above lifted and settled, lifted and settled, exposing light between the foundation and wall. Cold rain came in horizontally through the broken window, soaking them. The violence seemed to go on forever. The building groaned as if in pain, crashing sounds echoing from above. Trudy pressed herself against Mr. Ott's shoulder. She was aware only of the thumping of her heart and her fear for Bert as the dragon breathed on the unsuspecting town.

And then the monster retreated and left behind an eerie quiet. "Is it over?" Trudy asked Bob.

"I think so," he said. He lifted his face toward the exit. He stood and tried to peer out the window, but it was blocked by debris. "Are you okay?" he asked Trudy.

Trudy nodded mutely.

"Let's see if we can get out of here." He shoved a shoulder against the door, and it opened a few inches. "There's something in the way."

"Let me help." Trudy stepped gingerly over the broken glass, and together they pushed at the door. It budged another inch. "Maybe I can squeeze through," Trudy said. She turned her thin body sideways and edged one foot out. "If only I didn't have Grandpa Ploog's big head," she joked nervously. But she could move no farther. She twisted every which way, but it was no use.

Over and over again they called for help. What if no one heard their cries? The way the building had lifted and settled during the storm, Trudy worried it would collapse on top of them. Her cries became frantic.

Finally a voice answered, "Where are you?"

"In here!" Trudy and Bob said in unison.

Bob jiggled the door. Sounds of lumber being pulled aside were followed by bright light as the door opened. There stood Officer Jenkins with a ready hand. Trudy started crying as relief flooded her.

"You okay, Miss Ploog?" he said.

"I am now," Trudy said.

"How about you, Bob?" the officer said. Bob's mouth was agape. He gazed at the stairway his grandfather had built. It was a tangle of lumber. He ran his bandanna across the top of his head.

"It's all gone," he whispered as he walked through what had been a wall and into the pharmacy.

"I don't think this is safe," Officer Jenkins began, but Bob didn't seem to hear. The drugstore had been looted by the monster. The front window was gone, and the now-cool breeze wafted in. Glass was every-where—on the floor, stuck in the walls and furniture as if it had been shot from a cannon. It crunched underfoot. The warning siren ceased its wailing, replaced with sirens of ambulances and fire engines. Mr. Ott bent to pick up a bottle of Old Spice cologne untouched by the storm, still sitting on its shelf waiting to be bought.

"Would you look at that?" Trudy said.

Mr. Ott smiled sadly. "Better get out of here," he said. "This is dangerous."

The devastation that met them outside was incomprehensible. The east end of town, where many of the businesses had stood, was a pile of collapsed rubble.

Clusiau's Clothiers had entirely vanished from Ferry Street. A freakish mound of lumber and clothing racks sporting men's dungarees and white T-shirts jutted skyward. Hardware Hank was missing one wall, and the large oak that had shaded its sidewalk now stretched across Main Street; its rootball had ruptured the cement into an eight-foot mound, leaving an equally huge hole where it had stood. The Chuck-wagon had lost its big plate-glass windows. Yet the Farmers' Elevator next door still scratched the sky, dented but intact, a mere observer to the travesty.

Up and down the street, people gathered, some crying, others struck mute by the horror. Trudy walked to the side street where her car had been parked. Although leaves and papers had settled on the hood, her Pacer had somehow escaped the storm's fury. Her gaze rose to her apartment above the pharmacy. The old brick walls, broken in jagged lines, remained, but she could see blue sky through what had been her kitchen window. The gingham curtains flapped. Trudy stared, uncomprehending.

Mr. Ott tentatively patted her shoulder. "I'm sorry." It dawned on her like waking from a bad dream only to discover it was real. Everything she had worked so hard for in life—her art, her collection of purses, the letters she'd gotten from her father as a girl—had all been blown away by the wind.

Trudy sobbed into Bob Ott's mustard-colored cardigan.

Peter was in the field planting corn when the dark clouds had brought their villainous guest. He saw them hulking on the western horizon, plotting their advance, and somehow he knew this was no storm to dally with. Leaving the planter where it was along the dirt road, he ran toward the house. As he ran up the drive, hail pelted down, stinging his body. He covered his head with a hand and jumped the steps to the wraparound porch. The winds began their howl. They screeched at him, angry that he'd escaped their grasp.

"Mae!" he shouted.

"I'm down here." Her muffled voice came from the basement. Peter met her under the stairs.

"Are you okay?" she asked. She ran her hand along his arm as if to be sure he was uninjured. "I was so worried about you." She threw her arms around his wet shoulders.

"I'm fine." He held her as the winds wailed and moaned outside the clapboard walls. The old house shuddered and creaked. Peter gazed at the floor joists overhead. Mae rested her head on his shoulder. The light bulb that swung from a cord above shook and then dimmed as a loud crackling noise lit the air. Mae sat up straight.

"Took out a transformer, I'll bet," Peter said. They stared at each other, wondering what this invader was doing to their home. The battery-powered radio sputtered beside Mae, the signal from the radio station gone. Peter flicked it off. Then slowly all grew silent, even the storm. Peter stood first, listening to be sure the worst was truly past. "I'm going up," he said.

"Are you sure?"

"It's over. May as well assess the damage." They

walked slowly, dreading what they would find.

The house seemed okay. Peter opened the back screen door. It squeaked on its hinges. Mae followed close behind.

The murderous sky was now an innocent pale gray. The air was cool and fresh. They examined their island—the house and each outbuilding—to see what damage they had sustained. Aside from a tree that had fallen in the windbreak, everything was fine.

"Took a few shingles off the chicken coop," Mae observed, pointing.

They circled the big yard, then walked to the barn where the cows gazed at them with liquid-brown eyes rimmed in long black lashes. "Passed us by," Peter said. He put an arm around Mae's shoulders.

"It sounded awful," she said. A siren blared on Highway 36 in the distance. They turned as an ambulance raced toward Lake Emily.

"Grandma," Peter breathed.

"Let's go," Mae said.

The roads into town were a tangle of fallen trees, downed power lines, and twisted metal. Mae wrung her hands until her knuckles grew white as visions of Trudy and Virginia in the tornado's path tortured her mind. One patch of woods was otherworldly—sheets of metal torn from a turkey shed wrapped around trees bare of branches. Dead turkeys from the devastated operation lay amid the carnage. One bird that had managed to survive wove drunkenly through the chaos. Its long neck bobbed back and forth as it staggered and blinked curiously at Mae.

They neared a house they had always admired, a beautiful red two-story colonial. Peter slowed the Jeep. All that remained of the home was a stairway in the center of the foundation. Mae couldn't keep her eyes off of it.

"It's only a mile from our house," she said.

Peter sped up. Telephone poles along the road leaned progressively closer to the ground until finally they reached those that had snapped completely off, leaving a tangle of twisted live wires in the fields along Highway 36. Mae sat silently, staring, praying as they neared Lake Emily. At first everything seemed normal. The park still wore its tall oaks and elms. The fountain at its center was untouched, although it wasn't spraying as it usually did. The Methodist church was intact, but as they came down Main Street, it was obvious where the tornado had touched down in its cosmic game of hopscotch. It started at the Catholic church next to Lion's Park. The tall spire had disappeared, and the stained-glass windows were shattered. The twister had then knocked hard on the flower shop's and insurance agency's doors, reducing both places to rubble. The landmark maple tree, down. The upper branches had crashed through the post office's front door across the street. Peter parked the Jeep before the downed tree, and they got out, climbed over the thick trunk, and headed toward Trudy's. The used-book store and shoe repair were untouched.

In an attempt to clear the street of a tree that had been downed in front of his store, Marty Hayes from

Hardware Hank manned a Poulan chainsaw. Peter watched him working alone on the massive oak when he heard Mae's gasp.

He whirled. "What is it?"

She pointed to the pharmacy. "The roof is gone!" At first Peter didn't notice the damage, but then he saw it—daylight through the street-side windows. Mae began running up the street. Peter followed right behind. They rounded the corner. Trudy's car sat in its usual spot.

Mae started for the back stairs, but he pulled her back. "You need to calm down," he said.

Mae was crying hysterically. "But Trudy." They walked to the back and saw that the stairs were unusable. In fact, the back wall of Trudy's apartment was gone, revealing its stripped innards.

"She was probably in the basement." He held his wife by the shoulders and spoke firmly to her. "Don't assume the worst. We'll find her."

Mae pressed the palms of her hands to her eyes, wiping the tears away. Peter held her tight.

"Trudy!" Mae called when they released their embrace. Peter began calling for Trudy too as they searched around the century-old drugstore.

Jim Miller from the Chuckwagon came over. "Are you looking for your sister, Mrs. Morgan?" Mae nodded. "She's over by the diner."

"Oh, thank you!" Relief flooded Mae as they raced to the Chuckwagon's parking lot. The broad, slanted windows of the restaurant were gone, and as they neared the lot around back, Peter saw that a tree had fallen through the roof of the stockroom. Trudy ran to Mae. Both sisters sobbed as they embraced. "You're okay," Mae kept saying over and over again. "You're okay. When I saw the roof gone from the pharmacy . . ."

Trudy stroked her younger sister's hair. "Of course I'm okay. Mr. Ott took good care of me." She nodded toward the older man, who stood talking to Rosemary Johnson across the lot. "Rosemary's place had some damage too," Trudy said.

"Have you seen Grandma?" Peter asked Trudy.

"No, and the streets in town are impassable with all the downed trees."

"Let's walk then," Peter said.

The three of them headed toward Virginia's house six blocks away, on the south edge of town. Shocked neighbors stood in yards now filled with rubble that had once been homes. Those whose homes were untouched banded together to help others, removing downed trees, covering holes in roofs with plastic tarps, giving compassion and shelter. The Fire and Rescue from St. Peter was arriving, cautiously peering into houseless basements, clearing the roads, directing victims to the hospital or high school depending on whether they needed medical attention or shelter.

Lake Emily's citizens clustered together, wept, told the stories of where they'd been when the siren blared, and wept again. No one seemed to know exactly what to do, how to get past this one moment in time.

Trudy felt on the edge, teetering. And it scared her.

"Are you okay, Trudes?" Mae placed an arm around her sister's thin shoulders.

"It's all gone," Trudy said. "Even my letters from Dad. Everything."

"Letters from Dad?"

Trudy started to cry again. "I never told you. I was afraid you'd be hurt that he never wrote to you . . ."

"What did he write about?"

Trudy sniffed. "Oh, mostly how sorry he was for leaving us but then all his excuses for not coming back too."

"You kept that a secret from me all these years? Why would you—"

"I don't know . . . I'm sorry."

Mae stopped walking and gazed at her sister full in the eyes. "Trudy, I love you. I'm happy you're okay, but don't try to protect me anymore. I'm a grownup. I don't ever want any secrets between us. Okay?"

"I love you." Trudy kissed Mae's temple, then voiced the thought that wouldn't leave her. "Do you know if Bert's okay?" Mae turned to Peter for an answer.

"From what we can tell, the tornado didn't hit their farm," Peter said. "I'm assuming he's okay. But he could've been in town."

"No. He would've been milking," Trudy said. "It was five o'clock." She hugged herself tight. She smiled through her tears at Mae. "Good. At least he's okay. That's one bright spot."

Glass and debris and downed trees carpeted Virginia's street. Peter's sense of dread grew as they walked. Shade trees that had lined the boulevard like the entrance to a southern plantation were toppled like dominoes. Sheds leaned at precarious angles. One was completely flipped on its side. Another house had lost its roof, though the potted plants still rested peacefully on the steps to the front porch.

The windows of Virginia's Cape Cod had been blown out. They saw only darkness within. "Grandma!" Peter called as they approached.

"In the backyard," came her reply. Peter breathed in relief. She came down the driveway. He leaned over her in a bear hug.

"Are you okay?" Peter asked, not letting her go.

"I'm fine, dear. Waited it out in the cellar. Wasn't as bad as the Minnesota-Iowa twister of '67 or the one that hit St. Peter in '98. I'm afraid the house is going to need some work though." She opened the back door for them to go in. Inside, glass crunched underfoot and was stuck in the walls and furniture. "All my windows are gone," Virginia said. "Every single one. And the heater isn't going to be any help tonight, I'm afraid, with the power out. They're saying temperatures are going to drop into the forties. Who knows where Snip is. Hiding somewhere. Or gone."

"We'll get some plywood up if we can get ahold of some today. Otherwise I'll camp out in the basement," Peter said. "You'll stay at the farm until we get this fixed and talk to Chad at State Farm. He'll tell us what to do next."

Mae reached for Virginia's hand. "You stay with us

for as long as you need," she said.

"With the phones out," Virginia said, "I haven't been able to find out how Jessie is."

"I'll go make sure she's okay, Grandma." Peter nodded at Mae and Trudy to stay with his grandmother and took off for the Wise home.

JESSIE WISE

There was no month like September—it was a month when eternity lifted the curtain for a glimpse of its joys. Days stretched into forever. The grass was greener. Five-year-old Jessie Wise lay in the wide hammock that swung low between two maple trees and watched the sunlight play among the branches.

Jessie and her parents had been outside all day. It was too nice to stay in. A warm breeze blew, and robins hopped and chattered along the grass of their front yard. Jessie's mother was hanging clothes on the line next to the pasture's fence while her father pushed the loud lawn mower.

The hammock swung. A squirrel scolded her from the treetop.

"Jess," her mother called, "what are you doing over there?"

"Watching a squirrel," the five-year-old said. "I think he's mad at me."

"Come over here. I want to show you something." Jessie thought her mother was the most beautiful mother ever. She had long shiny blond hair, and she smiled with pretty white teeth. She was smiling at

Jessie now. "Look at that." She pointed to a plant that came almost to Jessie's waist. "It's a milkweed plant, but do you know what's special about milk-weeds?"

"They're weeds that have milk?" Jessie guessed. Her mother laughed. "Not exactly. See that?" She lifted a black, yellow, and white caterpillar from its leaves. "It's a monarch butterfly."

"It's a worm," Jessie said, scrunching up her nose.

"It's a caterpillar, but someday it'll be a butterfly."

"Really?" Jessie gazed into her mom's eyes. "Can we keep it until it changes?"

Her mother nodded. "Go get a Mason jar and a screwdriver. We'll have to collect more of these leaves too." Jessie ran to the house and was back with the needed jar in a few minutes. She watched in amazement as her mother poked holes in the lid with the screwdriver and made a home for the caterpillar in the glass.

"Will it really be a butterfly?" Jessie asked. She stared at the creature, wondering when the change would take place. "Mom, how do you know so much?"

Her mother chuckled. "Someday you'll know just as much. And more."

"What are my girls up to over here?" Jessie's dad came up, wiping the sweat from his forehead with his sleeve. He was tall and handsome, with dark hair cut short. Mom said it made him look strong against his square jaw line. That was always when he'd pull Mom close for a snuggle.

"An experiment," Jessie's mom said, lifting the jar for him to see.

"Wow!" He gazed at Jessie with wide eyes, then turned toward the lawn. "So, what do you think of all my hard work?"

Jessie's mom reached for his hand and gave him a kiss on the temple. "It looks wonderful."

Jessie frowned, and her dad asked, "What's wrong, punkin?"

"You cut off all the dandelions," she complained.

"They're weeds," he said. "Don't you think it looks better all green rather than having those fluffy heads poking up?"

"I think dandelions are pretty," Jessie said.

"They make nice bouquets in the spring," her mother said. "Don't they, Jessie?"

thirty-four

The Wises' neighborhood looked to Peter like an Orwellian village in shades of gray. Trees raised naked, twisted limbs as if their worship had been cut short. Everything was covered with a mulch of broken glass, cracked shingles, and splintered wood. Cars were upended, overturned, and somersaulted as if Henry Ford had taken up modern sculpture.

The Wise house had stood on Elm Street, a few blocks from Virginia's. Peter scrambled over downed trees as he cut across backyards to the unassuming cottage. Thick white smoke rose ahead of him, and as he drew near he realized Jessie's house was ablaze. He quickened his pace. A small crowd had gathered. "What happened?" he breathlessly asked a fireman. When the man turned his head, Peter recognized Jake Jenkins, a fellow usher from the Methodist church.

"The gas line ruptured," Jake said. "The ambulance took the father and daughter to the hospital."

"Hospital?"

Jake nodded. "The father was burned. I'm not sure about the girl."

Peter thanked him, then ran back to his grandmother's. He knew she would want to go to Jessie. He prayed they'd find the girl and her father still alive.

The ER was an uproar of urgent sights and sounds. Nurses and doctors rushed past Virginia, Mae, Peter, and Trudy. Someone was crying behind a curtain, and a baby joined the chorus from the waiting area. Family members and those with minor injuries stood, sat, and paced in the halls, the lobby, wherever they could find a spot. Virginia searched frantically, glancing at faces as she tried to find Jessie.

And then she saw her.

Jessie stood in the corner of the waiting room, frightened and alone. Tears streaked her dirt-smudged face, and her hair was filthy with soot. When her eyes met Virginia's, she ran to her embrace. She hugged Virginia tight around the waist and cried. "Daddy got hurt," she said. "I didn't know what to do. I didn't know what to do."

"Shh," Virginia cooed. "You're okay. Thank God you're okay. Shh." Jessie's small frame shook. Virginia rubbed her back and held her for a long time.

Finally Jessie lifted her head. "Can we find my dad?"

"Of course," Virginia said.

"You wait here, Grandma," Peter said. "I'll ask." He disappeared into the chaos.

"Are you hurt?" Virginia stared into Jessie's blue eyes.

Jessie shook her head and swiped at her nose with the back of her hand. "We were in the basement, like we learned at school," she said. "It got so loud. I didn't think it would ever stop. I could hear banging. Then there was a fire and smoke. It was black, and I couldn't breathe. I couldn't see through it. My daddy carried me. He was breathing so hard . . ." She sobbed while Virginia held her.

A woman in a nearby chair tapped Virginia on the shoulder. "Why don't you take my seat?" she said, then dipped her head toward Jessie. Virginia thanked her and held Jessie on her lap. Every time someone walked past, the nine-year-old looked up expectantly.

It seemed an eternity since Peter had disappeared into the dimly lit halls. Whenever a doctor entered the room, everyone would grow silent, waiting to see who would be chosen for his news.

Finally Peter returned. He squatted in front of Jessie and Virginia. "Your dad's going to be okay, Jessie. He's had a rough time, but he'll make it."

Her face broke into a smile.

"He breathed in a lot of smoke," Peter said, "and got

some burns. They want him to stay in the hospital for a while." He said to his grandmother, "The burns aren't bad, considering. But it might be a week or two, the doctor said."

"I guess we'll have a house full," Mae said from behind Peter. "You wouldn't mind staying with us, would you, Jessie? Virginia and Trudy will be there too."

"Okay." Jessie's voice sounded so small, so fragile.

"It'll be like a big slumber party," Trudy said. She tucked Jessie's blond hair behind her ear.

"Your dad wants to see you," Peter said. He reached for Jessie's hand.

"We'll wait here," Mae said, with a nod toward Trudy.

Their shoes clicked on the tan and white tiles of the antiseptic-smelling hall. Jessie reached for Virginia's hand.

Peter had mentioned burns. Virginia wondered how Jessie would react to her father's injuries. She squeezed the girl's hand. When they reached the door, Peter said, "I'll go back too so you can visit."

Virginia and Jessie entered the quiet room. The first bed held a sleeping man with white hair. When they passed the curtain that separated the two beds, Steve Wise turned his head. He had a bandage on his right cheek and another on his left upper arm that peeked from beneath the pale blue hospital gown. His face crumpled as his eyes touched his daughter's.

"Oh, baby." He held out his arms. Jessie ran to him and hugged him, careful not to touch his injuries. She pulled back and gingerly, tenderly touched the bandage on his cheek.

"Does it hurt?" she said.

His eyes filled with tears, and he nodded. "I'm so sorry, baby." He ran a hand along her short blond hair. "You must've been really scared."

"I thought you were . . ."

Virginia felt a lump in her throat.

"Thank you for being here with her," Steve said to Virginia.

"I had to be. You're family," Virginia said.

He smiled. "We haven't had family in a long time, have we, punkin?"

"We have each other," Jessie said. She turned and bumped his arm, and Steve winced. "Oh, I'm sorry, Daddy!"

"It's okay, punkin." He held his daughter, his eyes closed tight. When they pulled back, he said to Jessie, "Do you mind if I talk to Virginia alone for a minute?"

Jessie kissed his unbandaged cheek and went into the hallway. Virginia waited for him to speak. He leaned his head back against his pillows, and when he spoke, his words were halting, his expression deeply troubled. "We could've died today," he said. "Jessie could've . . ." His eyes searched. Virginia touched his hand. "I thank God I wasn't drunk." He started crying then; he cried until his cheeks and nose were red. She handed him a tissue. He blew his nose and said, "I've been a poor excuse for a father since my wife died. Things . . . I . . . used to be so different. Sometimes I wonder if Jessie would be better off without me."

"You mustn't say that," Virginia said. "Jessie loves you. She needs you as much as you need her."

"She's so happy when she's with you."

"But I'm not her parent." She paused as a realization struck her. "I'm afraid I owe you an apology. I made you think you weren't needed, made it easier for you to abdicate your responsibility. It wasn't intentional, but it was still wrong."

"I chose to turn to the bottle. I had other choices . . . but I didn't take them."

"You *still* have choices. To be Jessie's father, to love her and let her love you."

"I'm not worthy of that love," he said. The tears returned then, silent witnesses.

"Love—real love—is given when we least deserve it," Virginia said. "It's the love God has for you too, like Jessie."

"God?" he said, his gaze turning to Virginia. "He hasn't always been so kind to me."

"He's never left you or stopped caring about you," she said. She placed a hand on his. "He shows his love in so many ways—Jessie, for one. He loves you as you are. He doesn't care about your weaknesses."

"I've got a lot of those."

"We all do," Virginia said. "Every last one of us."

Then Jessie peeked around the doorjamb. "Can I come back in?" Her father nodded and mouthed *thank you* to Virginia. Jessie climbed up onto the bed, but Steve said, "I'd love to hold you, punkin, but my legs are hurting." She slid back to the floor, pulled a chair close to the bed, and took up her post.

"Mae and Peter have invited Jessie to stay with them," Virginia said to Steve. "That is, if it's okay with you. You're invited too, I'm sure, once the hospital releases you. You can stay as long as you want while your house is being rebuilt. My house is in need of some repairs from the tornado, so I'll be there."

"I don't know what I would do—" His voice broke. "Thank you."

The din of the waiting room cocooned them. Peter and Trudy talked in one corner while Mae watched people. She had seen the woman before. She was sure of it, but she couldn't remember where. The woman was in her thirties, and she held her infant son close to her breast as her eyes darted to the chaos around. A blanket was tucked snugly around the baby's round face. Finally a doctor came out to talk to her. Mae overheard him tell the woman to keep an eye on the child for the signs of a concussion as he handed her a sheet of paper and left.

"Hello," she said when her eyes met Mae's. "Are you the new receptionist at the county?"

"Yes," Mae said.

"I'm Janelle. I used to have your job." She held out her free hand to shake.

"I thought I recognized you. I'm Mae Morgan. Did your baby get hurt?" She motioned toward the sleeping child.

Janelle nodded. "Bumped his head. I was pretty scared, so I decided to bring him in. I hope it doesn't cost an arm and a leg. The storm took my house and car. He's all I have left. With the phones out I can't even call my family in Brainerd—" Her voice cracked. "Everything's gone from bad to worse. I thought I could get a fresh start here, you know? I have no idea what I'm going to do now."

Mae's heart reached out. "I know this is going to sound forward," she said, "but . . . we have this big farmhouse with lots of rooms. You could stay with us. Until you get everything worked out."

"That's very generous," she said, "but I don't even know you."

"You and your baby need a warm place to sleep," Mae insisted.

Janelle smiled tentatively. "Okay," she said. "Until I can figure out what to do."

thirty-five

B ert stared up at the missing second floor of the pharmacy, a shell of broken bricks with no roof. His heart hammered in his chest. Where was Trudy? He lifted his green seed cap and ran a hand through his curly hair.

He'd been in the barn when the storm had hit. It had come so fast and furiously that he hadn't had time to run for the cellar. The cows had stamped and bellowed in agitation as the rafters and siding on the big building shook. Nature had huffed and puffed, but in the end the only thing that had been damaged on the Biddle farm was the tree house Bert and Fred had built in the grove as boys. A dead oak had fallen on it and crushed its aged roof.

He could picture Trudy's face lined with fear, her beautiful eyes filled with tears. He had to find her. Even if she didn't want to marry him, he had to know she was okay.

Had she been in there when the winds had taken the roof and emptied her place? Was she lying injured or dead in some field? His breathing quickened, and he ran to the back of the building to see that the steps had been demolished.

"Bert, is that you?" It was Bob Ott. Bert whirled to see the older man's weary-looking face.

"Is she okay?"

"Trudy?" Bert nodded. "Last I heard she was going up to Virginia Morgan's."

Relief flooded Bert. He took off at a run, up the street toward Virginia's Cape Cod. Trudy was okay. She wasn't dead in a field somewhere, but she was alive and well.

He stopped suddenly. What would he say to her when he saw her? Nothing had changed. A storm had passed overhead. That was all. Sure, he loved her. He'd always love her. But their differences remained. There was no point. He'd found out what he'd come to find out.

The phones and electricity were out for almost an entire week. Thankfully Peter had the generator to run essentials like the milking machine and holding tank. He arranged for another creamery from Blue Earth to pick up his milk while the Lake Co-op Dairy was out of commission in Lake Emily. Many farmers weren't so lucky and ended up having to dump perfectly good milk.

Many of the buildings in town had been condemned. The flower shop and insurance company's remaining walls would have to be dozed, as would Ott's Drugstore and Clusiau's Clothiers. Hardware Hank had received a good thrashing, but the inspectors said the basic structure was still sound, as long as they could get the sidewall back up soon. Two massive trees had burst through the roof of the second-grade hall at the elementary school, creating instant sunroofs. The high school was unscathed.

Classes had been canceled for the week; nonetheless, the parking lot was crowded with busloads of volunteers from towns all across Minnesota and the Midwest—one bus from Hibbing, others from Duluth, Brainerd, Rochester. A large Red Cross truck was parked in the lot, offering assistance to victims. Volunteers handed out blankets and basic supplies that came from the good people of Minnesota and the Dakotas. The Federal Emergency Management Administration had set up an office trailer to help people with the paperwork to receive federal aid.

The local radio station, its broadcast antenna jury-rigged to keep them on the air, had set up an information booth where they gave away radios to those who needed them and kept the citizens informed. Pastor Hickey, Father O'Leary, and the Lutheran pastor came by to talk on the radio and offer comfort and counseling to the community. The Catholic church, devastated by the storm, was now meeting at the Methodist church during the late-service time slot.

St. Peter had set up a laundry program so those without power could bring a basket of clothes to the library and receive it at the end of the day, washed, dried, and folded by an anonymous benefactor.

Trudy stood still for a moment and watched the kindness of small-town America unfold. It was unlike anything she'd ever seen. It left her breathless.

Chuck Wilbee and Lydia Lindstrom filled black garbage bags with trash from the school's front lawn. Trudy waved, then went inside the school, which hummed with the murmur of voices. Grief counselors at one end of the cafeteria talked one-on-one with families who'd lost everything.

Inside the large gym doors more citizens mingled, held their children tight. These were the families who'd spent the night on the gym's hard floors but who were nevertheless grateful for a warm, dry place to sleep.

"Trudy?" a woman's voice said. It was Rosemary. The two embraced. "How are you?"

"I'm doing okay," Trudy said. "At least I have Mae and Peter to fall back on."

"Do you have any idea what you'll do?"

"No." Trudy shrugged. "It was just stuff, you know? Maybe now's my time to move back to St. Paul."

"You're considering that?"

"I've been thinking about it." She paused. "I saw Chuck and Lydia outside. Is the play called off?"

"No. We're Minnesotans. A tornado can't stop us.

It'll be a little later than we'd planned, but we'll make it happen," Rosemary reassured her.

"Do you think people are in the mood for something as frivolous as a musical?"

"They'll be ready before you know it. In the meantime we work on cleanup. Are you here to find out about FEMA or to get some counseling?"

Trudy smiled. "Neither. I came to help. I don't exactly have anything of my own to clean up. My renter's insurance will settle all that. For now, I may as well do my part." Trudy shrugged.

Rosemary glanced around, then said in a low voice, "I have something to tell you."

"Oh?" Trudy leaned in closer to hear.

"Well, first I need to apologize for overreacting about the whole Bob Ott thing—"

"You already apologized, and anyway it was my fault."

"I know, but . . ." She took a breath. "Bob asked me out yesterday. I guess he didn't feel the same way I did about your setup. He said he's liked me for a long time; he never had the courage. So . . ."

"So with help from a pushy broad and a tornado, he thought he'd take a chance?" Trudy finished with a grin.

Rosemary blushed and said, "Who knows? Maybe it wasn't such a nutty idea."

Trudy was sent outside with three big black trash bags to pick up debris on the football field. She figured it was God's sense of the ironic.

She ambled to the athletic field where a line of boys and girls worked. Soon she, too, was bent over, picking up scraps of wood, glass, and paper. When they found photos, they set them aside to place in a box at the library so owners could reclaim them. They found car parts, a scratched jewelry box missing its contents, hangers, clothing, and dirt-smudged toys, mostly broken. It was as if someone had taken a gigantic wooden spoon and stirred up the entire town's contents, redistributing everything down to the last paper clip. It didn't take long for Trudy to fill her first bag.

"Hey, Miss Ploog." It was Ken, the boy with the rich baritone voice who played Curly. He picked up a Coke can that had a stick run through its side like a skewer and held it up. "Look at that," he said.

"You see all kinds of odd things after a tornado," a man's voice answered from behind Trudy. Glen Miller was staring directly at her. "Doing some community service time, I see," he said.

"Helping out," Trudy said. She bent back to her work.

"Did you hear that the school board has rescheduled their meeting for next week?" He stepped in front of her, and she straightened up.

"Have I done something else?"

"No," he said, but there was a smirk on his lips.

"Listen." Trudy held up her hands. "I tried to find you last week. I wanted to apologize. I got carried away, and I was wrong."

Glen crossed his arms over his big chest and grinned

at her. "So now you're going to play nice?"

"I know I said some pretty mean things. I was rude and judgmental, and I was wrong for that. I'm going to write a letter of apology to the paper too. You know, we're after the same thing, helping students achieve their best. Even if their best is on a football field. But I'm not wrong for pointing out the inequity of the budget cuts. What are you grinning at?"

The coach uncrossed his arms. "I had a little talk with Officer Jenkins."

Trudy's face flushed. "What did he say?"

"Just that you were very . . . remorseful." The coach paused. "Bert was right about you. You do care about the kids, but I think you underestimated me. If you knew all the sacrifices and cuts the school board has already made to the sports program—"

"I didn't know," Trudy said.

He held out a hand, and they shook. "You and I should have a talk about the Gifted and Talented program. Maybe it's not too late to figure something out," he said.

Trudy had filled her three bags and was lugging them to the big blue Dumpster in the parking lot when she saw him. His back was to her, but she'd know that tall, lean frame anywhere. He turned, and their eyes met. Trudy sucked in a breath.

"Hey," Bert said. The sound of his voice made her feel like crying. "I'm glad you're okay. I saw your place . . ."

"I'm staying with Mae and Peter," she said, wishing

she could say what was truly on her heart—*I love you. I was so stupid. Please give me another chance.*

"Oh. Good." He ducked his head. "I gotta go." He pointed with his thumb over his shoulder.

"Okay," she said. And then he was gone.

Mae heard the water running in the shower at about the same time Janelle's baby began to cry in the bedroom. They'd borrowed a crib from Annette Pulaski at Extension, and she had insisted that Janelle keep it. "I'm long done having babies," Annette had said. "You may as well get some use out of it." It was a gorgeous white wooden crib with turned spindles and brightly colored bedding. Janelle had been overwhelmed by the simple kindness.

Mae crept into the bedroom and gazed at the rosy-cheeked infant. He stopped crying the instant he saw her, and his face erupted in a toothless grin. Mae's heart constricted.

Janelle was humming in the shower. Mae thought to get Peter but decided she was being silly. She bent over the white side rails and lifted the chunky five-month-old. He giggled and rubbed his face against her shoulder, snuggling close. Mae sat in the rocking chair in the corner. The baby stared at her with huge blue eyes and reached for Mae's long dark hair with a chubby finger. Mae rocked and sang to him. His body was warm and soft. The feel of him in her arms comforted her. Why had she been so afraid? The baby cooed, and Mae let him grab her forefinger in his tiny fist.

"Was he crying?" Janelle stood in the door in Mae's fuzzy pink bathrobe and wore a towel like a turban around her hair.

"Uh, yeah, I hope it's okay," Mae said.

"Of course," Janelle said. She sat on the white chenille bedspread.

"I lost a baby last year," Mae confided.

"Virginia told me." Her eyes were turned down as if she were avoiding Mae's gaze. "It must've been hard."

Mae nodded. "It was."

"I can't even imagine it. I . . . gave a baby up for adoption when I was sixteen. That was the hardest thing I ever did. I knew it was right, for her sake, but it was still hard. That's why I'm so determined to keep my son."

"I'm glad you came," Mae said. Janelle had a puzzled expression on her face. "We both needed this." Mae gazed back down at the baby boy, who had fallen asleep.

She laid him back in the crib, but he squirmed. "I'll rock him downstairs while you get ready," she whispered as she picked him back up.

She tiptoed down to the living room where Virginia and Jessie were playing a game of Go Fish.

"He looks happy," Virginia said. Then, "So do you."

"I am," Mae said. "Who would've thought a good thing could come out of a tornado?"

"I expect many good things will come. We had a good visit at the hospital, didn't we, Jessie?"

"Daddy gets out in a few more days," Jessie said.

Her face glowed with joy.

Bert parked next to the Morgan barn. May sunlight filtered through the green branches of the cedar and maple trees. Chickadees hopped on the gravel drive, flying up and settling down, warming themselves in the spring sunshine.

A car passed on the dirt road. Bert waited for the dust to settle before he got out. He had come on the pretense of helping Peter fix the fuel pump on the tractor, but he really wanted Peter's advice about Trudy.

He climbed out of the truck and walked into the barn. The side doors were open to the pasture so that sunlight filled the tall space. A barn swallow darted between the rafters. A pair of pigeons swooped out of the opening with a clatter of wings.

"Hey, Bert," Peter called from the tank room. "I'm about done."

Shafts of yellow light warmed the barn's interior. Bert breathed in the sweet smell of hay and milk, manure, and disinfectant—a smell that said *home*.

Peter wiped his hands on a rag. "Let's head to the shop," he said, leading the way to the round-roofed Quonset shed. "I appreciate your coming. With Dad gone and Mae working, I'm having a time of it keeping up." He flicked on the light in the big shed, and they stooped to examine the inner workings of the slumbering tractor.

"Should be an easy fix," Bert said. He fidgeted with the wiring, running a hand along its length. He straightened and an awkward silence descended.

When Peter saw his friend's face he said, "Looks like you have something on your mind."

"I must confess . . . ," Bert said.

"Ah," Peter said. "I was wondering when you'd want to talk about Trudy."

"What has she told you?"

"Not much really. Talks more to Mae than to me."

"Do you think she still—"

"Cares about you?" Peter finished for him. "I have no doubt."

"So why did she break up?" Bert said.

Peter ran a hand through his blond hair and said, "Have a seat." He pointed to the tall metal stools beside the long worktable.

"I want to give it another try," Bert said, "but it seems every time we get close, something happens. I don't even know what it is. One little comment, and we're into a full-blown argument." He sighed.

"Trudy's famous for that," Peter said. "You're going to have to find a way to work around it, I'm afraid. Marriage is give-and-take. And I have to tell you, Bert, I didn't do so well living with my mother-in-law, so I can sympathize with Trudy on that one."

"She didn't even hear me out. It was about the farm, not Ma."

"I guess I can see your point. I know that I'd want to live on the farm rather than in town. I know that with Mae there are times when I give her what she wants because I love her. I wasn't thrilled by her wanting to go back to work, but I felt she needed to build her self-confidence, get out of the house. It's probably good you and Trudy are learning these things now."

"Because?"

"You need to decide what's important. Where you can give in and where you can't. What you're willing to sacrifice in order to be with her—"

"Shouldn't she have to give some too?"

"If you're always keeping track of how much the other person is giving, it'll never be enough. Trust me on that one. I've learned the hard way."

Bert sighed. "I don't want to always be fighting her about the farm and Ma."

"If you want to marry her, Trudy needs to be number one."

The school board "requested" that Trudy attend the next meeting to discuss her problem with the police. School was set to resume its final month of classes next week, and they wanted to "settle this little matter before that," were Don Lind's exact words. Rosemary had offered to go with her as moral support. Mae had too, but Trudy had told her she wanted as small an audience as possible at her execution. The sick feeling in the pit of Trudy's stomach only grew worse as the hour approached. She placed a hand across her flat belly as she studied herself in the mirror. She had borrowed a dress from Mae for the occasion since hers had all been blown away. It was simple in style, subdued mousy brown—hardly Trudy's taste. But, she decided, being demure and boring would probably be a good thing.

A knock sounded on her bedroom door at 6:45 PM. Rosemary stood there in a peach wool jacket and slim-fitting black capris.

"Don't you look cute?" Trudy said.

Rosemary touched her darkened hair. "Thanks. I guess you and Bob have given me some confidence. We had a great time at the Fitzgerald Theater last Saturday, and he asked me out again. He's taking me to a Neal and Leandra concert up at Gustavus Adolphus."

"Goody!" Trudy smiled. "I'm so glad for you!"

"Oh, I got this for you." She handed Trudy a small, brightly colored beaded bag. "So you can start a new purse collection."

"Thank you!" Trudy held it to her chest.

Rosemary glanced down at her watch. "Come on," she said. "We have a firing squad to face."

"Do you have to word it that way?"

By the time they got to the high school cafeteria where the meeting was about to start, the room pulsed with activity. Coach Miller sat on the left of the room. He waved at Trudy. Arvin from the *Herald* was mingling with the crowd, his monster camera slung over his neck. He gave Trudy a they're-going-to-eat-you-alive smirk. She raised an eyebrow and turned away from him as she and Rosemary made their way to two seats at the front.

"Let's get this meeting started," Don Lind began. The crowd quieted. "I called this meeting before the tornado. Now that school is about to resume, I felt it essential that we deal with a certain matter." His eyes moved to Trudy. She wished she could melt into her hard plastic chair. "One of our teachers—Trudy Ploog—was arrested by the police for vandalism . . . on school grounds. This is a serious allegation, one that we plan to deal with appropriately. That's why I've invited Miss Ploog to speak with us about the circumstances surrounding this matter. Miss Ploog."

Trudy slowly moved to the podium in front that faced the school board. She felt very small, very foolish.

The police officer's words came to her—"If you apologize . . ."—and she remembered the hand of comfort she'd felt that night. Taking a deep breath and sending a prayer for help skyward, she began, "I must confess, I have no excuse to give you. I was way out of line. I apologize to you again, Coach Miller." She faced the coach, before turning forward. "I apologize to you all and to the school board for embarrassing you. I let my ideals get away with me, but I was wrong to think I knew better than everyone else."

"So it's true that you damaged his vehicle?" Don said.

"I let the air out of his tire and took a Minnesota Wild sticker off his window."

"Why would you do that?" His lips formed a grim line.

"I was upset. Like I said, there's no excuse." She shrugged and lifted upturned hands. "I'm hoping to keep my job."

Rosemary came to stand beside Trudy. "If I might say a word?" Rosemary leaned in toward the microphone. Don Lind nodded, and Trudy stepped back. "In the past months since Miss Ploog came to work with us, I've seen that she is a hardworking, dedicated teacher. She truly cares about students and often stays after school to help interested pupils learn more about art. She's been an invaluable help in getting the sets and costumes ready for the high school musical. All this she's done on her own time, sometimes paying for needed items from her own pocket—all for the sake of the students." She glanced at Trudy, who nodded.

The school board members whispered to each other. Finally Don Lind spoke again. "Being arrested on school property *is* a big deal. You are a teacher, Miss Ploog." His dark eyes bored into Trudy's. "In this situation, you set a poor example for your students. When they see you being taken away by the police from the front of their school . . . This is not something to trifle with."

"Could I?" a male voice behind Trudy spoke. It was Coach Miller. Trudy swallowed and moved aside so he could address the school board. He gave her a wink, then began to speak. "Miss Ploog and I have certainly had our differences, as most of you know. Yet I strongly believe that we would be doing ourselves a disservice to dismiss her. She's a good teacher. We need teachers like her to help our children believe in themselves. We all make mistakes. I know I have. I also know that giving someone a second chance is the right thing to do. As a community, we have more important things to think about these days." He shrugged and said, "I guess that's all I have to say." He returned to his seat.

Don Lind was quiet for a long moment, then he said to his fellow school board members, "Since Miss Ploog has admitted her error and Coach Miller has not pressed this matter, I propose that Miss Ploog should continue as our art teacher on a probationary status for the next six months. Principal Rosen will report to us every two months as to any issues. If something like this should happen again, Miss Ploog, dismissal would be immediate."

Sweat trickled down Trudy's neck. Rosemary gave her hand an encouraging squeeze.

"All in favor?" Don said. A chorus of ayes resounded. "Opposed?" There was silence.

Rosemary smiled and whispered, "Yeah!"

Trudy hadn't felt this happy since . . . since she and Bert had made their kite in the back of the pharmacy. His face flickered in her mind like an image from a silent film. She had one more person to make things right with. Time to give Bert that chance Mae had spoken of.

As they filed out of the crowded room, many came to talk, to offer words of encouragement and healing. The room emptied, and Trudy was moving toward the doors when she saw him. Bert. He stood next to the back wall. His eyes were on her and her alone.

"Hey," he said.

"Hey, yourself. What are you doing here?"

"I thought maybe you could use a friend."

Trudy smiled. "I'm sorry, Bert. I've been so stupid." She teared up. "I still love you. I've always loved you.

I don't want to hurt you." She noticed he was smiling. She wiped her cheeks with her palms. "For crying out loud in a supermarket bucket, why are you grinning?"

"I've never seen you cry before."

"I must look awful."

"No." Bert shook his head. "You're beautiful." He took her hand and led her outside. The sun was a burnished copper glow on the horizon. They settled on the hill overlooking the football field. "I've missed you," Bert said. "I want you to be happy. If you want me to quit coaching, move to town . . . whatever, you are worth it."

The sun sank lower, and copper turned pumpkin. Trudy took a deep breath, determined to finally risk her heart. "When I was a little girl, I adored my father. He was tall and strong. Then one day he left us— Mom, me, and Mae. I didn't understand how someone who said he loved me could leave like that. Mom was devastated. Mae was too little to even know what she was missing, but I knew." Trudy sighed and reached for Bert's hand. "I guess I've been afraid you would leave me. I was testing you to make sure you weren't like my dad."

"Trudy, I won't ever leave you," Bert said.

"That's something I have a hard time believing, so I didn't even give you a chance. I beat you to it. My dad wrote to me until I was fourteen," Trudy went on. "Not to the rest of the family, just me. Those letters were my little secret, but the tornado took them all away. I know now that secrets are a bad idea." She searched his eyes and found acceptance there. "I don't want to keep anything from you. Not anymore. Not if you'll still have me."

"I'll still have you." Bert grinned.

"So can I still have the ring then?"

"I'll have to see about that. I think I left it in the truck."

LILLIAN BIDDLE

Residents of the Owatonna State School filed into the hollow-sounding gymnasium. They were only children, orphans hoping for a chance. Each child stood behind a chair that held all his or her earthly belongings. A bag tied on the back of the chair held a change of clothes, toothbrush, those few reminders of a life before.

"Children," the principal began. Lillian Kluge held tightly to the back of her chair, afraid the stern man brought news of yet another funeral in the little cemetery outside. There were too many funerals. "We're going to have visitors, and I want you to be on your best behavior." He circled the room, a general inspecting his troops. Lillian shrank back. She wanted to be as small as possible so he wouldn't notice her. It was never good to draw attention.

Finally a man and a woman came in. They were both tall and skinny. The man—Mr. Swenson, the principal called him—had a bump in the middle of his nose, and the woman wore white gloves. They moved past the children, eying each critically like a good cut of steak. When they stopped in front of Lillian, she smiled at them tentatively. "This is Lillian Kluge. She came to us two years ago," the principal said.

The woman turned her around and felt the muscles in her upper arm. "Is she a good worker?" she said.

"Complains a bit, but good," he replied.

"Do you want to be adopted, Lillian?" Mrs. Swenson said. Lillian nodded, hope kindled inside her.

"Speak up, girl," Mr. Swenson said in a scratchy but kind voice. "You need to answer when spoken to, you understand?"

"Yes sir," Lillian responded. That brought out a smile from the old man.

Mrs. Swenson's gaze flicked around the room one last time before she said, "We'll take her."

"You're being adopted today," the principal said. "You have a mother and a father now."

thirty-six

Trudy pulled the Pacer into the Biddle driveway. The brilliant afternoon sunshine made the flower beds of purple Russian sage and yellow daffodils pop with color. No one was in sight, which was just as well since Trudy had no idea what she was going to say. She was determined to make a new start with Lillian no matter what.

Fred's obnoxious dog, Bullet, came around the corner barking and snarling, showing teeth in need of a good brushing.

"Chill out, would ya?" Trudy said as she walked to the back door. She knocked three times and waited.

Finally Lillian came.

"What are you doing here?" Lillian said. "Bert isn't home if—"

"No, I came to see you," Trudy said.

"What would you have to say to me?"

"May I come in?"

Lillian sighed and stepped aside for Trudy to pass. Trudy led the way to the parlor and took a seat on the floral couch with the doily across its back.

"Looks like your ankle healed nicely," Trudy said. "Are you happy to have your cast off?"

"Of course I am," Lillian said. She folded her arms. Trudy took a deep breath.

"I was hoping we could negotiate a truce," Trudy said. Lillian raised her eyebrows.

"The thing is," Trudy said, "I love Bert and you love Bert. So we have that in common. To be honest, I think we have a lot of things in common. I'd like to get to know you better. For Bert's sake, I would like us to be friends."

Lillian harrumphed as if what Trudy suggested was comparable to scaling Mount Everest.

"I know I've made a horrible impression on you. I've been rude and let my big mouth . . . carry me away more times than I can count. I've apologized to so many people I could give lessons."

"I heard Coach Miller spoke up for you at the school board meeting," Lillian said. "So your feud with him is over?"

"It wasn't a feud. I was trying to make a point, not start a war. We've mended fences, though. The way

I'd like to do with you."

Lillian stopped and stared at her. Her expression softened a bit. Then she said, "Trudy, you haven't done anything to me."

"So, what are you saying?" Trudy said.

"I guess we'll have to get used to each other." But there was a smile behind her eyes.

Mae watched from the front porch as Peter pulled Virginia's Oldsmobile into the driveway. Steve Wise seemed like a frail grandfather, stooped as he was in the front seat. Jessie's face glowed in the backseat; Mae could see that even from here. The nine-year-old bounded out of the car and opened her dad's door.

"Daddy's home!" Jessie called to Mae.

"I can see," Mae said as she drew near.

He moved slowly, evincing the pain of his burns. Sterile white bandages covered the side of his face and his forearm. Peter reached an arm around him to help him stand.

Mr. Wise put a hand to his face and said, "Whoa."

"You okay?" Peter said.

"Everything went black for a second." He gazed down at Jessie. "You're going to have to help me get back in shape, punkin."

"Let's get you to your room," Virginia said. Mae took Jessie's hand, and the women followed the men inside. Peter kept his arm around Mr. Wise as they slowly made their way up the stairs to the sunny room that overlooked the western fields. Afternoon light bounced off every corner. It was cheerful with its white chenille bedspread and sheer curtains, the only color in the room a thick bouquet of dandelions in a jelly jar on the nightstand.

"What's this?" Mr. Wise said as he settled onto the bed.

"Do you like them?" Jessie said. "I picked them myself, like I used to for Mom."

He was quiet for a moment, and Mae was certain she saw a tear glisten in his eyes. "I know they're weeds," Jessie said. She bit her lower lip.

"No, punkin. They're beautiful."

With the initial cleanup complete, the rebuilding of Lake Emily began in earnest. Ott's Drugstore was now a hole in the ground. But Bob had found the blueprints at home from when the store had been remodeled in the fifties and was determined to recreate the same place, complete with a few improvements to the soda fountain and upstairs apartment. Clusiau's Clothiers closed its doors for good. The insurance agency and flower shop were already being rebuilt, and the post office sported a new door and plate-glass window. A volunteer group of Hutterite carpenters arrived to assist in the rebuilding.

The high school had been emptied of its residents as most had found hotel rooms in St. Peter or Mankato. The churches of Lake Emily had found many willing homes for those without insurance to cover the cost of a hotel room.

The kindnesses continued long after the television cameras left the small town, and as contractors and construction companies came in to remake Lake Emily, the town slowly healed. Houses that had once had back decks now sprouted front porches with swings where neighbors could greet each other on warm summer evenings. Hammers and saws sounded up and down Virginia's street. The plywood Peter had nailed up was taken down window by window and replaced with new glass. Insurance paid for new furnishings and for a cleanup crew to take care of the glass that seemed to be everywhere in the house. Still Virginia and Mae and Trudy went every day to clean and move those valuables that had survived so the workers could patch holes, sand, and repaint the walls. It was tedious work, like moving all over again. Only this time the house was being rebuilt in the process. Virginia was glad to have the farm to escape to for respite from the reminders of her losses and from the overwhelming task of reclaiming her home.

"Virginia, are you okay?" Mae asked from the doorway to the den.

"What, dear?" Virginia said.

"I asked where you wanted this." She held up a box of Hummels; some of them had been chipped, but most were miraculously intact.

"I'm sorry," Virginia said. "I'm preoccupied, I guess. Life throws us curves." She stretched and patted Mae's hand. "Not even old ladies are exempt. But we do the best with what we're given and refuse to let it make us bitter—that's our choice."

"I'm learning that. Slowly, but I'm learning."

"No slower than the rest of us," Virginia said.

"Some lessons get taught over and over."

"Until we get it right?"

"No. I don't think learning to trust God is something we can ever perfect, at least not in this lifetime."

"That's something I've been learning too," Mae said. She sat down. "I've been so afraid since I lost the baby," she confided. "I didn't want to risk again."

"Life is risk, honey. Taking the risks instead of hiding in the closet—that's living."

Peter had decided that the fields could wait no longer. He had to finish planting the last few acres, although heaven knew what his crop would be like this year. He didn't know if his peas and corn plantings had been washed away by the storm, but he reasoned the twister's path had crossed north, so he'd probably be okay.

The tractor moved across the late-May landscape. Blackbirds swooped in a shifting cloud before him. They'd settle and blacken the ground with their dark presence, then take off again like a wraith searching and waiting.

Peter lowered the long guide arm and started up the row as the planter dispensed the seed behind him. The sun was warm through the enclosed green cab of the John Deere. It felt right to be back to his routine. Life resumed its patterns. He thought about his father and wondered what his patterns were in Arizona. He'd seemed so happy on the phone, talking about his new job. It was obvious that the joy had returned. But, oh, how he missed him. Every day he missed him.

David had called to see how everyone was after the tornado. He'd offered to come help, but Peter had assured him that they were all well cared for.

He turned up the next row, aligned the front tire with the arm's mark from the previous pass, lowered the arm, and began again.

His dad loved him. Peter knew that. He also knew that he wanted his father to be happy, even if that meant his leaving. Peter realized he was feeling what his grandfather must have felt all those years before when he'd sent his only son off to music school.

The light from a floor lamp cast an amber glow. Mae's feet were tucked under her as she nestled in the stuffed chair in their bedroom. She and Peter had come up to read and spend some time alone after supper dishes were put away. Peter sat in the matching chair, examining the latest *Farm Journal*.

"Honey," Mae said tentatively, unsure how Peter would respond to her news.

Peter lifted his eyes from his magazine. "Yep."

"I quit my job today." She kept her voice calm as if she were telling him about buying a pair of pantyhose.

"You what?"

"We'd agreed that it was only temporary. Besides you need my help with Dad gone."

"Yeah, but—"

"What do you think of trying for another baby?"

Peter tilted his head. "Are you sure you're ready?"

"How does anyone really know when they're ready?" She set her knitting in her lap. "I've been learning a lot about risking my heart." She shrugged. "I want a baby. I was afraid everything wouldn't be . . . perfect."

Peter reached for her hand. "Life is a risk. I can't guarantee perfection or even happiness. But I do know we have plenty of love to go around."

"I've heard that before from a very wise woman," Mae said. "I love you, Peter."

He lifted her to standing and said, "Come here, Mrs. Morgan."

They kissed, and the knitting slid to the floor.

The high school auditorium echoed with applause as the curtain opened to the third act of *Oklahoma!* The room was filled to capacity. Even people who'd lost everything to the tornado were there to support the kids. Jessie and Steve Wise. Coach Miller. Trudy could see Bob Ott's shiny head in the front row, no doubt so he could have a clear view of Rosemary as she conducted the musicians.

Trudy nestled her shoulder closer to Bert's. His face turned red, and she slipped her hand into his.

"Hey," she whispered. He smiled, his eyes trained forward as Laurey scolded Ado Annie for dating two men.

"Mae," Peter whispered from the other side of his wife who sat next to Trudy. He had a bothered expression on his face. "Did you toss all that fiberglass underwear?"

"I don't know. You did the laundry," Mae whispered back. "Why?"

Peter squirmed in his seat.

Trudy tried not to bust up laughing. She was going to tell Bert when she noticed that he seemed preoccupied. He pulled out the burgundy ring box and slowly lifted the lid. Trudy put her hand over her mouth and gazed into his tender face. Ado Annie began her song.

"I couldn't think of a better time," Bert said. "Will you wear this again? Be my wife? I promise not to let you get away. Ever."

Trudy glanced around. The rest of the audience was transfixed by the play, but she wanted to shout. She gently lifted the ring and put it on her finger, then she leaned close to Bert's ear and sang along with Ado Annie, "I'm just a girl who can't say no. Kissin's my favorite food."

Bert put a hand over his face as it became a darker crimson.

Trudy reached up and kissed his cheek.

"That means, yes, Mr. Biddle. I'll marry you."

Center Point Publishing
600 Brooks Road • PO Box 1
Thorndike ME 04986-0001 USA

(207) 568-3717

US & Canada:
1 800 929-9108